"SHIRLEY ANN GRAU IS ONE OF THOSE RARE WRITERS WHO CREATE A WORLD, DRAW THE READER INTO IT, AND MAKE HIM SOMEHOW HAPPY THERE, NO MATTER WHAT GOES ON."

—*Newsweek*

"SHIRLEY ANN GRAU IS AN ASTONISHINGLY GIFTED WRITER WITH A POWER TO STUN AND SHATTER."

—*Kirkus Reviews*

The Wind Shifting West

Shirley Ann Grau

A FAWCETT CREST BOOK

Fawcett Books, Greenwich, Connecticut

THE WIND SHIFTING WEST

THIS BOOK CONTAINS THE COMPLETE TEXT OF
THE ORIGINAL HARDCOVER EDITION.

A Fawcett Crest Book reprinted by arrangement
with Alfred A. Knopf, Inc.

ISBN: 0-449-23349-9

Portions of this book originally appeared in *Atlantic Monthly,
Cosmopolitan, The New Yorker, Redbook, Reporter, Saturday Evening Post, Shenandoah, Southern Review,* and *Vogue.*

Printed in the United States of America

10   9   8   7   6   5   4   3   2   1

Contents

The Wind Shifting West

THE WIND blew out of the south, cold and wet as southern winds always were. It had been blowing for a week, not hard but very steady. And the fog got thicker every day. Makoniky Head and the old gray house perched on its back got dimmer and dimmer, day after day, until by Thursday morning they had disappeared completely.

"Well," said Caroline Edwards cheerfully, "there they go."

"What, honey?" Robert Edwards squatted in the far corner of the porch, his black hair glistening with damp.

He was doing something with a length of rope. Caroline asked: "Is that the new anchor line for the *Chère Amie*?"

"*This* line?" He didn't look up, but his tone was startled.

"Wrong?"

"Jib sheet."

"Oh. Yes, I suppose it would have to be."

"Honey, you'll never make a sailor."

"Well, the Head has disappeared, that's all I was saying."

He glanced up, not at her, but across the bay, briefly. "Yep. Glass dropping, Guppy?"

The lanky nine-year-old, who had been crouched down beside him, galloped across the porch to see. "Nuh-uh."

"You're not taking Godfried?" She hated her son's nickname and never used it.

"Sure," Robert said. "Why don't you come?"

"Because it's wet and cold and I think both of you are crazy."

"It's a new boat, Mama," Guppy said, his round brown eyes bright and eager.

"You sound just like your father . . . And how could I help knowing it's a new boat? It's all I've heard for months."

"Just enough wind . . . We can put a lot of canvas on her, and we'll make it in no time." Robert grinned at her annoyance.

He already had that expectant, shivery, exalted look, Caroline noticed. The one she called his holy boat look.

"Make it in no time," he repeated.

They would sail directly across the sound to the little cove on Boar Island, a gentle little cove with soft beaches and freshwater streams rising right in the sand. Up the high bluff there was a small yellow house, fluttery with gingerbread.

"We'll see if Homer has his fleet in the water yet."

Caroline sighed. Every year the same game. Sail over to Homer Delatte's and criticize the care of his boats.

"You've been doing that for ten years," she said. "Don't you get tired?"

Robert said calmly, "Been doing it since I was a kid."

"Doesn't it worry you to keep coming back to a place where your family has been coming for years?"

"Only in the summer."

"But I mean, you've come here all your life, and don't you want to try something new?"

"I like it here," Guppy said.

"Oh, hush."

"Your mother wasn't talking to you, Guppy," Robert reminded him. "Please be polite."

"Why?" Caroline said.

Robert looked at her and winked. Then he began coiling his line with crisp, precise movements.

"All right," Caroline said, "if you want to kill yourself and your son . . ."

He winked again, this time at Guppy. "Your mother," he said, "has a great flair for the dramatic."

And Caroline gave up. "All right," she said, "I know you're a great sailor."

He was, of course. The mantel in this summer house, the closets of their winter place were jammed with the hideous trophies he had won, ugly shiny gold boats and engraved water pitchers and cocktail pitchers they had never used.

"Okay, loves." Caroline shrugged. "Sail on! I bet there won't be a dry spot on that stupid little boat, except maybe way up forward in the cuddy."

"Mother, we've got foul weather gear."

"Oh shut up, Guppy," she said before she remembered she did not approve of that name.

"Go get the compass, old man," Robert said, and as the long legs scrambled away, he said, "I've got to get him some new Topsiders, those he's wearing have about had it."

Robert did not kiss her good-by. They did not kiss in front of Guppy any more, it embarrassed the child. ("Wait it out," Robert advised. "It's the age; he'll get over it." And how long ago had that been: a year, year and a half . . .)

When they were gone, Caroline began to carry the small flats of geranium plants to the front deck. They had opened this house only two days ago and the windowboxes were still empty. Robert had been so busy with the new boat that he (who usually set them out) hadn't found time. She set down the frame with a little twinge in her back, and a little twinge in her soul: I'm not so young any more. Time was when I could manage a frame a lot bigger than that and not think twice about it. Now I'm going to have to start remembering exactly how it is you lift without straining . . .

She got the trowel and began work on the first of the boxes. As she did, she saw the *Chère Amie* glide out from the dock, moving silently in the light wind that always blew across the bay. She stopped for a minute and watched. The sails seemed almost slack, but they must actually have been drawing very well: the boat was getting dimmer and dimmer and there was a little frill of white water for a wake. They saw her, too, saw the bright coral of her sweater against the dark shingles of the house, and gave a sharp blast on the fog horn. She waved with her trowel, and a damp wad of mud splattered down on her forehead.

It was then barely eight o'clock. By eleven the geraniums were done. She washed her face, combed her hair, and drove half a mile along rutted, washed-out roads to her mother-in-law's for lunch.

Matilda Edwards lived in the house on the very highest point of Makoniky Head, a house that had belonged to her parents, big and gray, with turrets and bay windows and narrow balconies. A noisy house, always shaken to its very beams by the constant winds that battered it.

The last few yards of the drive were very steep and covered with loose gravel. Caroline jammed down on tht accelerator and the car lurched up, swaying from side to side wildly, caught in the ruts. She popped over the edge into a flat space, dodged among the other cars parked there, and stopped a bare six inches from a beach plum, pinkish white with the burden of its flowers.

From the tennis court at the back of the house a young man came up to meet her.

"Hello, Archie, I didn't know you were here."

He was a nice boy, Robert's nephew, red-haired and freckle-faced, lean and gay. "Yesterday." He grinned. "I don't know why we have to pretend we're surprised. I'm always here, just about this same week, and you're always here, just about the same time."

A quick peck on the cheek. "You're taller than last year, aren't you?"

"Six one."

"Good for you."

"Everybody's up at the house."

"Like every other summer too. Can you really play down there on those courts? I always meant to ask."

"Too much wind . . . You never played there?"

"I hate sports, child . . . But your Uncle Robert married me anyway."

("Well," Robert said doubtfully, "you're rather old to begin, you know, but I guess you might be able to do it."

"But, Robert darling, I don't want to learn tennis."

He looked amazed.

"And I don't want to play golf. The only thing I want to do is swim when it gets warm. Then mostly I want to float on top of the water."

Robert began to laugh, with the warm friendly chuckle that she loved. "And you look so athletic, you know."

She did. She was tall and slender and long-waisted. In those college days she wore her hair shoulder length and severely straight. The first time she met Robert's family—they had driven up here, to this same house— Robert's mother had nodded approvingly, making the same mistake. "You've found a lovely girl, Robert," she said immediately and aloud. "She's pale from the winter, but nothing a bit of sun can't fix up."

And that was the other thing. Caroline hated to tan. At parties she always counted the bare brown backs and sleek sun-bleached heads and felt thoroughly content. Her own hair was black and unstreaked, her face and arms as white as she could manage to keep them with lotions and long-sleeved shirts and big floppy beach hats.)

Archie was looking at her approvingly. "You look great this year, Aunt Caroline."

Abruptly she asked him, "How old are you?"

A short pause while he considered lying and gave it up

because she would know better anyway. "Eighteen in two months."

"Seventeen." She let her level brown eyes pass over him impersonally. "Little pitchers have big eyes . . . Now tell me who these cars belong to."

"The Jeep is Grandma's."

"Of course." It was at least ten years old. Mrs. Edwards roared back and forth along the roads with it, invariably in four-wheel drive, the huge snow tires whining along the paved stretches and churning through the sandy ones. A battered green hulk, on the tail gate a half-faded stencil of a fish that somebody had put there when the Jeep was new.

"I'd know that Jeep if I met it in Australia. Who else?"

"The Olds is my mother's."

Of course. Black. Conservative. No vulgar dash like the Cadillac.

"She had that last year."

"No," Archie said. "It was another one, but it was black too."

"And who has that monster?" A cream-colored Corniche perched on the bleak reindeer-moss-covered hill like a dab of buttery mashed potatoes.

"Giles is here."

"Now? Is he going to be here this summer?"

Giles van Fliet, half English, half Dutch, had married Mary Edwards some twenty years ago. He was a handsome man, no doubt of that, though he was only moderately tall (much shorter than his towering in-laws) and only moderately muscular. But his face had a crisp, clean handsomeness, his eyes were an icy blue that sparkled the way glass does in the light.

"Pretty boy," Mrs. Edwards sniffed when she first met him. "Now let's see what he can do."

He did very well indeed. He was an engineer with a passion for gadgets, and within a few years of his marriage he had produced a dry photocopy process and an absolutely perfect patent to protect it.

That, Caroline thought, was the story of Giles.

"Sure he's here," Archie said. "Special invitation from Grandma. She wants him to hire Phillip."

"Phillip?"

"Cousin Julia's boy, the one got thrown out of all those schools. *You* remember."

Giles van Fliet had done so very well that he had taken over the strays and waifs of the family. He was very cheerful about it, and always managed to find jobs for them somewhere. "They can lick stamps," he said cheerfully. "And we can get rid of one postage meter. We'll do our bit to turn American business around and send it the other way."

"That's why he's here," Archie said. "Where's Uncle Robert?"

"Sailing. Boar Island."

"Wet day."

"I'll go up to the house." Caroline climbed the damp, sparsely covered slope, stumbling slightly over the suckers of the rugosa roses.

They were waiting, three of them, on the enclosed porch on the west side. "I hate the sight of that water, all day every day," the old Mrs. Edwards was saying. "I don't know why I keep coming back here. Probably because I don't know any other place to go."

Ann Magnasen, Archie's mother, saw Caroline first, and waved a lazy hand toward her. "We saw something sail out, sweetie, and we wondered if it was Robert."

"It was." Caroline kissed her mother-in-law dutifully. "How are you this morning, Mother?"

"I've been on the roof," the old woman said abruptly. "You should see the state of those shingles."

"She will kill herself but it will be gallantly." Giles was standing politely. "How are you, Caroline, I haven't seen you since last summer."

She noticed that he did not offer his hand until she had extended hers. How very nice, she thought; so few people bother with that any more.

"Did I ask you for lunch?" Mrs. Edwards demanded.

"Do you want me to say yes or no?"

Giles laughed, his usual brief snort. "She has you there, Mother."

"Of course I did," Mrs. Edwards decided.

"Yes, you did." There were cards on the table, scattered. "Go on with your game. I'll watch."

"We're finished," Ann Magnasen said. "Giles doesn't like to play."

"And why does Giles decide everything?" Caroline sounded more peevish than she had intended, and she felt his cool blue eyes shift to her.

"He doesn't . . ." A shrug. "Not even his hiring policies."

"Okay, no fighting," Ann said. "Mama, how about a drink?"

(How do you suppose that happened, Caroline wondered. Her children called her Mama and her in-laws called her Mother. Just a family way, she answered herself.)

"You drink too much, Ann."

"I've thought of that, Mama." And she was gone in search of ice.

"Will you have one, Mother?" Giles asked. After her abrupt no, he turned to Caroline. "And you?" The blue eyes fringed by their dark lashes, absurdly curly, like a girl's, touched her coolly.

"Yes, thank you . . . Where's Mary? Isn't she here?"

"Mary stayed home to receive the boys. They come home today and she thinks she should be there, a welcoming committee."

Ann was back, drink in hand. Her mother's eyes flicked over and checked the color. It was dark. "Is that bourbon?"

"No," Ann said. "Scotch."

"Anyway," Giles went on, "the *Mariner* has just come off the ways at Indian Bay and I wanted to see her."

"You fished on that boat," Mrs. Edwards said. "You should never fish on a nice boat. It smells forever after."

"It smells," Giles said gently. "But we have to use these things while we have them."

"That's what Robert said," Caroline told him. "Just before he left this morning."

The afternoon drifted through the inevitable stages of family lunches. Even Archie came in from the courts and sat politely at the table with a vague and abstracted look on his face.

"He's doing isometric exercises," his mother said.

"Needs some prune juice," Mrs. Edwards said.

"When I'm your age," Caroline told her, "I will, like you, say just exactly what I want to."

"That is something to look forward to," Giles said, "is it not?"

At the end of lunch, when they were idly peeling oranges they didn't want, the south wind abruptly shifted into the west.

Mrs. Edwards noticed it first. She always noticed wind; even from her sleep she could have told you the precise quarter. "It's come around," she said. "Good weather."

They went outside, glad of any excuse to leave the table. The wind was blowing from the west, clearly, and the clumps of fog were racing overhead, blotchy gray and white.

"Clearing," Giles said. And went inside to take a nap on the wicker couch in the corner of the porch.

The three women followed him back. Mrs. Edwards did a Double Crostic, Ann picked up a book, and Caroline called Archie to get her knitting bag from the car. He brought it and then disappeared. The house was quiet, except for the steadily increasing wind-borne noises. Once Mrs. Edwards got up to look at the anemometer. "Half a gale," she said quietly, "increasing."

"Robert's all right, don't you think?"

"He's been at Boar Island for an hour or more. Way this wind is, he'll be sailing back and forth across the cove, racing himself."

"Always was queer for boats," Ann said. "And Guppy's going to be just like him."

By the middle of the afternoon there were two finished Double Crostics on the table, and a half-finished sock dangled from Caroline's needle. But it was Ann who got restless and slammed shut her book. "I don't know what I'm reading any more." She rubbed her eyes. "I'm going to wake Giles," she said. "I need somebody to talk to."

"Irritable alcoholic," her mother said calmly.

The phone rang, and Caroline picked it up automatically. For the first minute or two she did not understand; the window right by her ear was rattling so badly that she had trouble hearing. It was Robert shouting irritably, "Are you there? Are you there? Over."

"Of course I am, Robert. Where are you?"

Again the distorted and muffled voice. "Didn't you hear the operator's instructions? Don't talk when I'm talking or I can't hear you. Say 'over' when you're finished and then I'll know. Over."

"I'll try, Robert. Where are you?" A hesitation while she felt very silly. "I feel like something in a war movie. Over."

"Listen now. I'm at Homer's. Don't worry about me. Guppy is here with me and we're perfectly all right. Do you understand? Over."

Caroline said, "It's a ship-to-shore phone, isn't it? Of course I understand. You want to tell me that you'll be at Homer's until the squall blows over, and then you'll be home. Over."

"God," Robert said, "don't talk so long when I can't stop you."

"Sorry," Caroline said automatically and then realized that he hadn't heard her and he was still talking.

"So the mast went—at the spreaders—with only the jib on—you don't know what I'm talking about, do you?" A hiss of exasperation. "Anyway, it was a defective fitting somewhere—couldn't take even this little bit of weather. Over."

"You're all right, and what do you want me to do? Over."

"Phone the insurance company and tell them what's happened and where the boat is. Over."

"I will," Caroline said. "Do you want me to wait dinner? Over." She giggled again. She couldn't seem to get used to it.

"That's the trouble," Robert said testily. "None of Homer's boats is in the water, not one of them."

So you beat him this year, Caroline thought, that should be of considerable comfort to you. You won the race with Homer.

"And the launch is gone, you know the one that brings the mail and the groceries. It went to Mare's Head, and it won't be back until tomorrow, on the regular schedule."

"So you're stranded at Homer's until tomorrow," Caroline said, forgetting that he wouldn't hear, that he was still explaining how an experienced sailor had ripped the mast off his new boat.

Giles said: "Trouble?"

"Robert is at Boar Island without a way of getting home."

Giles reached for the phone, waited patiently for the signal. "Listen, Robert. This is Giles. My boat is in the water at Indian Bay. I will come over this afternoon and pick you up. It will be easier than waiting for the launch. Your wife will feel better. Over."

Even through the distorted transmission, Robert sounded very embarrassed. "I don't want to be a lot of trouble. The wind is dropping right now and tomorrow I'm sure we could get a tow back. Over."

"Maybe," Giles said practically, "we can give you a tow now if we are careful. Or maybe we'll have to come back for the boat tomorrow or the next day. In any case, we will come late this afternoon. Caroline will show me where it is. What do you think of that? Over."

"Great," Robert said. "I'd rather sleep home tonight. Over and out."

"So." Giles put up the phone. "We go for a ride."

Caroline said: "Now?"

Ann Magnasen said: "Not me."

Mrs. Edwards said: "Lost his mast? His father would never have done that."

"Leave your car here," Giles said to Caroline. "We'll use mine."

As they eased over the sharp drop and down the rutted road, Caroline caught a glimpse of bright red hair. "Oh dear, we should have asked Archie if he wanted to come."

"I'd rather have you all to myself for a change."

"I haven't seen you all winter, have I?"

"No." He shrugged. "I've been working. And my mother has been sick."

"Oh," Caroline said, "I'm sorry, I didn't know. You didn't tell us."

"She is very old." He shrugged again, looking at the road. "After the Germans killed my father, I did not think she would live to see the end of the war. She is the sort of woman who has only one man in her life."

"But she's still alive?"

"She had no other men."

"I didn't mean that," Caroline said, and then, "Look, Giles, you know perfectly well that I didn't mean that, and if I'm going to fight with you and be watching every word, I'm not going. Robert can catch the launch tomorrow."

He reached for her hand. "I am sorry. I suppose I have —what do you call it?—an Oedipus complex."

"Of course you don't."

He turned into her road and drew up before her house.

"Here?"

"I thought you would want to change. That dress and those shoes wouldn't be very comfortable on the boat."

"You're always right. I'll just be a minute."

"Take your time." He followed her inside. "The longer

we wait, the smoother the trip. The wind is dropping every hour."

She changed quickly and found him waiting in the living room. He had fixed himself a drink. "I'll finish this in a minute. You want one?"

"I'll fix it myself; don't bother." He had not asked, she thought, but then after all, he was her brother-in-law. And maybe he figured he had done enough for the family so that he was entitled to move easily in and out of their houses . . . I must ask Robert, Caroline thought, if Giles has ever helped him. And I will be so very glad if he has not . . .

"That is a very stiff drink," Giles said behind her.

She turned and because she was used to much taller men, she looked above his head.

"Your drink, it's very stiff."

"I'll pour some out." Her hand shook. "Damn," she said softly.

Giles steadied her, as the yellow whiskey ran back into the bottle. She was aware suddenly of the slightness of his body, willowy like a boy's, of the small muscles that ran hard and hidden among the delicate bones.

"There," he said, "that is a good drink."

She sipped, wondering why she had taken Scotch. She did not even like the taste.

"I did not know you were a Scotch drinker."

"A change . . . How could you remember from one summer to the next what I drink? You couldn't."

"With you I remember, not with everybody."

"Thank you, sir," she said politely. And drank.

"Bring a bathing suit," he said, "if you want to swim. The water in a lot of those coves is very warm."

"No, thank you," she said. "I would rather just pick up Robert."

And he laughed. Put back his head and laughed aloud.

"Whatever is the matter with you?"

"Nothing," he said, "nothing at all."

The boat smelled of paint and disinfectant. "To clear the smell of fish," he said. "It will disappear when we are underway." He worked silently, shaking his head in answer to her "Can I help?" He started the blowers, took the canvas covers from the brightwork, checked the bilge, connected the fuel line. Then he tossed his lines aboard and ran lightly up to the flying bridge.

Caroline got her scarf and joined him. He was skillfully finding his way out of the crowded harbor.

"That *was* fast."

"We'll go the long way round," Giles said. "It will be smoother."

"Whatever you say."

They came out of the harbor, into the wind-speckled stretch of ocean. Giles pushed both throttles open. The wind grabbed the edges of her scarf, fluttering them into her eyes. "The wind is higher than I thought."

"You're not afraid?"

"For heaven's sake . . ."

Compared to a sailboat the ride was rough. The motors thumped and the hull danced on the surface of the water.

"There's none of the deep smoothness of a keel," she said. "You can feel all the surface motion."

"We haven't got a keel," Giles said practically. "And some of that motion is because this bridge is so much higher than the deck of a sailboat."

She sat very still and noticed little things, the freshly varnished trim, the new canvas covers on which she sat, the wheel pockmarked by salt.

"That isn't steel?"

"Aluminum." He nodded to the compass directly in front of him. "No steel around that."

"Of course . . . You know, I've been on this boat with you before—you remember when you took that big party up to Howards Creek; it was somebody's birthday . . ."

"Mine."

"Was it? . . . I never found out."

"It got lost," he said quietly, "in the crowd and the confusion."

"What I wanted to say was—I've been on this boat before and I didn't even notice you had a compass up here."

"One needs it."

"Of course," she said. "I just was too stupid to notice."

He regarded her carefully, eyes invisible behind sun glasses. "Sometimes things are right there and one does not see them."

"Silly, isn't it?" She settled back, legs stretched. "Lord, what a day!"

Then there was only the steady sound of the motor, the low whine of the wind, the nervous surface of the water, and every now and then, a dash of spray. She took off her glasses and closed her eyes. She thought she could feel Giles looking at her, but she did not open her eyes to be sure.

Time passed, unmarked, unnoticed. She did not care. She felt Giles move occasionally—she supposed to switch on the depth finder to check his course against the charts.

"Let me know if you need any help finding it."

"I will," softly, so that the wind almost carried the words away.

Then the engines slowed. She jerked upright.

"We are not sinking," he said.

They were in the lee of an island; she squinted and tried to recognize it. "That's Mattox Cove, isn't it?"

"Precisely . . . you do know the waters."

"I've sailed here often enough with Robert."

He swung the bow in, slowed the engines even more, flipped on the depth finder and left it on, watching the needle indicate shallower and shallower bottom.

"What are you doing here?"

"Take the wheel, will you? When I say to, push both throttles in."

He swung over the ladder. "What are you going to do?" she shouted after him.

He was already on the forward deck. "Put the anchor over."

He waited, looking down, as the bow edged closer to

shore. "Now," he said. She pushed in the red plastic tops of the throttles. He tossed the anchor away, the line falling smoothly. He payed out slowly, letting the arms catch, then secured with a quick hitch to the cleat. "Okay," he said, still not looking up. He went into the main cabin and turned off the motor.

Caroline climbed down slowly and followed him. "What on earth are we doing here?"

"Change of plan. You were asleep and I did not want to wake you."

"Damn it, Giles, what are you talking about?"

"It's a warm day, more warm than it ever is this time of year, the sun is hot, there is no wind here in the lee, so I anchored to have a drink and a swim."

"Robert will be furious."

"A sailor who has just lost his mast because he is an idiot can't complain if rescue is delayed a little while."

And Caroline shrugged. "That's so true."

He pulled off his sun glasses. "I've been plotting for years to get you all to myself on a desert island."

"Oh for heaven's sake . . . Now I wish I'd brought a suit."

"There are some in the lockers below."

"Well," she said, "you go first."

"Sure thing." He hesitated. "Is that the way the slang goes these days?"

"I don't think so. If Godfried was here, we could ask him, or I bet your boys could tell us . . ."

"Yes," he said, "yes . . . But I do not think my sons would tell me. I am a proper European father, you see. One must speak properly to me."

"Even yes sir?" Caroline teased, until she saw that he was not joking.

"I have had them speak very properly to me, always. And I have had them wear ties for dinner. I suppose they are different with their mother. Mary tells me that they are . . . "

"I don't think that American children show enough respect for their parents," Caroline suggested lamely.

"Yes?"

For a moment he seemed about to say something else. (What, Caroline wondered, what?) But instead he turned and went below.

As Caroline waited for him to change, she thought slowly: There is something wrong.

And she answered herself: Don't be so silly.

Giles came back, in bathing trunks this time, his slight, almost hairless body reflecting the sun smoothly.

"You need a tan," she said.

"You never tan."

"I don't want to."

He had a good body. Really amazingly good when you remembered his age; he must be close to fifty. No, not that old.

"I'm forty-four," he said.

She jumped guiltily. "What?"

He put his dark glasses back on. "I was twenty-three when I married Mary in 1943."

"Giles, you're a mind reader."

"No," he said. "I just know by now how the family thinks."

"Now really, Giles, stop thinking of me as the family —anyway not in that tone!"

"My apologies, madam. I have never thought of you as my sister-in-law or my brother-in-law's wife or the daughter-in-law of my mother-in-law . . . I have always thought of you as something else . . . Now go put on your bathing suit." He swung a towel to his shoulder. "While you are finding one that fits you, I will have a bit of sun on the foredeck and then we will have a swim together."

She went below and began to rummage in the lockers there. She heard his bare feet pad along the deck, check the anchor line. He began to whistle softly, a tune she did not recognize.

She found three suits that were about her size, a black and two blue prints. She thought about them for a moment, then she lifted the forward hatch which was right over her head. "Giles, are these the only suits?"

"I suppose so."

"One is new, it still has the tag."

"Somebody did not like to swim."

"And they are all bikinis."

He chuckled. "I will promise to look only in admiration."

She tried on the black, looked in the mirror, and then put on the larger of the blue prints. She pinned up her hair, decided not to wear a cap, and swung through the hatch to the deck. He opened one eye. "Giles," she said, "this is not my size."

"You have a lovely figure," he said quietly. "You should wear suits like that always."

"Robert wouldn't hear of it."

"I remember the one you had on the trip last year—for my birthday. It was greenish—with a lot of pleats."

He was right. "How on earth did you remember that?"

"I told you—I always look at you. It was a terrible suit."

"Oh don't be so silly . . . Let's swim in now."

They put the ladder over the stern and climbed down into the water. It was cold and salty and absolutely clear. Caroline shivered and puffed and then started off for the beach, easy regular crawl, keeping her head high, and her hair out of the water. Giles paced alongside, popping up and down like a gray porpoise.

It was a longish swim, and she was unused to any exertion. Her neck began to hurt from the unusual way she was carrying her head. She gave up the crawl, and rested a moment, treading.

"Are you all right?" Giles asked immediately.

"Yes," she said disgustedly. "It's just old age."

She shifted into a breast stroke, and felt better. The bra slipped to her waist and hung there. Well, stay there, she thought furiously. Just stay there.

She concentrated on the water and the motions of her body. The soft smooth flow of the water, the soft aching motions of her muscles, the labored pulse of her breathing. She was so busy with this that she swam straight into the sand shallows. Startled, she tucked her legs under her and jerked up the bra.

This early in the season the beach was empty. Later it would be rimmed with boats and echoing with the shouts of drunks and the roar of outboards.

"It's a beautiful cove," she said, and her voice was shaky and breathless.

"You *are* winded."

"I told you—I'm an old lady . . ."

"I've never known why there are not any houses on this particular island. There are on all the others."

She settled herself back against a dune and pulled a pink flower from a beach pea vine. "There used to be houses," she said, "until that big hurricane in '38. They were all washed away then, not even a foundation left. And there wasn't a single survivor—I'm not sure they ever found the bodies. It was like there never had been anything here. And nobody has ever come back."

"Ah," Giles said, "yes."

He built himself a chair of sand, scooping out the seat and building up the back. Finally he settled himself down in it, tipped back his head and closed his eyes. "The sun *is* warm . . ."

"That's a lot of trouble for a few minutes' rest . . . I just flop down on the sand."

He turned his head slightly and looked at her, but did not answer. His pale hard body gleamed with the salt water.

I shall have a terrible sunburn, Caroline thought, as she slid down, put her hands behind her head, and, closing her eyes, stretched carefully and slowly, like a cat.

Then only the speckles of the sun behind her closed lids. The small sounds of water at the rim of the sand. The far-off screech of gulls. And the smell of the beach, of all lee beaches, the sun-perfected odor of decay from useless things along the tide line, sea wrack. Of seaweed, of barnacles and sea snails left by the tide. Of tiny black mussels and white clams. Of half-empty shells of spider crabs, dropped by the gulls. She strained to hear the rattle of stone on chitin, but heard only waves and the easing wind.

Giles was sitting up, close to her. "Did you hear me?"

"No," she said, "I was thinking, I'm afraid."

"Of what?"

"The smell of beaches, mostly."

"Millions of little dead things."

"I know. The useless things . . ." She rolled over. "I'll get some sun on my back . . . Giles, these aren't Mary's suits; she's bigger than I."

"No," he said.

"You don't care if people know?"

"Know what?"

"That you're not happy with Mary?"

He chuckled. "What a puritan you are; no wonder Robert married you. Of course I am happy with Mary."

"Oh," she said. "Giles, have you ever helped Robert?"

"A change of subject!"

"I want to know. Have you ever got him a job or lent him money or put him through school or anything like that?"

He looked amused. "No, madam. Your husband is one of the members of my family who has never needed help. He is a very able man."

"And a bad sailor."

"Overeager," Giles said. "He would be a good man in a race."

"Well"—Caroline was matter-of-fact—"all he's got now is a broken mast."

Giles said abruptly: "Come back to the boat." He took her hand to help her up, held it as they waded into the water. She said nothing until they were waist deep and then she asked: "Why rush back now?"

"Because," he said quietly, "it is too difficult making

love on the sand." He pushed her off. "Now go!"

All the long swim back she thought of nothing, nothing at all beyond the slipping of the water past her body.

"Let me go first," he said at the ladder, "then I will give you a hand."

He was up quickly, leaning back over the cowling to grasp both her wrists. She put her feet on the ladder rungs and swung up. As the hot sun hit her body she realized that the bra had slipped to her waist again, but he still held her wrists and she did nothing about it.

"Aphrodite from the sea," he said lightly, "all you need is a seashell."

You are disturbed, she thought, you smooth gray and blue and white creature, you are disturbed and your voice is not steady.

She stood very quietly before him, salt water running down her naked body, cold and hot at once, water and sun. She did not make the slightest motion.

Robert has never asked for anything from you, she thought. And I will never ask either . . . It is the other way around, you will ask me.

Caroline looked over the open empty waters of the cove. "How silly we'd feel if another boat appeared."

"Sex is what boats are for."

"What your boat is for. Not everybody's."

"Yes," Giles said, handing her a folded towel. "Robert's boat would be for sailing . . . Of course it would."

Caroline shrugged. "Robert would never make love on a thin cushion on a blazing deck . . . no. He never went in for sex in the raw."

"Do you think that's what it is?" Giles was standing directly in front of her. She went on drying her arms, and then pushed him away so that she could bend over and rub the towel along her legs.

"Some people call it a tumble in the hay," she remarked to the deck. "I am going to be sunburned, for the first time in my life."

"You are a very strange woman."

"Your sister-in-law, so it's all in the family."

For one moment she thought he would slap her, but that moment passed and nothing happened. He only began to button his plaid shirt. And sat down to put on his shoes.

"I don't understand," he said. "Are you sorry?"

"No, no indeed."

They raised anchor. Caroline worked the shiny electric winch while Giles maneuvered the boat, then they were clear of the cove and running eastward.

She settled down on the flying bridge, next to him. They said nothing until the hazy shape of Boar Island appeared.

"The west end," she said. "There's plenty of water, right up to the dock there."

Giles nodded.

Abruptly she put her hand over his on the pitted aluminum wheel. "Poor Giles . . ."

"Not if I see you again."

"Poor me then."

He was looking steadily ahead, not turning. She found herself staring into the gray hair that curled behind his ear. "I never noticed that your hair was curly," she said softly. "I suppose I haven't looked."

He said, "You must." His eyes were following the coast, looking for the cove where Robert and Guppy waited.

"I expect to," she said.

He turned then, and the level blue eyes (dark and quiet now) watched.

"The anchor is still wet." Caroline nodded to it.

"Robert will not notice."

"I didn't mean that. I meant that's all there's left," Caroline said, "some weed on the anchor and some salt dried on our skin."

"There isn't ever much left, when it's done."

I know, Caroline thought. I know that. But why should it bother me.

The Householder

❦

THE BABY woke at two, stirred and chirped, the twittery nervous sound of morning birds. Without turning on a light, Nora swung herself over the edge of the bed, picked up the small limp bundle, and settled it next to her, pulling the covers over them both.

Quietly Harry listened, as he had every morning these last three weeks, ever since the child had come home. He knew every movement and every sound by now—same sounds, same order every night. The little puffs of breathing, almost like pain, when Nora roused herself: Uh, uh. Little whistles of breath, in and out, shivering in the cold room. And the soft rubbing of the sheets across his own body. The squeak of the plastic cover on the baby's mattress, as her hands slipped under the little body. She probably didn't once open her eyes, Harry thought.

"Shush, shush," she said, "take it now." It was the only thing she ever said at night. As soon as the baby fastened on the nipple, she was silent again.

It seemed to him sometimes that he could feel the tension in that fragment of flesh, feel the muscles flex and strain with the effort of sucking. He had given the child his finger once, and had been surprised by the strong pull. But then he'd been surprised at a lot of things.

He opened his eyes in the dark, but saw nothing beyond the shadowy window and the arc of the curtain across it. Nora was completely out of sight in the covers. She would be lying on her side, turned toward him, the child nuzzling into the swollen flesh. He marveled at her breasts, now heavy and blue-veined. She'd been such a slight woman with small high breasts, tight breasts that changed abruptly into bulging udders. You could almost see the milk inside them, ready to run out at the first touch. Whenever he was home he sat and watched her feed the child. "What's the matter with you?" she said. He only shook his head, not trying to explain.

Only one other thing had ever fascinated him this much. Once in the country, when he was eight or so, he had spent all of his time staring down into an open spring, stretched flat out on the tiles that surrounded it, staring down through the clear water to the stone-lined bottom where the source was.

The child was finished. Nora put it in the crib, covered it, and slipped back to bed.

She moved a lot quicker at night, he thought, than she did all day long . . . She was asleep in less than a minute. He just never seemed to fall asleep until she was finished and back under the covers. He'd never done that before the baby. In those days she could get up to read or knit, and he would not even stir. It was different now . . . My god, he thought, I'm going to be a good father. You better believe it.

He scrunched down farther in the bed, pulling his knees up to avoid the chill at the foot. Then there was just her light breathing, and the quiet cold air around his face, and the distant sound of traffic on the interstate highway. That was half a mile away, nothing but woods and grass in between. Not even cattle in the old pastures now, which were waist high with weeds. All that would be a housing development—he would be sorry when they started building and the nights were full of people sounds. He liked the quiet and the emptiness. He liked the sense of no one being near his house. Especially on nights like these, clear and starry.

An occasional truck whistled its air brakes at the interchange, then shifted three or four times as it pulled away. Some nights when he didn't sleep well, he counted the gears. Tonight there were hardly any trucks, just the occasional brush of tires, once a squeal of brakes. Little sounds with long silences between. Nights like this you could sometimes hear the trains in the switching yards way across town. When they first moved to this house, he'd taken the sounds for distant thunder, and gotten up and closed the windows against a sudden storm. It was the engines humping cars together, long strings of cars, so that the crashes rolled out on the night air, muted and hollow with distance. But not tonight. The yards did not work on Sunday. He knew their schedules now, they'd lived here almost a year. Sunday nights were quiet, just a little pulse of highway traffic. Now and then.

The heavy sleepy air was all around him, thick and gentle. So comfortable that he did not really notice the sound until he had heard it for quite a while. A different sound. He lifted his head off the pillow, just a bit, to break contact with the sleeping world. He hung his head there in mid air, until his tense muscles ached and quivered. He was awake and the sound was gone.

It hadn't been a sound anyway, he thought dully. It had been like a creak. Like a shift in the house timbers. Almost but not quite.

His heart began knocking against his ribs. There was a tremor in his fingers as if the hairs on the back of his hands were standing up. A nightmare, he thought, I'm having a nightmare.

The sound again. This time his ears pinpointed it, his mind saw it. The kitchen window. Somebody was forcing it open.

He shook his wife's shoulder. "Somebody's breaking in," he said quietly.

She always woke up slowly, and this time she did too. She lay silently rubbing her eyes. "Call the police."

"The phone's in the kitchen, honey." He spoke gently as if he had all the time in the world. "That's where he is."

She sat up, her eyes round and shiny in the half light. He reached for his robe, found a sweater and put that on. "Where'd we put the gun, Nora?"

"I don't remember . . . The bottom drawer, under the pajamas, I think."

The floor boards were cold. There was no rug in the bedroom. Nora had bought an expensive one for the living room, and they were waiting to afford another. The drawer slipped open. It works a lot better in cold weather, he thought. He felt the lump under the pajamas: the .38 Special his father had given him. He swung open the cylinder and felt for the cartridges he couldn't see in the dark. He'd never fired this gun but his father said it had a very stiff trigger. He remembered his father's always intending to have it eased.

The dull blue steel was almost invisible in his hand. He hadn't even wanted the thing, but his father insisted. "Every householder's got to have a gun." Well, he had one now, and he didn't quite know what to do with it.

He walked back to the bed, fingers curved around the trigger guard. His wife was tucking another cover over the baby. Funny, he thought, as if the burglar were going to make the house colder.

"Where'd I leave my glasses?" he whispered.

She shook her head. "I don't know."

"Well," he said, "I don't need them. I just want to give that guy the scare of his life."

She finished with the baby and stood up, waiting.

"Lock the door to the hall," he said softly, "but don't turn on the lights. I'm going out on the porch." It was a small sun deck off the bedroom. "I'm going to shoot down into the ground and yell my head off. So don't you get scared."

She nodded.

As he felt his way toward the porch there were more sounds below. Metallic sounds. What would that be?

I wish my night vision were better, he thought. But then if it were I'd have an air force commission and I'd be off flying somewhere instead of standing here freezing like a brass monkey while I try to figure out sounds.

His wife seemed to be standing in the bedroom doorway, looking down the stairs. He motioned to her silently. Why didn't she do what he asked and lock that door? It was bad enough sneaking around in the dark, without glasses, holding a gun you weren't even sure you could shoot.

And all this on the coldest night of the year, he thought. Great night for playing cops and robbers.

He turned the doorknob and nothing happened. Oh God, he thought, God Almighty. They didn't use the porch this time of year and the new paint had stuck the door closed. He shifted the gun to his left hand. He wanted to kick the door open, but instead put his shoulder to it and pushed, thumping softly to jar the paint free.

I've got to be making a hell of a lot of noise and if that guy is right below he's got to hear me . . .

He squinted through the breath-misted glass. Something moved in the side yard, across the frosty grass. Something quick, like a cat, and shadowy. Something leaving.

I scared him away, he thought. I can turn on the lights now and go down and have a cup of coffee and turn up the heat and laugh about it. How quick that guy moved, I never really did see him, never once, just his shadow. I felt him more than heard him.

But his skin went on twitching. And he knew there had to be something else. Something else.

Then he remembered. The metallic sound. That hadn't come from the kitchen directly below. It had come from the side of the house. There was a door there, into the little room they called a study.

He went on remembering. That door had a knob lock. You could put a wrench to it and twist it and it would open . . . Something like that. It had to be something like that.

So there wasn't one man, Harry thought, there were two. One is gone, but the second one didn't hear anything. He's got the door open by now and he's inside the house.

Harry's brain moved so slowly he could see it shaping the thoughts. Like stringing beads on a string. One after the other, each examined carefully and placed in its spot.

He's inside my house . . . And Nora's just standing there, she hasn't even *closed* the door. He's downstairs right now . . .

He was turning around when she screamed. Not loud, but shrill, a siren sound.

Afterward, he never could remember exactly what had happened. He was running; he noticed how numb his feet were as they pounded against the boards. He knocked over the bedroom chair, stopped to pick it up and fling it aside. It must have hit the crib because the baby began shrieking. The bedroom lights went on, but he never remembered who touched the switch. Then he was running down the stairs, shifting the gun from his left hand to his right, following the sounds. The other man made a wrong turn, missed the door, and went straight through the house. He was running too, confused and blundering in the dark. In the dining room something fell and broke. The swinging door to the kitchen fluttered and creaked.

Something heavy sailed past Harry's shoulder and smashed into a wall on his left.

He threw something at me, he thought. I almost caught him.

The thought of that closeness elated him . . . *Almost got him . . .* That and anger . . . *He's in my house, breaking my furniture!*

The other man found the kitchen door, flung it open.

Harry, still following, squinted nearsightedly into the dark yard. He saw the other man then, saw him as a blur at the far corner of the yard, couple of hundred feet away. There was a metal fence across there, fairly high. On the other side were azaleas—with just the beginning scatter of blooms this time of year—gone wild, grown taller than a man; and clumps of ligustrum and hackberry. A thick tangled cover.

For an instant the man stood perfectly still, one hand on the top of the fence, ready for the swinging leap to the other side.

Later, Harry wondered why the man had hesitated. Was he checking his directions? Looking for the second man? Catching his breath? But why do that when he was, even in his dark clothes, visible in the light from the upstairs bedroom?

Afterwards, Harry was sure he used his revolver only because he saw a still figure. He would never have fired at a running target; that was an impossible shot. But a figure stationary even for a second . . . his arm swung up and the gun fired.

He thought: I missed, I was way off. At night people aim too high. Always aim too high.

The figure rose and swung horizontally over the fence. In Harry's mind, it hung there, suspended there, a line across the fence. He fired again. As his hand squeezed closed on the now warm metal, he thought: This time I'll hit.

The figure disappeared into the bushes, down under the covering tangle. He blinked and stared but couldn't see. He tried to listen but all he heard was Nora calling: "Harry, Harry! Where are you, Harry?"

She snapped on the outside light. He squinted in the glare but still couldn't see clearly. He just couldn't manage without his glasses; he would have to go back and get them.

"Harry, you need this!" She was standing in the door, the baby in one arm, his overcoat in the other. She held the coat out to him; standing on the top step he put it on, then he went inside.

The oven door hung open. He closed it silently.

"Harry, I opened that to warm up the place a bit."

"Oh sure." He had supposed somehow that it had

come open during his dash through the room.

The kitchen window was splintered. "We'll have to fix that," he said.

"The side door will close, but it won't lock."

So she'd had time to see to that. And light the oven. He'd been outside longer than he'd thought, staring at that one spot in the brush.

"Did you see him?" he asked.

Nora shook her head.

"You started screaming."

"But I didn't see anything." The baby was asleep again. She put it down.

Shivering, he stood by the open oven. "I have to call the police," he said. "I think I hit him. I'm sure I hit him."

"I'll call them," she said, "while you get warm."

He held his hands in the open oven, feeling sensation come back with a sharp sting.

She finished with the phone and gave it a quick wipe with a dishcloth. She always did that. She liked the shiny white surface.

"You know the Lalique vase in the dining room, Harry—well, it's broken."

It was their only good wedding present. She dusted it every day and washed it carefully in ammonia every Monday morning. "I'm sorry, honey," he said, "maybe the insurance will cover it or something."

"I could hear it breaking. I knew that's what it was."

"We ran through there. I guess that's when."

"There's a wrench on the dining room floor. And a big gash on the wall."

How had she had time to see so much . . . "I'll look in just a minute, honey." If it had hit him he'd be lying on the floor now.

"The coffee's hot enough."

"Okay," he said. "Fix me a cup while I get my glasses."

He got his shoes too, and as soon as he finished the coffee, he began putting them on. He'd forgotten socks and the laces knotted; he stood up and stamped them on his feet.

"You're not going out, Harry?"

"I shot at him. I ought to go see what I did."

"Out there?" She pulled her robe tighter and walked to the kitchen window, the one with the splintered frame. "He tried to kill you, Harry."

"No. He didn't."

"He threw that wrench hard or it wouldn't have left a hole like that in the plaster. It could have killed you."

She didn't miss much, he thought. "Well, he didn't, honey."

She kept on staring at the dark outside. "There were two men, Harry, weren't they? And if you did hit one and he's still out there, he'd try to kill you again."

He shook his head stubbornly. "No."

"Or while you're out, he could sneak back here."

"With all the lights on and the police coming?"

"If he's desperate, he might." She folded her arms under her breasts tightly, as if she were holding on to herself. "I thought," she said to the night-glazed glass, "that a man wanted to protect his wife and his child."

He put down the coffee cup. That was it. Of course that was it. He couldn't leave her and the child while he went chasing shadows. He had to stay with her.

"Okay," he said.

She turned around then, still holding to her body. "I'm scared now. Just think what it would be like if you weren't here."

"I guess I'm too mad."

"Yes," she said, "I guess you are."

"Because somebody was sneaking around in my house. And because he woke me up, and I was cold. I really tried to hit him with that second shot because I was just plain mad . . . Does that make any sense to you?" he finished.

"Well," she said, "maybe." And that was her way of saying no. "You ought to have something to eat."

"The police'll be along."

She made fresh coffee. He stood at the window, looking out across the back yard, wearing his glasses, staring as hard as he could at the darkness beyond the circle of light.

"Can you see anything?" she asked.

He shook his head.

"Not even the police?"

"I don't know how long it's been since you called them. I didn't look at the clock . . . maybe I didn't hit him," he said. "I never was a good shot."

"If you wanted to hit him," she said, "you did." She said it with such certainty that he left his window to give her a hug and a kiss.

And it was then the police came. Three prowl cars parked outside the front door, four policemen and a state trooper.

"It looks like an army," she said quietly, "now that we don't need them any more."

Three policemen went through the house. "Want to be sure he isn't hiding in here somewhere."

She shivered. "I didn't think of that."

The fourth policeman and the state trooper went outside. Harry stood in the kitchen door and watched them. "There isn't any gate in the back fence," he called, his voice loud in the silent cold, "you have to jump it or go around by the side of the house."

"Go ahead, boy," the policeman said to the trooper, "jump it."

"Always got to be a comedian," the other said. They came back across the yard, right hand on holster, as rules required, left slapping thighs for warmth.

They were about the same size, and they looked pretty much alike to Harry. "What's the other side of the fence?" one called.

"Brush and there's a little spring in there," Harry said.

"A swamp," the trooper said disgustedly. "Every place I go, I got to find a swamp."

"It isn't very close to the fence," Harry said quickly.

"The ground's dry for a hundred feet the other side of the fence."

"I'll still end up in the swamp," the man said.

The others came out of the house. "Nothing in there, mister."

Harry said, "He went over the fence, one of them. I don't know where the other one went."

"We'll take a look."

"Close the door, Harry," Nora said when they were gone. "You'll freeze the baby."

"All right," he said and moved to the window.

They were on the other side of the fence. He could see the little points of their flashlights flickering in the brush. They'd be shouting to each other, but he couldn't hear anything with the window closed. He got tired standing and, not shifting his eyes, he hooked a chair with his foot, dragged it to him, and sat down.

He was trying to count the lights. There should be five, but he never could seem to see them all at once. They seemed to be keeping pretty close to the fence. He hoped they'd remember about the swamp, the water was always highest in winter. With the irregular ground you could step in before you realized where you were. He'd been down there only once—last year right after they moved in. Then the swamp was filled with sprouting yellow-green pitcher plants. They were supposed to be fly catchers, those plants. He wondered if that was true. He'd never got around to finding out.

Behind him, Nora sat down in the rocking chair that she used when she was feeding the baby. She sat quietly in it, waiting, with only an occasional creak when she shifted her weight.

After a while the state trooper came to the door. She jumped in her chair. "Oh," she said, "It's you. I'm just edgy."

The trooper came inside, slapped his hands together four or five times before he pulled off his gloves. "Cold job this time of year."

His tone is different, Harry thought. His tone is different. Not louder. No, the other way around. He's speaking perfectly quietly. But there isn't a lift to his voice, there isn't any intonation to it at all. And if he were speaking naturally there'd be something, there always is. One word wouldn't come behind the other, so neatly, so closely, one after the other, sheep jumping a fence, beads on a string.

Nora didn't seem to notice. "Would you like some coffee, officer?"

"No ma'am." He turned abruptly, his cold-reddened face showing bright blue eyes. "The man who was in the house, where did you say he was when you shot at him?"

You've found him, Harry thought. Aloud, he said, "He was standing by the fence in the back corner, right where that little azalea bush is. He must have run across the yard, after he took the wrong turn and went into the yard instead of out the side door."

"He was running when you shot?"

"Well"—Harry hesitated—"he stopped for a minute, I think. I shot and he jumped just about the same time, I guess."

"There was a lot of crashing around, and things breaking," Nora said, "when he tried to hit Harry with the wrench and smashed my vase instead."

"It happened pretty fast."

"They always do," the trooper said. "He tried to kill you with the wrench?"

Harry hesitated again, not liking the sound of those words. "Maybe he could see more than me—I don't see much in the dark and I didn't have my glasses anyway—so maybe he did mean to hit me, and I guess the wrench could have killed me."

He could see two flashlights outside, they were swinging back and forth, crossing the yard. The police were coming back. He was so busy watching them he forgot to listen.

"—if you make a formal statement," the trooper was saying. "And your wife too."

"Did I hit him? You mean I hit him?"

"You killed him," the trooper said.

The rocking chair had stopped creaking. There was just the dripping tap at the kitchen sink. Harry reached over and pressed it closed, so even that sound stopped. He could hear muffled voices outside now. They must be very close to the house; he hadn't been able to hear them before.

"I can't even see very well at night," Harry said, "that's why I couldn't be a flyer in the navy."

"It happens like that," the trooper said. "You didn't go out after him?"

"No," Harry said, "I stayed here."

"I was afraid to have him go," Nora said abruptly.

There's something different in her tone, too, Harry thought. All of a sudden everybody's different with me.

"I begged him to stay here with me."

"I'd have stayed too," the trooper said. "You got to protect your family."

Harry asked: "Why did you want to know if I'd gone out? Would it have made a difference?"

"We were a long time getting here," the trooper said. "The town didn't have a unit to send and by the time they got around to calling headquarters and headquarters got me, I was way over by the county line on Dowman Road. Must have taken us near an hour to get here."

"It was pretty long."

"You never know. You probably couldn't even have carried him out of the brush, not alone."

"We don't have any near neighbors," Nora said. "No one to help."

"I don't know how I hit him," Harry said. "I haven't fired a gun in years."

The other police hadn't come into the house at all, they must have gone around to their cars. Nora and the trooper seemed to be talking, but Harry didn't listen. There was a funny shaking in the middle of his chest and he concentrated on that. Nora touched his arm. "You're supposed to sign this, Harry." Not reading it, he did.

"One unit'll stay," the trooper said. "You might see

their lights out there, so don't worry about it."

He began pulling his gloves back on. "One of the men thinks he recognized him. He was a kid out on bail from Winn County. Looks like he went back to work too soon."

"I'm not that good a shot," Harry said. "I never have been."

"You were just lucky," the trooper said. "Happens like that. People make lucky shots all the time."

Harry did not notice when he left. But when he looked around again, the trooper was gone. The room seemed extra quiet and very empty. It was getting warm now too. He could feel beads of sweat in the creases of his neck. He poured himself a cup of coffee. He didn't really want it, but he couldn't think of anything else, and he wanted to be doing something. He wanted his hands to keep moving.

"What are we going to do about locking the door?" Nora asked. She was still sitting in the rocker; she had begun to move it lazily back and forth.

The side door, where the lock was wrenched open. "I'll fix it tonight after work."

"When you've finished with the police, you're going to work?"

"Yes," he said, "this time of year, I got to be there."

"I'll be scared here alone."

"Go by your mother's and I'll pick you up at five-thirty."

The rocker creaked some more. "No," she said, "I'll stay. If you've got a house you got to look out for it."

I did, he thought. I sure did.

"You don't feel bad about not going after him?" she said. "You can't."

"No," he said, "I had to stay with you."

"You heard what the trooper said. You couldn't leave the baby."

The coffee was much too hot. It was scalding his lips. He put it down abruptly, so that it clattered on the counter, and grabbed some butter out of the refrigerator.

"What, what," she was asking, "what happened?"

He didn't answer. Just went on smearing the butter over his aching lips, until the soft cool grease had relieved the pain.

"It's almost daylight," he said. "We'll feel better when it gets light."

He sat down on one of the stools at the counter and waited. It would be a while yet. Though he didn't want to, he began thinking. At first he pushed the thoughts away, but then he stopped and let them come.

I didn't even see him, not real clear. But I pulled the trigger, and I meant to kill. He'd been in my house, and my wife was screaming, and I was mad. He shouldn't have been in my house . . .

"You had a right," his wife said, "you had a perfect right."

She could almost read his mind. Almost, but not quite.

It was a question of the cost . . .

"You were protecting your home," his wife said, "you have to do that."

Householder, that was his father's word for it. When he gave him the gun.

I ought to call him and tell him, he thought.

He'd started for the phone when he changed his mind. He was a grown man and he didn't go calling up his daddy.

His wife was looking at him; her face, already thin and pale from the baby, was more gaunt and blue-tinged than usual. He pulled his lips into a smile. "It's all right, honey. Maybe we can even go back to sleep for a while."

And he sat back down at the counter, hooking his legs around the stool's chrome legs. He stared out the window pretending he could see something more than the reflection of his own face.

Homecoming

❦

THE TELEGRAM was in the middle of the dining room table. It was leaning against the cut-glass bowl that sometimes held oranges, only this week nobody had bought any. There was just the empty bowl, lightly dust coated and flecked with orange oil. And the telegram.

"Did you have to put it there?" Susan asked her mother.

"It's nothing to be ashamed of," her mother said.

"I'm not ashamed," she said, "but why did you put it there?"

"It's something to be proud of."

"It looks just like a sign."

"People will want to see it," her mother said.

"Yes," Susan said, "I guess they will."

She took her time dressing, deliberately. Twice her mother called up the stairs, "Susan, hurry. I told people any time after three o'clock."

And they were prompt, some of them anyway. (How many had her mother asked? She'd been such a long time on the phone this morning . . .) Susan heard them come, heard their voices echo in the high-ceilinged hall, heard the boards creak with unaccustomed weight. She could follow their movements in the sounds of the old boards. As clearly as if she were looking at them, she knew that the women had stayed inside and the men had moved to the porches.

Wide porches ran completely around two sides of the house, south and west. "Porches are best in old houses like this," her mother often said. "Good, useful porches."

The west porch was the morning porch. Its deep over-hang kept off the sun even in these July afternoons. There was a little fringe of moonflower vine too, across the eaves, like lace on a doily. The big white moonflowers opened each night like white stars and each morning, like squashed bugs, dropped to the ground. They were trained so carefully on little concealed wires up there that they never once littered the porch . . . The south porch was the winter porch. The slanted winter sun always reached that side, bare and clear, no vines, no planting. A porch for old people. Where the winter sun could warm their thin blood, and send it pumping through knotty blue veins. Her grandmother sat out there, sightless in the sun, all one winter. Every good day, every afternoon until she died . . .

Susan always thought one porch was much bigger until she measured them—carefully, on hands and knees, with a tape measure. How funny, she thought; they seemed so different to be just the same.

On this particular afternoon, as Susan came downstairs —slowly, reluctantly, hesitating at each step—she glanced toward the sound of men's voices on the south porch. Looking through the screen into the light, she saw no faces, just the glaring dazzle of white shirts. She heard the little rattle of ice in their glasses and she smelled the faint musty sweet odor of bourbon.

Like a wake, she thought. Exactly like a wake.

Her mother called: "In the dining room, dear."

There was coffee on the table, and an ice bucket and a

bottle of sherry and two bottles of bourbon. "Come in, Susan," her mother said. "The girls are here to see you."

Of course, Susan thought. They had to be first, her mother's best friends, Mrs. Benson and Mrs. Watkins, each holding a sherry glass. Each kissed her, each with a puff of faint flower scent from the folds of their flowered dresses. "We are so sorry, Susan," they said one after the other.

Susan started to say thank you and then decided to say nothing.

Mrs. Benson peered over her sherry glass at the telegram propped on the table next to the good silver coffee-pot. "I thought the Defense Department sent them," she said, "that's what I always heard."

Susan's mother said emphatically, her light voice straining over the words, just the way it always did: "They sent me one for my husband."

"That's right." Mrs. Watkins nodded. "I saw it just now when I came in. Right under the steps in the hall. In that little gold frame."

"When I read that telegram," Susan's mother said, "I got a pain in my heart that I never got rid of. I carried that pain in my heart from that day to this."

And Susan said, patiently explaining: "The army told Harold's parents."

"And the Carters sent word to you," her mother said firmly. Her hand with its broad wedding band flapped in the air. "There on the table, that's the word they sent."

All of a sudden Susan's black dress was too hot and too tight. She was perspiring all over it. She would ruin it, and it was her good dress.

"I'm so hot," she said. "I've got to change to something lighter."

Her mother followed her upstairs. "You're upset," she said, "but you've got to control yourself."

"The way you controlled yourself," Susan said.

"You're mocking now, but that's what I mean. I had

to control myself, and I've learned."

"I've nothing to control," Susan said. She stripped off the black dress. The wet fabric stuck and she jerked it free. Close to her ear, a couple of threads gave a little screeching rip. "I've got to find something lighter. It's god-awfully hot down there."

"White," her mother said. "White would be correct."

Susan looked at her, shrugged, and took a white piqué out of the closet.

"Are you all right?"

"I'm fine," Susan said, "I'm great."

She put the white piqué dress across a chair and sat down on her bed. Its springs squeaked gently. She stretched out and stared up at the crocheted tester and felt her sweat-moistened skin turn cool in the air. She pulled her slip and her bra down to her waist and lay perfectly still.

Abruptly she thought: If there were a camera right over me, it would take a picture of five eyes: the two in my head, the one in my navel, and the two on my breasts. Five eyes staring up at the ceiling.

She rolled over on her stomach.

It was a foolish thing to think. Very foolish. She never seemed to have the proper thoughts or feelings. Her mother now, she had the right thoughts, everybody knew they were right. But Susan didn't . . .

Like now. She ought to be more upset now. She ought to be in tears over the telegram. She'd found it stuck in the crack of the door this morning. "Have been informed Harold was killed at Quang Tri last Thursday." She should have felt something. When her mother got the news of her father's death in Korea, the neighbors said you could hear her scream for a block; they found her huddled on the floor, stretched out flat and small as she could be with the bulging womb that held an almost completed baby named Susan.

Susan lifted her head and looked at the picture on her night table. It was a colored photograph of her father, the same one her mother had painted into a portrait to hang over the living room fireplace. Susan used to spend hours staring into that small frame, trying to sharpen the fuzzy colored lines into the shape of a man. She'd never been quite able to do that; the only definite thing she knew about him was the sharp white lines of his grave marker in Arlington.

"That picture looks just exactly like him," her mother would say. "I almost think he'll speak to me. I'm so glad you can know what your father looked like."

And Susan never said: I still don't know. I never will.

And this whole thing now, her mourning for Harold, it was wrong. All wrong. She hadn't even known him very well. He was just a nice boy from school, a tall thin boy who worked in the A & P on Saturdays and liked to play pool on Sundays, who had a clear light tenor and sang solo parts with her in the glee club. His father worked for the telephone company and they lived on the other side of town on Millwood Street—she knew that much. He'd finished high school a year ago and he'd asked her to his senior prom, though she hadn't expected him to. On the way home, he offered her his class ring. "You can take it," he said. She could see his long narrow head in the light from the porch. "Till I get out of the army."

"Or some other girl wants it."

"Yeah."

Because she couldn't think of anything else, she said: "Okay, I'll keep it for you. If you want it, just write and I'll send it to you."

That was how she got the ring. She never wore it, and he didn't ask for it back. She didn't even see him again. His family moved away to the north part of the state, to Laurel, and Harold went there on his leaves. He didn't come back to town and he didn't call her. He did send a chain to wear the ring on—it was far too big for her finger—from California. She wrote him a thank-you note the very same day. But he didn't answer, and the ring and the chain hung on the back of her dresser mirror. He was just a boy she knew who went in the army. He was just a boy whose ring she was keeping.

Maybe he'd told his parents something more. Why else would they wire her? And what had he told them? All of a sudden there were things she couldn't ask. The world had changed while she wasn't looking.

And Harold Carter was killed. Harold was the name of an English king, and he was killed somewhere too. Now there was another Harold dead. How many had there been in between? Thousands of Harolds, thousands of different battles . . .

Her mother opened the door so quickly it slipped from her hand and smashed into the wall. The dresser mirror shivered and the class ring swung gently on its chain. "Susan, I thought, I just thought of something . . ."

What, Susan asked silently. Did you forget the extra ice? Something like that? Will people have to have warm drinks?

"You're acting very strangely. I've never seen you act like this . . . Did something go on that shouldn't have? Tell me."

Susan tossed a hairbrush from hand to hand. "Maybe it's me," she said, "but I just don't know what people are talking about any more."

"All right," her mother said, "you make me put it this way. Are you going to have a baby?"

Susan stared at the broken edges of the bristles, and she began to giggle. "Harold left a year ago, Mother."

"Oh," her mother said, "oh oh oh." And she backed out the door.

Susan said after her, sending her words along the empty hall where there was nobody to hear them: "That was you who was pregnant. And it was another war."

She put on some more perfume; her flushed skin burned at its touch. She glanced again at the photograph of her father.

You look kind of frozen there. But then I guess you

really are. Frozen at twenty-three. Smile and crooked cap and all.

And Susan remembered her grandmother sitting on the porch in the sun, eyes hooded like a bird's, fingers like birds' claws. Senility that came and went, like a shade going up and down. "He don't look nothing like the pictures," she said. She always called her dead son-in-law he, never used his name. "Never looked like that, not dead, not alive." The one hand that was not paralyzed waved at an invisible fly. "Died and went to glory, that boy. Those pictures your mother likes, they're pictures of him in glory. Nothing more nor less than glory."

The old woman was dead now too. There weren't any pictures of her. She'd gone on so long she fell apart, inch by inch of skin. All the dissolution visible outside the grave . . .

Susan breathed on the glass front of her father's picture and polished it with the hem of her slip. The young glorious dead . . . like Harold. Only she didn't have a picture of Harold. And she didn't really remember what he looked like.

She could hear the creak of cane rockers on the porch, the soft mumbling of men's talk. She stood by the screen to listen.

"I'll tell you." Harry Benson, the druggist, was sitting in the big chair, the one with the fancy scrolled back. "They called us an amphibious unit and put us ashore and they forgot about us. Two weeks with nothing to do but keep alive on that beach."

That would be Okinawa. She had heard about his Okinawa.

"And after a while some of the guys got nervous. If they found a Jap still alive they'd work him over good, shoot him seven or eight times, just to see him jump. They kind of thought it was fun, I guess."

"Hold it a minute, Harry," Ed Watkins, who was the railroad agent, said. "Here's Susan."

They both stood up. They'd never done that before.

"We were talking about our wars, honey," Mr. Benson said. "I'm afraid we were."

"That's all right," Susan said. "I don't mind."

"It was crazy, plain crazy," Mr. Watkins said. "Like that guy, must have been '51 or '52."

"Ed, look," Mr. Benson said. "Maybe we ought to stop talking about this."

"Nothing so bad . . . This guy, I don't think I ever knew his name, he was just another guy. And in those days you remember how they came down in waves from the North. You could hear them miles away, yelling and blowing horns. So, this time, you could hear them like always, and this guy, the one I didn't know a name for, he puts a pistol right under his jaw and blows the top of his head off. The sergeant just looked at him, and all he can say is, 'Jesus Christ, that son of a bitch bled all over my gun.'"

"Hard to believe things like that now," Mr. Benson said.

"I believe them," Susan said. "Excuse me, I have something to do in the kitchen."

She had to pass through the dining room. Mrs. Benson still had a sherry glass in her hand, her cheeks were getting flushed and her eyes were very bright. Mrs. Watkins had switched from sherry to whiskey and was putting more ice in her highball. Susan's mother poured herself coffee.

Susan thought: Mrs. Benson's going to have an awful sherry hangover and Mrs. Watkins' ulcer is going to start hurting from the whiskey and my mother's drunk about twenty cups of coffee today and that's going to make her sick . . .

She only said, "I'm just passing through."

But she found herself stopping to look at the telegram. At the shape of the letters and the way they went on the page. At the way it was signed: "Mr. and Mrs. Carter." She thought again how strange that was. They were both big hearty people—"Call me Mike," Mr.

Carter said to all the kids. "We're Mike and Ida here."
Now all of a sudden they were formal.

Like a wedding invitation, Susan thought suddenly.
Only just the opposite.

She reached out and touched the paper. It crackled
slightly under her fingers. She went on rubbing her thumb
across the almost smooth surface, watching the sweat of
her skin begin to stain the yellow paper. A little stain, a
little mark, but one that would grow if she kept at it.

That was the end of Harold Carter, she thought. He
ended in the crisp, crunchy feel of a piece of paper. A tall
thin boy who'd taken her to a dance and given her a
ring that was too big for her. All that was left of him was
a piece of paper.

She'd send the ring back to his parents. Maybe they'd
like to have it.

Or maybe they'd rather she kept it. But keeping it
would be keeping him. All of a sudden she saw the
ring hanging on the side of her dresser mirror, and she
looked into its blue stone and way down in its synthetic
depths she saw a tiny little Harold, germ-sized and far
away. As she looked he winked out.

She put the telegram down. "I really was just going
to the kitchen."

"You're not wearing your ring," Mrs. Watkins said.

"No," she said, "no, I never did wear it."

"You must be so upset." Mrs. Benson sipped delicately
at the edge of the yellow sherry. "Just like your poor
mother."

"I wasn't married to him," Susan said, "it's different."

Her mother was standing next to her, hand on her
shoulder. "You would have married him."

"No," Susan said, "no, I don't think so."

"Of course you would have." Her mother was firm.
"Why else would he have given you the ring?"

Susan started to say: Because he didn't have anybody
else to give it to and he couldn't give it to his mother.

Her mother went on patting her shoulder. "We should
be proud of them, Susan. Harold was a fine young man."

Was he? She didn't have the heart to say that aloud either. Did he shoot people to see them squirm? Did he pull the trigger against his own head with fear?

"The young men are so heroic," her mother said. The two women murmured consent. Her mother would know; her mother had lost a husband in a war, she would know.

All the brave young men that die in their glory, Susan thought. And leave rings to girls they hardly knew, and pictures on mantels in houses where they never lived. Rings that don't fit and pictures that don't resemble them.

"Harold was an English king," she said aloud.

"Yes, dear," her mother said patiently. "That's history."

Harold Carter didn't get to sit on porches and remember, the way Watkins and Benson were doing now. He hadn't got to do anything, except go to high school and die. But then, you didn't really know that either, Susan thought. You really didn't know what he did out there, what memories he might have brought back inside his head.

Mrs. Watkins repeated, "All the young men are so brave."

"No," Susan said abruptly. "Not my father, and not Harold. They weren't brave, they just got caught."

In the silence she could hear the soft wheeze of their astonished breaths, and, as she turned, the creek of old boards under her heel. "They don't die in glory." The words came out sounding like her speech at the Senior Debating Society. "They just die dead. Anyway, I was on my way to fix a cup of tea."

Nobody followed her to the kitchen, just the little ribbon of sound from her high heels on the bare boards and the linoleum. She flipped on the fire under the kettle, decided it would take too long and began to heat some water in a pan. Her feet hurt; she kicked off her shoes. The water warmed and she poured it over the instant tea. There were no lemons in the refrigerator; she remembered suddenly that there weren't any oranges on the dining room table either, that today had been marketing day and nobody had gone.

She put sugar in the tea and tasted it. It was barely warm and nasty, salty almost. She'd forgotten to rinse the dishes again. She would drink it anyway, while she made another proper cup. She put the flame back under the kettle. She pushed open the screen door and went out on the kitchen porch.

It was very small, just wide enough for one person to pass between the railing and the garbage can that always stood there. She'd often argued with her mother over that. "Put it in the yard, it just brings flies into the house." "A clean can," her mother said, "does not attract flies." And the can stayed.

She sat down on the railing, wondering if it would leave a stripe on her white dress. She decided she didn't care. She sipped the cold tea and stared out into the back yard, at the sweet peas growing along the wire fence, at the yellow painted boards on the house next door.

She was still staring over there, not seeing anything in particular, not thinking anything at all, when Mr. Benson came around the corner of the house. He walked across the back yard and stopped, finally, one foot on the bottom step.

"You left the girls in quite a state back there," he said.

So they had rushed to the porch to tell the men . . . Susan didn't take her eyes off the sweet peas, the soft gentle colors of the sweet peas. "They get upset real easy."

"I reckon they do," he said, "and they quiet down real easy too."

She began to swing her leg slowly. I shouldn't have left my shoes in the kitchen, she thought. I'll ruin my stockings out here.

"I take it he wasn't even a very good friend of yours," Mr. Benson said.

"You'd take it right." Because that sounded rude, she added quickly: "Nobody understands that. He was just a boy I knew."

"Shouldn't be so hard to understand."

"It's like a wake in there, and that's silly."

"Well," Mr. Benson said, "he was nineteen and maybe when it's somebody that young, you don't even have to know him to mourn after him."

"He was twenty." Susan looked at Mr. Benson then, the short stocky man, with a fringe of black hair around his ears and a sweaty pink skull shining in the heat. His eyes, buried in folds of puffy skin, were small sharp points of blue. My father might have looked like that, she thought.

"Twenty's still pretty young," he said.

"This whole thing is my mother. The minute she saw the telegram all she could think of is how history is repeating itself. She's called everybody, even people she doesn't like."

"I know your mother," Mr. Benson said.

"And that dying in glory talk." Susan hopped off the railing and leaned against it, palms pressing the rough wood. "That's all I ever hear. My mother knows those stories—the ones you were telling on the porch—she knows it's awful and stupid and terrible."

"No," Mr. Benson said, "it isn't awful." He pulled a cigarette holder from his pocket and began to suck it. "I gave up smoking and this is all I got left . . . You're wrong, child, but maybe the stories don't say it clear enough."

Susan said slowly, "You talk about it all the time, any time."

He nodded slowly and the empty cigarette holder whistled in the hot afternoon air. "Because it was the most glorious thing ever happened to us."

"Too bad you can't tell Harold," she said.

"Take Harold now." Mr. Benson's voice was dull and monotonous, singsonging in the heat. "He didn't have to join up right out of high school. Draft calls have been pretty low around here lately."

"He knew he was going to have to, that's why."

"It don't happen like that." He blew through the cigarette holder again, then tapped it on his palm. "Always seemed to me like men have got to have their war. I had to have mine twenty-five years ago. When you're in it, maybe it's different, but you got to go. Once you hear about it, you got to go to it."

"That doesn't make any sense to me," Susan said. "None."

"Even when you're in it, you know that if you live, you're going to remember it all the rest of your life. And you know that if there was another war and you were young enough, you'd go again."

"That's stupid," Susan said.

"Maybe. You forget places you've been and you forget women you had, but you don't forget fighting."

Behind her the tea kettle gave a shriek. He glanced up. "Sounds like your water is boiling."

"Yes," she said, "I'll see to it."

He nodded and walked away, leaving a light smell of bourbon behind him. He turned once, lifted his hands, palms up in a little shrugging gesture.

She made her tea. As if she were obeying a set of rules. Things were beginning to feel less strange to her. Even the talk about Harold didn't seem as silly as it had.

I'm beginning not to mind, she thought, but it's still all mixed up. He was the sort of boy I could have married, but I didn't even know him. And that's lucky for me. Otherwise I might be like my mother. His being dead doesn't really change anything for me. I'll get married after a while to somebody as good as him or even better . . .

She drank her tea slowly; she was sad and happy at once. Harold was a young man who had died. He didn't leave a memory behind, he didn't leave anything. He was just gone and there wasn't even a mark at the place where he had been.

Her mother stood in the door. "Do you feel well enough to come back in, child?' '

Susan chuckled, a quiet little self-contented chuckle.

"Whatever is funny, child?"

"You're having such a good time, Mother, you haven't had such a good time in ages."

"Well, really."

"You're alive and I'm alive and Harold's not alive."

"That's horrible."

"Sure."

She followed her mother across the waxed linoleum. "Wait, I've got to put my shoes on."

There just isn't anything, she thought. I'm sorry, Harold. I hope it wasn't too bad and I hope it didn't hurt too much. You and my father. I bet your parents have your picture on the mantel too.

Her shoes were on now and she straightened up.

"Good-by," she said in a very light whisper. "You poor bastard."

And she went inside to join the people.

The Patriarch

I, EDWARD MILTON HENLEY, was born eighty-eight years ago in the front bedroom of my family's five-story townhouse. There was great jubilation among the Irish servants: it meant whiskey and extra money for all of them. My mother, who'd borne a daughter six years previously, was reported to have whispered, "Thank God it's a boy, I won't have to do that again." Even my father must have been elated far beyond his usual stoical dignity. He promptly transferred to me (three days after my birth and some months before my christening) half of the family shares of railroad stock. It was a splendid gesture.

Their celebrations completed, they left me to endure through the ten years of my childhood.

In those days, our part of the city was a pleasant, clean place—narrow brick-fronted houses, plane trees growing in islands in the cobblestoned streets, cool parks where wicker governess carts with their cargo of silent, velvet-dressed children rolled through the heavy greenness. At night policemen walked their beats, sticks echoing hollow through the properly empty streets.

Our ways too were orderly and proper. Every May

we closed the house and went to the country. My father moved to his club; he would come later, in August, to spend two months with us. My mother, the children, and an assortment of servants took the train to our farm near Lancaster.

The farm itself was prosperous and well run, its manager a thin, hard-faced German who rarely spoke to anyone. But our life in the summer had nothing to do with farming or with him.

We lived in the Great House. So it was called: a huge, pretentious place (built by my maternal grandfather), vaguely Palladian, with many Gothic touches. Like the Great Lantern. It dangled from the arched dimness of the entrance hall—a huge tin lantern, pagoda-shaped, paneled around its sides with colored glass. Each dusk the house staff hung a series of kerosene lanterns within it. Light sprayed upward, like flower stalks from a vase. The glass panels threw down pools of green and red and blue light, a sifting of strange petals to the rugs below. Later, as the upper air heated, the lantern shivered, then swung in slow circles, while solemnly dressed people sat at my parents' long dining table and ponderously ate their accustomed dinner. Later still, when the ladies had twittered their way upstairs with a rush and rustle of skirts, men's laughter shook the dining room door and smoke from their cigars hung like banners from the eaves of the tin pagoda.

I never tired, evening after evening, of watching the shimmering display of lights in the gloom.

I've remembered all these years, and at the strangest times. When my second wife, Eleanor, was dressed for the opera one evening: "My dear, you remind me of a chandelier. All those colored stones like flashing lights."

I meant it rather kindly, but she was not impressed.

I can't claim Eleanor as a mistake of my youth; I was thirty-two when we married. She was plump even then, or so I seem to remember. At the end of a marriage it is difficult to recall the beginning. In ten years, oh, how she grew, how she puffed, how she threatened to fill my world. Her elaborate jewelry, reflecting her family's garish taste, rested on flesh as soft as lard and very nearly the same color. The only piece I'd ever given her, an extraordinary cat's-eye pendant, she often wore—poor soul, no doubt she thought to please me. But, alas, on her the stone lost its terrible animal gleam. It lay horizontally on her breasts, offered to me, the good husband, for all the world like a fried egg on a plate.

But it was her arms that most disturbed me, those perfect rounds of skin, so soft, so delicate that even bracelets bruised them.

As a relief from Eleanor, I found Guido O'Connor. Of course his name wasn't Guido, it was probably something like James or Sean, but he would never tell me. He was twenty, dark-haired and green-eyed. He was short and slight, very hard and very angular. His arms were ropy with muscle, his legs distorted with sinew. He was exactly what I needed after ten years of drowning in Eleanor.

Guido moved into the house as my valet, and Eleanor left in a rage. He was with me for less than a year, a foolish time for me. Men are not my taste at all. I've had only three or four in my whole long life, and Guido certainly was the worst. He knew nothing about the care of clothes and did not choose to learn. Eventually I tired of badly pressed suits, muddy shoes. Even those muscular arms, hairless as a woman's, no longer moved me greatly. Guido left.

I saw him only once, some four or five years later. He said he was having trouble finding a job and he needed money. Since it was then the middle of the depression, I thought he was quite probably telling the truth, so I gave him the money. He was surly and insulting about taking it, but of course he did.

All of that—all the two-legged annoyances who have passed through my bed—was years away from the small boy who sat and watched cigar smoke curl around the hall lantern.

I grew up alone, but I wasn't an only child. There was

my older sister, Priscilla, who became a beautiful woman and married a well-mannered and very rich man from Chicago. They did nothing unusual in their entire lives, except sail on the *Titanic*. And drown.

My sister's death affected me greatly. (A selfish feeling, I am sure.) The hand of God had struck close to me. I could smell the chilly ozone of eternity.

I decided to strike back; I fathered a child. A conventional thing to do, of course. Matter of fact, I was delighted to find I was so basically conventional—it is a pleasure to discover something unknown and unsuspected in oneself.

But I digress.

If, as a child, I often forgot I had a sister, so my parents often forgot they had a son. When my father's glance fell on me—when, say, he looked up from his croquet game (he was a great player, starkly handsome in his white flannels)—he would frown slightly, as if he were having trouble identifying me. I look exactly like him, and that perhaps was the trouble. It must have been like seeing himself through the wrong end of a telescope. "Oh yes," he would say finally with great effort, "it's you, Edward Milton . . ."

He always used my full name. My mother, on the other hand, would call me only Edward. "Milton," she said, "is such a dreadful name. If only your father hadn't read 'Paradise Lost' that year."

I was never aware of my father reading anything at all. Though I often spent rainy afternoons searching through the house I never found his copy. Well, as good a reason for a name as any other. And I have kept it all these years. Occasionally, even, my cards have read E. Milton Henley. One brash young man in the American consulate in London actually called me Miltie. Though he was at least half my age, I swung my umbrella, hooked it around his neck, and gave a sharp tug. He hit his face on the desk in front of him. After people had stopped being frantic at the sight of a little blood, I explained to him that I could not tolerate disrespect to the name of a great poet. His lip was so swollen he could hardly disagree.

In my tenth year, I finally managed to attract my parents' attention: I got very sick with brain fever.

It was May. We were ready to leave for the country. My father had moved to his club, my mother was finishing the last of her arrangements—she was a compulsively good housekeeper. The house was almost closed, and we were already officially out of town: no one would call on us now. I, who had been feeling terrible for some time, simply collapsed.

First my mother raged at the maids: in taking up the carpets, in packing our summer trunks, they had obviously released a noxious dust. Then she turned her attention to me; she closed my windows tight, hung curtains across them so that no harmful street airs could enter. The floor of my room was stripped of its rug and strewn with pine needles, fresh every other day, to dispel the dangerous miasma.

Nothing worked. I got sicker and sicker. At times it seemed I was floating in the air, at other times I was swimming. But the air was pleasant and the sea was warm, and I did not care. I talked constantly, my words complete gibberish. "The gift of tongues," my mother said. I can still hear the awe in her voice. She was, I suppose, in the midst of one of her religious revivals. She even brought my father to listen: "The gift of tongues!" I don't remember what he said. If he said anything. If indeed he remembered who the boy in the bed was.

The doctors (there were any number of them, they always arrived in pairs) told my mother that I was dying. I heard them.

That would be unthinkable today, but then—before the turn of the century—death was an expected thing. Children died, poor ones and rich ones, and they died of all sorts of different maladies. The only important thing was to prepare the soul for paradise.

Therefore, because they were responsible men, the doctors announced my impending departure for eternity.

I wasn't upset. After all, one of my recurring dreams was of already being dead. And from fact to dream and back again didn't seem particularly horrible. As for my mother, perhaps she shed a few prayerful tears, I don't know. But I do know what else she did. She called all the maids together and had them reopen the summer-stripped double parlors, wax the floors, put down the formal rugs, so the house would be ready for my wake. My room was over the parlors, I could hear the thumps of moving furniture, and my mother's steady barrage of instructions. It was, oddly enough, rather comforting.

Weeks later, when it was clear that I would live, the whole process was repeated in reverse. Thumps and thuds and constant commands meant that the funeral formality was coming up and summer mats and slip covers going down.

In any case, thinking about my funeral had started my parents thinking about my future. And so my education began. It started with three years in Paris, in the house of an ancient cousin and her equally ancient house-keeper, three years when my greatest excitement was watching balloons in the park. Finally, I caught a heavy February cold; my cousin immediately diagnosed it as tuberculosis and sent me to Switzerland. She'd had quite enough of me by then. I was growing up, and with her perennial visions of rape she was afraid to have a young male under her roof.

After Switzerland came England, after England, Germany. I grew tall and attractive, at least so women told me. I drank and traveled, considered acquiring a dueling scar and decided against it. My best friend, a Berliner named Ernst, had such a mark. Though it was almost a year old, it was still a liver-colored streak across his cheek. He was killed in 1915, and I often wonder if his scar ever faded to the pale distinction he wanted so very much.

I was in Europe, one place or the other, for some ten years. My sister was a very diligent correspondent; she even visited me. My parents, I suspect, simply forgot about me again. My allowance and all my extra expenses were automatically handled by my father's office. His letters sounded so completely unlike him that I suspect he merely delegated somebody in the office to "write a letter to my son" the first week of every month. My mother wrote even less frequently, and her letters were mostly newspaper clippings. I suppose that was easier than thinking of something to say to a son you can't remember.

(Perhaps I am just easy to forget. I myself have had periods of difficulty remembering who I am. Not factually, of course. I could always recite my name and current address. But there have been times when I did not feel like my name. Times when it took an effort of will to wrap my identity around me, to put flesh on the bones, skin on the skull.)

When my father died, my mother actually forgot to cable me. Discreetly my sister notified me. Her letter arrived the day before her cable announcing our mother's death (she'd survived her husband by only three weeks) and asking me to come home.

On the boat—the old *Majestic*, how clearly I remember —I met the young woman who became my first wife. Her name was Abigail and her father was "in cattle" in California. He had constant losses and was always badgering me for a loan. Still, Abigail and I stayed together for some ten years, no doubt out of mutual boredom. The one serious and finally fatal disagreement we had was over my son.

As I've said, I produced him very shortly after my sister's death. Though I'd been married only a few years, I knew I wanted a child with no attachment to any of my wives—even then I could predict a series of them. I selected an Irish girl, of no importance whatever, and paid her very well for her trouble incubating my child. She seemed delighted with the whole arrangement. My only requirement was that she disappear completely, and so she did. I bought her ticket to Pittsburgh and I presume that is where she went.

The boy I named Anthony and set up with nurses in

my house, intending to adopt him at once. My wife would not hear of it: she possessed the firm resolve of all very stupid people. The boy continued to live with me as my son in spite of his clouded legal status.

My second wife, Eleanor, was delighted to cooperate. (My wives are all most docile in the first three years of marriage; after that they become stubborn and opinionated.) She was genuinely fond of the boy; her maternal instincts were strong. She practically begged me to begin adoption proceedings. I did so the second day after our wedding.

Anthony was a quiet, self-contained child, perhaps because of those early years spent with my first wife. She had never been abusive toward him, but she had hardly been cordial either. The child could scarcely not be affected, though I myself tried hard to amuse him. One year he was infatuated with horses, so I bought him four ponies, beautifully matched roans. He considered them gravely, said thank you properly and without any warmth. To this day I don't know if he really liked them. And then the monkeys. For his tenth birthday, Eleanor and I built a large greenhouse as a tropical jungle for two pet monkeys. Anthony was often there, watching, playing with them. But so carefully, so gravely. As if he were afraid of breaking a single flower or bruising a single leaf.

My friends congratulated me on Anthony—I myself was never so sure. He was an excellent student, a calm, rational boy who refused to take part in prep-school athletics. "I cannot agree with the concept of an all-around man," he wrote me. "If I have only so much physical energy, I do not choose to dissipate it racing around a frozen muddy field." His school, impressed perhaps by the fact that he was the first serious Greek scholar they had had in a hundred years, agreed with him.

He wrote long letters to me—serious, well-reasoned discussions of subjects that interested him. There were no personal details at all.

Obviously he would never join me in business. (And perhaps that was lucky; I am as much a loner, in my way, as is Anthony.) With his passion for classical languages, his quiet, studious ways, I assumed that he would settle into a dusty chair at some university. I was not prepared for the letter that announced, in his last year of college, that he was entering the Unitarian ministry.

I took the next train to Princeton, my arguments ready. I was not objecting to the ministry itself—as a matter of fact I am devoted to fancy Episcopalian services.

"Anthony," I said, "if you must hear the call, why don't you hear it from a respectable church? Does it have to be Unitarian?"

Anthony smiled and said nothing. Only a slight clouding of his dark eyes told me that I had offended him.

I did not mean to. But would he know that?

In due course my son married and produced two children. A wretched number. I once told his wife that to have two children was the sobbing end of shabby gentility. "Father,"—she insisted on calling me by that name. Once I objected and she said: Shall I call you Mr. Henley? So Father it was for lack of anything else. English is a very limited language—"Father, we have two children because we can afford two children."

So it was simply a matter of money. I looked up my son's income, the bits and pieces of things he had been given on birthdays and Christmases in his childhood. It did not amount to very much. The salary from his church was even less.

So I had my lawyers transfer a block of five thousand shares of Potomac Electric to my son. It would pay well enough, I thought, to add another child to his household.

My gift went to them by messenger. And came back by messenger within a few hours.

That was my son. And his wife. And their two children.

I scarcely spoke to them for years afterward. I loathe that kind of righteousness. Also, I was unusually busy with a new interest. And a new woman. I was now a publisher of lavishly expensive art books; I also supported an equally expensive and ambitious quarterly review called *The Finer Arts*—its title sprawled across the cover in a tricky Gothic script nobody could read. A very serious magazine, full of high purpose, it was just exactly like its editor, Helen Reed. We were together four or five years—I actually took an apartment in New York, actually moved there, I was that much in love. She was a handsome woman, a little too tall for me, with thick gray hair pulled into a bun. A schoolteacher's face, a pedant's seriousness.

I did not marry Helen (she even kept her own apartment) though I was fonder of her than I had ever been of my fourth wife, who was her immediate predecessor. With age one becomes more wary, more eager to avoid trouble. After four attempts I simply stopped going through the farce of a marriage ceremony.

My affection for Helen faded, as my loves always seem to do. I really think she exhausted me into indifference. She herself lived at a high pitch of excitement, bounding breathlessly from interest to interest. I was overwhelmed.

She left, in furious tears, one afternoon. She crammed her belongings (how had she accumulated so many things here?) into three large suitcases, two of them mine. (They were Vuitton, and I did not expect her to return them. She did not.) I offered her my car and driver, she refused silently, turning her back on me. I therefore fixed myself a Scotch, kicked life into the living room fire, and began to enjoy the quiet.

Half an hour later, crossing the room for my second drink, I happened to glance out the window and into the rather miserable street. There she was, at the curb, with her suitcases, waiting for a cab, pacing up and down impatiently.

I began to work on my carving. It was a wooden figure, two feet high, an Indian in full ceremonial dress. I had started it merely to annoy Helen. Now it was very nearly finished, except for the elaborate headgear. I was doing each feather with absolute precision; I had little trouble with rachis and vane, but the fluff was very difficult indeed. After nearly an hour, my hand was tired.

Helen was no longer at the curb. I opened the window and looked down the street: there she was, no more than a hundred feet away. The taxi had never come, she was dragging a suitcase in each hand, and kicking the third along in front of her. As I watched, she stopped the paper boy, who'd finished his route and was on his way home. And so she found a way to exit with dignity, stalking behind a rattling newsboy's wagon.

I saw Helen again almost thirty years later. Someone introduced us; I would not have recognized the hunched old woman. Perhaps she felt the same about me . . .

MY SON is very fond of a quotation from Ecclesiastes about the alternations of opposites: war and peace, love and hate, life and death. He actually seems to take comfort in this instability. I may indeed have my seasons but I emphatically do not enjoy them. I prefer to think of my life as a pageant. Or a processional. Like that wonderful march in *Aïda* in which once, as a boy, I was a costume extra. I would parade across the stage, race around the back, exchanging my spear for a banner, then across the stage again. At one point I even rode in a chariot, my armor hidden under a hastily wrapped toga, on my head a garland of paper leaves.

Now in my old age many things seem more unreal to me than those costumed figures in *Aïda*. A trick of the observer's eye, no doubt, a senile astigmatism.

A concession to my years, perhaps, but I am no longer active in business; I now devote myself to philanthropy. It is, in its way, as amusing as making money. I built a school for my son's congregation; with their financing problems I didn't think they would ever have one otherwise. Anthony was very nervous about it; he didn't really approve, but he couldn't think of a reasonable objection. (I find it hard to believe that thin gray old man is my son.) I added a small wing to the children's hospital here. (My son was equally nervous about that; he doesn't care to have me in what he regards as his territory.) I am presently deciding upon the best way to endow a few neighborhood pediatric clinics.

All of it for children, you say? Yes, I know. I am fond of youth. That is probably why, after almost six years, I still keep Roberta. She is thirty now, which to me is a veritable infant. Her skin still has the glow of young tissue, and she is quite beautiful. She is indeed worth every penny she costs me.

And she is very expensive—her clothes, her apartment, her allowance. I even sent her young sister to college, then for two years to the Sorbonne. Did such a younger sister really exist? I doubt it. Still I am amused by Roberta, and her flaming beauty—she is a true redhead—fits perfectly into my processional view of life.

For some four years Roberta was my live-out mistress. I would often introduce her that way: it made her simply furious. She claimed it hurt her pride. Now, the very idea of Roberta with any pride is indescribably hilarious to me.

Two years ago the role of my live-out mistress abruptly changed. I was unable to prevent it at that time.

I had a coronary. One morning at my desk I had the most absurd feeling of not being able to breathe. I thought of heart—at my age who doesn't—but there was no pain, no pain at all. Quite automatically I rang for my secretary. Equally automatically I put my pen back in its holder. And then I stopped breathing completely.

Or so I thought. When I next remember, I was ensnared in a tangle of wires and hissing valves and surrounded by busy white-coated people. And oh yes, Roberta was there, her frightening hair pulled back into a bun, her face as free of make-up as any nun's.

Months later when I came home I found that she had moved into my house. For my sake, as she put it, she had sublet her apartment—furnished, of course—and had crammed all her most personal belongings into half the upstairs closets of my house. She had also taken over the bedroom next to mine, after doing a little work on it first—rug and bed were white fur, blue damask walls and curtains. Just a place to rest, she assured me, from the strenuous anxiety of caring for me.

She was, as a matter of fact, a very good housekeeper. She got on well with the three shifts of nurses, though they were all absolute harridans. She charmed my fretful, suspicious cook, soothed the feelings of the butler. And sought out ways to be gently amusing and totally delightful to me. It was in many ways her best performance. (I sometimes think that Roberta, like me, sees her life as a series of pageants. This was her Domestic Idyll.)

I recovered completely, though it was almost six months before I felt like moving about freely. First I discharged those white-capped witches who had so completely controlled me. Then I set about returning Roberta to her proper place.

One Wednesday she went shopping, promising to be gone all afternoon. She was, of course, meeting a man; I applauded silently: her true shopping expeditions left me only a mountain of bills. This way was far better.

While she was gone, I mobilized the house staff, very much the way my mother had done for my funeral so long ago. We, helped by the two strong Polish dailies, packed all of Roberta's things into large brown boxes, carried them down the front stairs, through the kitchen, past the pantry (this is an old-fashioned house), and into the small wing behind the second summer kitchen. It was originally the servants' wing, but since I do not keep that sort of staff any more, the four small rooms were empty and waiting. The two dailies chose the very first room—the boxes were heavy and awkward, and they were tired of carrying. (The butler, the cook, and I, being almost equally dottery and ancient, were of very little help.) We hung some clothes in the small closets, but most we left jumbled in the boxes. It was just too difficult to unpack her completely. I myself brought the flowers from her other room—a big sprig of purple California lilac. I knew she was very fond of it. I simply removed it from its blue vase (eighteenth-century Japanese, and very valuable) and put it in a more suitable container. In this case, a Mason jar.

She threatened to leave. How noisy she was, how that red hair flashed back and forth. Filled with the curious elation that follows a coronary, I ignored her. And she stayed. Of course, I know that she is now looking for another spot, that she will eventually go. I shall miss her too. She is so very decorative.

But I shall not miss her as much as I might once have done. I think perhaps I have finally grown tired of women and their ways. At last. And I certainly have grown very fond of my great-grandchildren. (My son's two children have each produced two children: I am haunted by that absurd number.) They are as curious about me as I about them—and I always censor the story of my life for their hearing.

THE REVEREND ANTHONY HENLEY, who ought to have been at work on Sunday's sermon, was staring idly out the window. There, in the violent green of the new spring, under a Bristol-blue sky, his father sat on the arbor swing, talking to the children. The grape vines had not yet leafed out; the sun gleamed brightly on his pink face and his white hair. He had, the Reverend Henley noticed, let his hair grow quite long, well past his ears. He has thicker hair than I do, the Reverend Henley thought wearily.

Forgetting the sermon, he went on looking out the window. He had never, he thought, seen the garden so pretty. It was a very ordinary plot of ground, just a few rhododendrons and the scattered tulips that his wife insisted on planting every year. Now it seemed dramatic, unreal—the gleam of his father's hair, the children's upturned faces, their complete immobility. Even the youngest boy was perfectly still.

I have seen that picture before, the Reverend Henley thought. His practiced mind worked backward, sorting through memories, until he found it: an illustration in a book of Bible stories he'd used years ago in Sunday school . . . the sort of maudlin illustration he had always

disliked. The sort you didn't find in textbooks any more
. . . And who? Some patriarch? Some prophet?

The Reverend Henley turned his chair slowly, con-
templating his study walls. Each book had its proper
place, and he knew them all. Nothing was ever moved,
nothing changed, the chairs fitted the holes they had worn
years ago in the carpet. But even here his father's presence
disturbed him.

Not a lack of understanding. The Reverend Henley
imagined he understood his father quite well . . . No, it
wasn't that. It was an uneasiness, a growing suspicion that
his father had succeeded where he had failed, that his
father understood many things in a way denied to him
. . . Such perfect and unconcerned assurance the old
man had. It was disquieting. He who had spent his life in
pursuit of understanding, who was on familiar terms with
the accumulated wisdom of five thousand years of human
existence . . . why should he be troubled, why should he
feel diffident and uncertain in the presence of a man whose
life had been devoted to the irrational, to the pursuit of
instant pleasure and selfish whims?

But what then, thought the Reverend Henley suddenly,
if truth lies beyond fulfillment of desire, in satiated
appetite . . .

He leaped from his chair, his back aching with the
violent motion. *No. Absolutely no.*

Furtively he glanced out the window into the garden.
His father was getting up. The two biggest children stood
behind the swing, steadying it. The littlest waited in
front, holding ready his cane. Then, children following
closely, the old man strolled across the small green skirt
of garden grass. He saw his son at the window and lifted
his hand in a slow careful greeting.

It was, the Reverend Henley thought with a shudder,
altogether like a blessing.

The Beach Party

❧❧

THE BRIGHT blue Jeep left the main road and plowed its way over the dunes, snow tires spinning out sand like a wake behind. Twenty minutes later it skidded side-wise down the last slope and stopped on the hard-packed sand of the beach.

Three young men got out, took out three shovels and a bright yellow-and-black-plaid cooler. And the Jeep roared back the way it had come. It was then about four o'clock.

The three young men jammed their shovels in the sand, sat down, backs to the towering dune, and each had a can of beer. They filled the cans with small pebbles and tossed them out into the ocean, beyond the ruffled line where the surf was breaking. Finally they took off their shirts and began to dig the pit. When it was knee deep, they collected round stones and lined the pit carefully with them. Then they sat back and had another beer.

The bright blue Jeep skittered down the dune again. This time it held five girls, several paper bags, three damp sacks, and a large wooden crate. Two of the young men carried the crate into the ocean, stepping carefully over the stony bottom, making their way to a pool the falling tide had left. They put the crate there, in the knee-deep water, and weighted its top with rocks. The others collected driftwood and began a fire in the stone-lined pit. Then they spread their blankets and stripped to their bathing suits and started their transistor radios. Some of them went swimming, picking their way carefully through the fallen boulders. And some merely stretched out in the last of the sun. It was slipping rapidly over the edge of the dunes, and the shadows of the eel grass and the beach peas edged farther and farther down the slope.

Frieda Matthews decided to go for a walk. She was already badly sunburned, and lying on the flat hot sand made her body itch and tingle all over. She switched off her green transistor radio and put it carefully in the middle of her towel.

It had been a present from her family, not six weeks ago. It was a good radio, an expensive one, a Zenith, far more than her family could afford with her brother Everett already in college and wanting to go to medical school, and her own college bills still to come.

She walked down to the edge of the water, and stared out beyond the rocks to the open Atlantic. The swimmers were there, splashing around the bright orange of an inflated mattress. She saw her brother's head, sleek and dark as a seal's. "Hi, Everett!"

He yelled: "Come on in!"

She waved and strolled off down the beach. She was afraid of the ocean. It had something to do with the dark color, with the sound and the motion of the surf. She swam well and happily in pools—the clean green and white tile was friendly and sparkling. But the unknown opaque distances of the ocean . . . no.

She walked toward the west, following the line of high tide, searching among the sea wrack. She found a string of whelk egg cases, wrinkled and joined like cardboard. With her fingernail she cut through the thick horny casing of one compartment and a dozen tiny shells spilled into her hand. She found a sprig of Irish moss, perfect and white, and she tucked it into her shirt as a boutonniere. (There was something her grandmother had made—in the old-fashioned kitchen of her big gray house—seaweed pudding. With this very same ruffled white seaweed.) She found a lobster pot marker, striped in its owner's colors. She did not recognize them. The marker must have drifted a long way, from some part of the coast to the south—the currents were that way—where she did not know the symbols.

She tossed it aside, annoyed. Feeling just the way she had when, as a child, she found a floating bottle and a message too blurred to read.

Frieda picked up the marker again anyway and carried it with her as she scrambled along a rocky spit that jutted out into the ocean, dividing the coast into two shallow coves. There seemed to be a picnic in the second cove too. She was surprised; this stretch of coast was so difficult to reach that few people ever came. But there they were, two Jeeps standing side by side. As she watched, three men struggled into their shiny black skin-diving suits and backed gingerly into the surf, holding their guns carefully. They were not carrying air tanks; they would be snorkeling close inshore. A cluster of women waited on the beach. With the wind in her face Frieda could hear the sound of their laughter. A half-grown boy was climbing the highest dune, sliding and scrambling in the loose sand. Two small children ran up and down in the slip of the ocean, splashing and screaming.

It was then about five o'clock, midway in a falling tide.

The sun went down, the light lingered, then faded. The blue Jeep made its final trips, and the beach party really began. There was a guitar now, and a second bonfire, and a washtub full of beer cans. The swimmers had come in long ago—about the time Frieda returned from her walk—and gotten dressed. The wind had dropped, and so had the surf. The ocean slipped quietly down into the low of the spring tides.

A couple of the young men were working on the pit. They dragged out the remains of the burning wood and sprinkled the rocks with water. Then they got a bag of rockweed and shook the shiny black strands down into the pit.

"Can't I do something?" Frieda asked.

Everett said, "Help me wet the corn."

They carried the sack of corn down to the edge of the water. She felt it swirl cold around her ankles.

"Don't dip it here," Everett said. "Too much sand."

She looked at the dark water. "You know I can't."

"Oh for God's sake!' He pulled the corn away from her, and she retreated to the dry sand. He came back in a minute, dripping sack on his shoulder. "Thanks to you I got my shirt wet."

She spread out her hands, miserably. "Everett, you *know* that . . ."

He walked away, to the pit. A dark girl with crispy curly black hair helped him slide the sack from his shoulder. As she bent to look inside he nibbled the nape of her neck. She giggled, without seeming surprised. Frieda looked away.

I shouldn't have come, Frieda thought. And she remembered: Everett, her mother said, you have simply got to see that Frieda makes some friends. Four summers at camp and she doesn't know a soul around here any more.

Okay, he said, I'll take her to the beach party. She's too young and it won't work. But okay.

Now Everett looked over at her, his face streaming sweat from the heat of the pit. "Where's your date, little sister?" he asked.

A tall thin boy who was in prep school somewhere and whose name was John . . . Everett had arranged it.

"I don't know," Frieda said.

"Looks like he's standing right behind you."

Frieda spun around.

"You don't have to jump out of your skin," John said.

"Oh," she said. "Oh. Haven't seen you for ages."

"Haven't seen you either. What've you been doing?"

"Nothing," she said uncertainly. "Nothing much."

"I saw you go running off down the beach."

"I was watching some skin divers over there."

"No!" Exaggerated unbelief.

"Don't be silly. Of course I did."

"Okay. We'll just go and have a look."

Hand on wrist, he pulled her along. She hung back, but he only squeezed tighter until little prickles of pain ran up and down her arm. Then she gave up, and with a couple of quick hops, came into step with him.

"Just to the point," she said. "Then you can see."

They looked. Even in the faint light they could see that the group was gone—the dogs and the children and the women. There was only a single boy sitting by a heap of towels and clothes. He was writing in the smooth hard sand.

"Okay," John told Frieda, "you get A for that."

"Let's go back."

"That shaky little girl voice . . . Will you please stop being scared of me?"

"I'm not," she said.

"For God's sake," he said, "I'm not going to rape you. I'm not even going to kiss you."

"I don't know what you are thinking," she said as formally as she could. "I may be the youngest person at this party, but I am not a child and I am not all that naïve."

"I'm going to go get a beer," he said.

And she had to admit that during the slow walk back across the sand the pressure of his hand on her wrist was not at all unpleasant.

The guitar player was standing up. "Seeger does it like this." He rattled off a bit of song. "And if I had a banjo

I'd show you the way Scruggs'd do it. With those pegs, man, it's terrific, great."

Frieda noticed all of a sudden that he had a goatee—it was so very blond that she hadn't even seen it before. In the soft light from the bonfire it gleamed with sudden brightness.

"Look what's coming," the guitar player said, waggling his shiny tuft of whiskers. "Lookee there."

Two young men carried the lobsters from the surf, staggering under the awkward crate, leaving a trail of water like blood on the sand behind them. They tumbled the crate to the edge of the pit, opened it. (Frieda saw that Everett was one of them. Strange, she thought, I almost didn't recognize him. He looks different.) They began pulling the lobsters out and dropping them on the steaming seaweed.

John came back, beer can in hand. "Do you know that there's a superstition that lobsters scream when you put them in boiling water?"

Frieda felt the back of her throat close, sharply.

"My mother says she's heard it, half a dozen times, only I don't know how she could have because they don't have any vocal cords, you see. But there are lots of people who say they've heard it."

Frieda turned away, found a sheltering dune, and settled herself there, back to the fire.

John followed her, dropped down beside her. "That bothers you, doesn't it? But it's a fact."

"I won't swim in the ocean either," she said stubbornly, "and that's just as much a fact."

"You'll be all right when you grow up," he said. "Want a swallow of my beer?"

She accepted the can, silently. The cool liquid ran over her aching throat.

He turned to watch the party. "They've put the tarpaulin on, and the sand on top, so if you want to go back it's all right."

"I think I'll stay here."

He slipped an arm around her, and she saw that he had misunderstood her answer. But she didn't feel that it mattered any more. His jacket smelled of sweat and the steel of the zipper pressed into her cheek, but even so it was better than being alone. Even so.

Frieda lifted her head. "I hear something," she said. "Something's going on." She had become aware of it gradually, imperceptibly, as the noise became louder. It seemed to have begun on the opposite side of the fire, a considerable distance away. "Look there," she told John.

People seemed to be drifting away, the way sugar runs out of a paper, gently, quickly.

"What's happening?"

John shook his head. "Want to go see?"

By then everyone seemed to be running down the beach, toward that rocky point. Except one—a boy who sat by the fire.

"Who's that?" Frieda asked.

"I never saw him before," John said.

"Hi," Frieda called, "what's the matter?"

He sat very quietly, didn't answer, didn't blink, just stared into the colored flames on the driftwood, as if he hadn't heard, really.

John said: "Let's go see."

The group had come to a stop and was milling around at the tip of the beach. Frieda found Everett and grabbed his arm, firmly. "Everett," she said, "do you know what's going on?"

He started to pull away, then stopped. "My little sister, for God's sake . . . did you see the boy, or were you too busy making out with John?"

"The boy by the fire?"

"Well, he turned up, asking us to help." Everett rubbed his chin, nervously. "He said that a diver didn't come back."

Frieda noticed that the full moon had swung itself over the horizon's rim, leaving a yellow buttery trail on the water, on the unexpected shiny rocks.

"We saw them," she said, "earlier. There were three or four divers and some children."

Everett said: "The way he told it to us, his brother went back for one more try while the others went home and he stayed to keep him company." Everett shrugged. "I guess we go look for him now."

Frieda said, "Somebody ought to go for help. Like the fire department or something."

"Somebody went."

Somebody lit two bright gas lanterns. Somebody brought all the flashlights. Somebody figured the shore-wise drift. And one by one they waded in to begin the hunt.

John let go of Frieda's hand, and in the sudden sweep of cool air across it, she realized that he had been holding it for quite a long time.

"Well," he said, to the rising moon as much as to anyone else, "I guess I'll go look too." He turned to Frieda and his blue eyes grinned at her. "What we were doing was more fun. Keep my place, huh?"

He slipped off his jacket and handed it to her. "Watch it. There's some money in the pockets." He put one foot in the water. "Jesus, it's cold." He hitched up the belt of his plaid trunks and squinted down, shrugging. "Well, I might step on him, but I'll never see him."

Frieda held the jacket carefully. "I should think you could see the color of his skin. Kind of white like."

"Honey baby," John said, "he'd be wearing a black rubber suit . . . Don't spill my money."

He waded out, and Frieda went back up the beach, rolling the jacket carefully, pockets inside.

Maybe I could go in just a little, and help, she thought. But even she did not believe it.

Then she remembered the boy. The boy sitting alone by the fire. I'll go back and keep him company, she told herself. I can do that.

She walked toward him briskly. He was sitting just exactly the way he had been when she last saw him.

Knees up. Arms wrapped around them. He must be the boy, she thought, who was climbing up the back dune when I first saw them, when the sun was still out.

"Can I get you something?" she said. He was wearing only a T-shirt, and she put a hand on his shoulder. Through the thin knit she felt the icy coldness of his skin, bone deep. "Can I get you a coat?"

He did not answer, but she hunted until she found an extra jacket that somebody had dropped. And she put it around his shoulders. He did not move—not even his eyes. They stared steadily at the tips of his white sneakers.

She gave up and wandered down the beach to watch the search.

Most of the girls were in close, in the shallow foaming water. The young men were farther out, barely inside the surf line. Their lights reflected off the broken surfaces of the scattered black rocks. As she looked, one was caught by a surf and rolled. He came up cursing, his flash still burning.

Like a horde of flounder fishermen, Frieda thought. All that was missing were the gigs . . .

All but one of the flashlights were out; the moon had slipped a couple of inches up in the sky; all but a few searchers had come ashore and were standing by the fire, shivering, when a changing tide brought him to them.

A muffled shout: "Here, hey!" And one of the gas lanterns swung in a signaling arc. The other lantern and the single remaining flashlight moved quickly to the same spot. Two young men left the warmth of the beach and ran out again. A few more shouts and they began their trip in, dragging something through the waist-deep water. They got past the largest of the granite boulders, into its lee, when a single heavy surf caught them. The lanterns went over, flooded, and disappeared. In the sudden dark the men tumbled into the rocks, dragged and rolled by the undertow. Three held on; they struggled to their feet, and, lifting their burden, scrambled the rest of the way.

They carried him up the wet tide beach to the dry

sand, black flippers dragging like a fish's tail behind. They left him there—left him to the others who crowded around—and hurried to the fire, their wet bodies huddled against the cold night wind. They found towels and scrubbed furiously at their bodies, jigging up and down for warmth. They coughed and slapped each other's back. They gulped cans of beer because their mouths tasted of salt, their stomachs were numb and their throats tight. "Damned if I saw it coming," they told each other. "First I knew was the crest coming over."

Everett, who'd been crouched over coughing, straightened up and took the sweater Frieda held out to him. Blood was running down the side of his jaw. He touched his ear gingerly, sucked in his breath with pain. "Jesus, all of that for a guy that's already dead. We got to be crazy."

"I think maybe I broke my hand," somebody said. "How do you know when you break your hand?"

"You sure he's dead?"

"Never felt anything heavier."

"Where's that kid? He still around?"

The boy was watching them. His eyes had lifted from the tips of his sneakers, he was watching them directly. He was sitting up quite straight and the borrowed jacket had slipped off his shoulders. He was looking right at them, and he was listening to every word.

Frieda did not remember too much about the rest of it. They tried to revive him, using the only method they knew, mouth-to-mouth breathing. John had been the first. When he was finished, he walked a little way up the beach, knelt down, and vomited. Then he kicked sand over the spot, washed his face, and scooped up a couple of handfuls of sea water into his mouth. When he turned, Frieda was holding a beach towel for him.

"Come to the fire," she said. "It'll make you feel better."

"Find me a beer," he said. Then as an afterthought, he added, "It's the idea mostly."

He was still scrubbing his fingers across his lips when Frieda held out the beer to him. "It was better when I was kissing you," he joked feebly.

She sat close by him, waiting to see what else he needed. Once she put her arm across his shoulder, but he pulled away. "I'm okay." And when he finished the beer, he got up himself and got another.

So there was nothing for her to do. She took her own jacket and climbed far up the nearest dune, twenty feet to the top, and settled there, spread herself out against the smooth whiteness, felt herself twitch and die under the moon, sucked and brittle like a shell.

No one noticed that she was gone. Everett would now be nursing his bloody ear. John would be crouched by the fire fighting down his nausea. And that unnamed boy would be sitting and waiting, staring at nothing.

As she watched, a police van came roaring and skidding along the beach. Two deputies popped out, almost before it stopped moving. They waded into the small crowd of people, like a pool of water, sending the individual drops flying off to the side. They lifted the black form—in the bright moonlight Frieda could see smears of sand on the rubber suit. Just before the door slammed Frieda caught sight of one deputy busily slipping something into the slack mouth on the floor.

Frieda lay back on her sand bed and forgot all about the scuffling and the crisscrossing pattern of headlights below her. There was nothing she could do. There was nothing in it that belonged to her.

She looked up at the moon-faded stars and began to count them carefully. She had gotten to fifteen before she lost her place and had to start over.

When she did bother to look down again, the cars were gone. And the people. The bonfire had been covered with sand. The pit was still banked and unopened, and there was a tiny bit of steam rising from one corner, brisk and frosty in the moonlight.

They forgot me, she thought. But then I wasn't really there, was I?

She slid down from her dune. And stood on the level sand, scuffed by rushing feet and the deep treads of snow tires.

She saw the dark mark on the sand where the diver had lain. She wondered why that did not bother her more, but it seemed no more horrible than everything else. Than the lobsters—screaming or silent—still steaming in the pit. Than the surf grinding the chitinous bodies of uncounted animals to bits on the shingle. Than the sharp smell of a man's sweat, or the angular pressure of another body.

Standing alone on the trampled, littered sand, she talked to herself, silently.

I wish that boy hadn't heard their talk . . . But of course he sat so still that you didn't really notice him . . . But he still didn't have to hear it. Not like that.

She wished that the boy had listened to her. She wished she'd been able to put her arms around him and tell him gently.

But, in the empty hollow of the dunes, after a while, she realized how useless it was, that the surge of protection was just a part of her sex. As natural as her ovulation. And as useless as the ova which had ripened and decayed for these eight years past in her own body.

She noticed that the moon was high and white in the sky now. The tide had come in; the spume from its breakers drifted over the dunes like fog. The ocean itself was black and still, rollers rising and falling like breaths.

The others would remember her and they would come back for her. All she had to do was wait. And that was what she couldn't do.

No. She couldn't wait for them.

She wanted to run, but she did not allow herself to. She saw that her radio still lay on her beach towel, which was still spread out carefully. She walked over to it. There was sand blown or trampled across the towel, sand frosting the top of the radio. She picked it up, blew

it clean, and turned it on. It worked. Then she picked
up the towel, shook it, folded it carefully. She put her
back to the ocean and began to think of the long walk
ahead of her. She would have to find a path through the
poison ivy and the spiny clumps of rugosa roses. It would
be slow going in the sand until she reached the road, and
from there it was three or four miles home. Unless she
met someone, she thought it would take her most of the
night.

She put her towel across her left shoulder, and her
radio in her left hand. And she began her walk. The sound
of her radio was a small mark in the sea-beaten dark, but
she was grateful for it, and she moved along confidently,
safe inside its tinny shell.

Three

✠

BECAUSE SHE was very glad to have him back, she asked no questions. No questions at all.

She didn't think he'd answer anyway. He was so moody these days. Quick to take offense, silent for long stretches of time. So changed that sometimes she wondered if this were really the same man—until, in his brief flashing smile, she recognized the husband she'd loved. When he was alive.

Perhaps apparitions (she hesitated at the word ghost —no, not Jerry) were like that. Perhaps . . . She spent one long day in the university library, a day when she ought to have been finishing her economics term paper, searching for an answer. Methodically she read book after book, until her red-rimmed eyes were ready to leap from her head and her very fingers ached.

Apparitions, she learned, had messages. But Jerry did not seem to want to talk. Indeed he rarely glanced in her direction. It was she who stared at him . . . Apparitions, the books also said, were restless. Jerry spent most of his time in the big chair in the living room, as comfortably as any man come home from work . . . Apparitions returned to the places they frequented in life. But Jerry had never been to her apartment, knew only what she'd written to him, had seen only the photographs she'd sent.

I have wasted my time, she thought as she left the library that evening. It was almost eight o'clock: she was sick with hunger because she'd forgotten lunch. "Jerry," she called as soon as she got home, "Jerry!" He was not there.

She snapped on the living room television, then walked into the kitchen to fix dinner. She ate at the counter, listening to the chatter of TV voices, watching the campus lights wink and shift in the wind-shaken trees eight stories below.

Where do you go, Jerry? she thought, half-expecting an answer from him. When you're not here with me, where are you? Were you annoyed with me for being late?

The kettle whistled; she poured her tea.

Over two years, she thought. And Jerry, you never come close, you stay across the room. Do you want to be here at all?

Ann Martin Richards drank her tea, forehead pressed against the cold window, following the aimless crisscrossing of traffic lights below. It was an evening like any other.

HE HAD NOT come back at once. For at least a month after his funeral, she had been alone, totally alone, in a vast, obscuring, mistlike pain. She had no will, no strength, no control. Her eyelids twitched and she could not stop them. Her fingers danced along tabletops. Once, crossing a street, her legs refused to carry her, and she sat there in the middle of traffic while people screamed. When she tried to explain to them, she found she hadn't the words either.

She was, she thought, like a balloon collapsing. There was nothing inside her. She was disintegrating, the world was pulling away, she would fall off on one of its vertiginous spins . . .

She went back to college. Her mother came with her, stayed with her. Ann seemed to remember days that passed without a word between them—that couldn't be so, she thought. The silence must be inside her own head.

Then, suddenly, the emptiness disappeared. And she asked her mother to please go home. Definitely. Firmly. Because Jerry was back.

It happened like this.

Late one afternoon she was walking home, classes finished for the day. (She did not remember which classes —she remembered nothing these days. She had to look at the books in her arms to discover where she'd been.) She saw her husband standing at the corner of her apartment—saw him perfectly clearly. "Jerry," she called, and began to run, dodging through traffic. But the sidewalk was empty; he was gone. She peered through the glass doors into the lobby: plastic plants and shining marble floor and nothing else.

She leaned against the building, breathless, heart shaking her ribs. A snow of small black flakes clouded her sight. He is here, she thought, he is back. He found me.

After that a sense of him trembled in the air, hung like smoke, to color her days. She found herself looking for him among the dizzy falling tree leaves. She found herself searching crowds, to see if he were not hiding among the unknown bodies.

He is here. A vast yellow light shivered across everything, detaching objects from their bases so that they floated, an inch or so in the air.

She often caught glimpses of him. Each time she ran; each time he was gone.

She began to realize that she could never catch him by running, could never find him by looking, could never surprise him around a million corners. He would come when he was ready.

So when she saw him again, walking briskly toward the campus through the winter-stripped trees, she only smiled after him. And watched his precise military steps carry him out of sight.

She saw him more and more frequently. It was as if he had to accustom himself to the neighborhood, which he had never seen. As if he had to learn the streets and houses one by one. As if he had to be sure of his ground . . .

One gusty November afternoon, when the last football game filled the stadium and parked cars jammed the streets, he opened the locked apartment door and walked into the living room.

THEREAFTER HER LIFE ran smoothly. She went to classes, cheerful and smiling, saw her credits mount and the date of her graduation draw closer.

She was home every evening, except for an occasional movie. She wanted the company of neither men nor women. After a bit they left her alone.

Except for Ted Langley.

She had, she supposed, dated him a few times, in a manner of speaking. Ted never called her, never asked directly. But outside a classroom, crossing the campus, he would join her. Casually. No sweat, she thought, not with him. Occasionally they went to the zoo to watch the seals feeding. The scarred gray bodies leaping through the air vaguely disgusted her. And amused him—"They look just like people I know," he said.

He never asked her to dinner, but after an hour or so of walking along the ammonia-smelling zoo paths, he would say abruptly, "I'm hungry, aren't you?" Sometimes they perched on stools, elbows up, like frogs on a log, and ate hamburgers. Sometimes they went to one of the Mexican restaurants that surrounded the campus. And once they went to a Japanese steak house—"You got to see this," he said, "the way they slice the meat, right in front of you, the way they sort of pet the blade, it's god damned obscene." She went, saw, and didn't agree with him. They sat together at campus movies sometimes; he would spot her in the crowded lobby and wave to her.

It was one good thing about being so tall, she thought, he could see over the heads of most people.

Something was wrong with Jerry. These days he had long silences, when even the outlines and substance of his body would begin to fade. She discovered that she could will him back. She could feel him restoring himself upon her, drawing fullness and depth from her. When he was fleshed and shining again, she was exhausted. Her bones ached; she could feel her own skeleton beneath her skin.

I am sucked dry, she thought, my bones are hollow. Jerry lives from me. He is my baby and I suckle him, nurse him, sustain him . . .

But sometimes she was so very tired. Like today.

It was a beautiful day, summer heat gone, winter rains not yet begun. The trees were bare but there was a brilliant green in the experimental fescue grasses on the lawn of the agriculture school.

I will go for a walk, she thought. Exercise may stop my aching, and the air is so lovely. Purse on her shoulder, notebook in hand, she selected the long diagonal brick walk that ran across the center of the campus. At once she began to feel better; she lengthened her stride, the air swirling around her.

She'd walked this way with Jerry—it was almost three years ago now; these very same bricks held the echoes of their steps somewhere in their grainy interior. Those were the weekends Jerry came to visit her, before their marriage. They'd walked for hours—past the campus, through the town, out into the fields, along dirt roads stitched together with tractor treads.

Jerry, she thought, oh Jerry, how lovely, how exquisite those days were. You know, don't you? When every breath hurt with the beauty of things. When the faint touch of a rough Harris tweed jacket was shivering delight.

Though he was a professional soldier, he'd never once worn his uniform—he almost seemed to avoid it with her.

He hadn't even married in uniform, though he was fourth-generation West Point. "My family expects it," he said, "but only because of tradition. They haven't really thought about it. My uniform is a symbol of war. It's not appropriate in a ceremony dedicated to love."

He was, she thought walking alone across the autumn-browned campus, the most logical man she had ever met. The most intelligent, the most direct. Assurance clung to him like perfume around a beautiful woman. Absolute, unaffected assurance.

Jerry, she thought, even from this distance in time, *oh Jerry*.

She'd met him at the tennis club on Nantucket, her first summer there. His family had been coming for years to the same gray-shingled house at Siasconset. He'd watched her play, leaning against the wire fencing, openly laughing. When she'd finished—her face flushed bright red, her hair dangling in soaking strings from her white headband —he said, "It's too hot for tennis. Come sailing with me this afternoon."

Later he drove her home, the sound of the wind still in her ears, the smooth salt spray still on her face. He leaned across the front seat of his car, speaking to her through the half-closed door: "You don't know it yet, but you're going to marry me."

And that was that. They had only two days then, his leave was over. Occasionally on weekends he would fly to see her at college, but not often. He was saving his leave for their honeymoon. Yes, she found herself saying over and over again. Yes. Yes. She had a sense of rightness, of things fitting into their proper places.

When their honeymoon was over, and they moved into his tiny bachelor apartment, she gasped at the sight of uniforms lined neatly in the closet.

I had forgotten, she thought, I had truly forgotten . . .

Six months later his expected orders came, and he left to find the combat experience so necessary to his promotion. "A field command is part of the seasoning of an officer, Ann. It's what I should be doing."

She agreed smilingly. Jerry would be one of the youngest generals in army history, his family assured her; he had a great career ahead.

She closed that apartment, helped by his mother, and went back to college. There, helped by her mother, she found another apartment, furnished it, and settled down to the business of waiting.

She wrote every day. "You would like this apartment, Jerry. There's a nice pool I haven't had time to use. And the view from the living room is really quite remarkable. By the way, Mother wants to give us that de Kooning you admired so much when we were there. Shall I accept it or would you rather not?"

Daily letters from a young wife, waiting, cradled in money-lined comfort.

His letters were long descriptions of the country and the people. He was studying their language and making fair progress. He was trying to understand Buddhism but there didn't seem to be any really informative texts . . . He made no mention of the war. Nothing to disturb her perfect cocoon, her total security.

Ann Martin Richards, alone, walked briskly along the path, conscious only of the pleasure of her body moving lightly in the cool air. Tall, thin razor body cutting through the air like a ship.

"Ann, wait!" Ted Langley's broad pink face and thin blond mustache grinned happily at her. "I've been yelling at you for the last block."

She chuckled at her own nonsense. "I was pretending to be a ship."

"You what?" He slipped into step beside her.

"I'm taking a walk."

"Let's see how the seals are coming along. Maybe they'll even have a new young one that you can like."

The feel of his hand on her arm was quite pleasant and the short drive in his yellow VW was far more interesting than a walk.

She did not think about Ted, Ann admitted to herself, unless she was with him. But when she was, when his large angular body was next to her, she found that she liked him very much indeed.

He'd been around for such a long time, she thought, since those first months after Jerry's death. She'd become aware of him gradually, of his name, of his appearance. He drifted into her sight and her awareness. He was a gentle, firm pressure, unhurried, unchanging. When he was with her, she even felt the lap of a small tongue of desire. Muted and buried and frightened, but there.

There were no new seals in the zoo's pool. "Bad idea, lady," he admitted. "Let's go in search of dinner." They settled on a Chinese restaurant a half-hour drive from town through cut bare fields where swarms of blackbirds whirled. After dinner he said, "Did you know the music school's doing John Cage tonight? What do you think of the new music?"

One thing at a time, patiently, insistently.

They left the auditorium early to drink beer in a crowded student bar two blocks from her apartment. We have come home, Ann thought calmly. We have made a big circle of miles and miles but come back home at last.

She was slightly tired and slightly sleepy, and she could feel his warmth surrounding her, wrapping her, like a present in gold foil . . .

Ted said quietly to the foam in his heavy mug, "Ann, listen to me."

"Ted, I don't want to." She knew her eyes were getting wide and round and she hated that.

He went on talking to the beer. "There been any man since your husband?"

His eyes leaped up quickly and caught hers. She considered lying, then didn't. "No."

"I thought so."

For no reason at all she said, "He was killed in Quang Tri."

"I was in the north too," he said. "That little death detail come calling on you?"

"Very early one morning—I was still asleep." She'd never talked about it before, none of it, but now it was as if she'd just been waiting. "A captain and a sergeant, and their uniforms were so crisp and shiny I thought they must be made of plastic."

Ted reached across the table and took her hand. "Don't pass out on me."

"I have never fainted in my life," she said angrily, "I don't see why I should start now."

His lopsided grin twisted the new mustache. His teeth were widely spaced and perfectly even, like the teeth of some small animal. "You want to know what I did? Spent a year slogging around in the mud, trying to find decent cover while somebody called in air strikes."

Very faintly in the deep recesses of her mind she was beginning to hear all the things that Jerry's letters hadn't mentioned. All the bloody things she did not need to know.

Ted was still holding her hand; he began playing with the tips of her fingers. "Let's go to your place."

"No," she said as they went outside.

It had gotten much colder, she shivered inside her light coat. "Hurry," he said.

At her building the elevator was waiting for them; sliding doors opened and closed like wings before them. He took the key from her and opened the door himself.

"Ann," he said seriously, "I have waited one hell of a long time for this, ever since I saw you."

"Why, yes," she said, stopping suddenly in the middle of the floor, "I suppose I have too."

The apartment was perfectly silent with a churchlike emptiness.

THE NEXT AFTERNOON Ted waited at her economics class. "You miss me?"

It wasn't at all difficult for her to smile and nod and find her fingers on his arm. The wiry strength of his body was so familiar to her.

"Let's drive to Dauphin Island," Ted said. "It ought to be warm enough for a last swim or something like that."

So they went, driving all night to spend a weekend doing nothing on coarse yellow sands.

"You know," she said practically, "there's a heated pool in my building. We could have avoided that long drive."

"Old lady,"—Ted tapped her stomach through the slick nylon of her bathing suit—"old lady, you have to work to have fun."

So each weekend they drove somewhere, anywhere. At the long Thanksgiving holiday they drove to the Ozarks and walked through the bone-bleached hills while quail whirred up from their feet and deer stared at them over shallow screens of huckleberry bushes.

"You were beautiful when I met you," Ted said, "but you're incredible now. I must agree with you."

She could feel it herself, this happiness. Like a balloon floating, a cat stretching in the sun. The very tips of her fingers tingled now and then with the strength of her coursing blood. And Jerry stayed away.

AT CHRISTMAS, they each went home.

She thought once, briefly: Jerry, will you use the apartment when I'm gone? Jerry, why don't you answer me?

Ted phoned her every day, amusing chatty calls that soon included her parents. "He has such a nice voice," her mother said. And then she carefully and obviously refrained from saying anything else.

Early one morning, two days after Christmas, Ted's call woke her: "Let's go to Aspen for the rest of the holidays."

Ann blinked sleepily at the ceiling. It was not yet seven o'clock and the winter morning showed dark and blowy. "What?"

"Wake up, honey. And listen. There's a flight at noon,

you can make that. I'll meet you in Chicago and we'll fly together to Aspen. Okay?"

She shifted the phone to her other hand, thinking of powder snow and thin clear air and the feeling of love on all sides of her, enclosing her like the mountains . . .

"What's the matter?"

The snow and the cold dry mountain air blew away from her face, leaving only a tiny mocking echo of their presence. "Oh, Ted, I'm supposed to go to the Virgin Islands with my parents."

A small pause. She could hear him breathing; he had not expected her to say no.

For a moment she hesitated, then the thought of her father's pale, waxy face decided her. "Ted, my father needs this, he's been working far too hard after that last coronary last year. If I don't go, he'll decide he can't go either."

"Right," Ted said calmly. "Talk to you when you get back."

She went. And dreamt of snow mountains.

Afterwards, she was suddenly so very tired, too tired to go back to college. For four days she lay in bed, doing nothing. She held a book in her hand and did not read. The TV control lay on her pillow, untouched. The house hustled and whispered and busied about her. Her father brought breakfast before he left in the morning. Her mother brought lunch. She was always fast asleep by dinner. Ted still called every day; usually he spoke to her mother. She hung immobile, timeless, aching softly.

The lethargy passed. One morning her eyes opened wide and there was no more weight on their lids, her shoulders no longer clung to the support of the bed.

She flew back to college the next day, took a taxi through the rainy winter dusk to her apartment.

She nodded to the secretary in the office, answering her "Nice to have you back, Mrs. Richards," with "Did you have a nice holiday?" She collected her mail—nothing interesting: some circulars, the usual first of the month bills, now fairly well overdue; a dozen or so letters whose return addresses she did not recognize. She crumpled them into her coat pocket—morning was time enough. She glanced into the patio; it was rain-polished and winter-stripped, the iron furniture piled in sheltered corners and covered with green plastic. Hard to remember summer there. In the tiny foyer outside her door, she put down her bags and fumbled for the key. She'd turned the lock before she noticed: It's different. Something's different.

She lifted both suitcases inside, carefully closed the door behind her, automatically slipping the bolt.

"Jerry?"

"Here," he said.

He was sitting in the big chair by the window, his favorite chair. The lamp light fell on his yellow sweater, on the book in his hand. It glittered on the lenses of his glasses.

"I was waiting for you," he said.

"Jerry, I didn't know you wore glasses."

"We get older," he said, "we all get older."

She dropped her purse to the coffee table. "I'm glad you're back," she said. "It was lonesome without you."

"I know about that," he said. "I never said anything in my letters, but I was lonesome all those months."

"I wish you'd said more in your letters."

"So do I."

There was an edge to his voice, an anger. Abruptly she changed the subject. "I always did like that sweater, particularly with gray flannels."

He smiled at her, his steady confident smile. "You look rather tired," he said. "Have you been sick?"

"I'm just tired now. I think I'll unpack and not bother with supper. I never feel right until I've emptied my suitcases."

Methodically she hung her clothes away, then put the suitcases in the living room closet. Jerry went on reading. She couldn't quite make out the title. "What's that?" she asked. He seemed too absorbed to hear her. She stood looking at him, thinking that she had never seen him more clearly. There was a solidness to his figure—if she touched him she was certain she would be able to feel him. She was so sure . . . but he might not like it . . .

She would bathe now. As she undressed, the phone rang; she did not bother to answer, though there was an extension at her hand. She soaked in bubble bath and steam, slowly stretching, slowly easing herself into sleep. How comfortable it is with Jerry here . . .

Once she thought she heard the front door buzzer, but she ignored it. Eventually, water-logged, wrinkled, and sleepy, she toweled dry in front of the mirror.

We get older, she thought, we do get older. I'm heavier than I was and hollows are beginning to appear on my thighs and my skin isn't as shiny as it used to be, even with the bath oil; there isn't such a glow to it any more. In a little while I'll have to wear glasses too.

She fell asleep at once. And woke to find Jerry sitting on the side of the bed. He'd never come this close before, not ever. In the dim light from the open window she saw that he'd changed to pajamas. Elbows on knees, he sat there, having a last cigarette before coming to bed.

"Jerry," she said sleepily, "I have to tell you. There was somebody else, did you know?"

His handsome profile shivered for a moment. It was, she thought, a sigh.

When she woke again, the window was still opaque with night. He was no longer sitting on the side of the bed, but she was sure he had touched her on the shoulder. She could still feel the press of his fingers. "Jerry, are you there?"

He answered from the shadows in the far corner. "I suppose I'll always be here."

THE INSISTENT ringing of her door bell woke her— somebody was standing outside, finger pinned to the buzzer. She pulled on a robe and, hair uncombed and eyes heavy with sleep, she went to answer.

Ted walked into the room. "I called you last night.

Where have you been?" He yanked open the curtains. It was a brilliant sunlit morning. "I was about to go for the police."

"I've been here, Ted."

"I *know* you've been here. I talked to your mother yesterday. So why didn't you answer your phone?"

"I was taking a bath I guess. I thought I heard the phone when I was taking a bath."

"You could have called me."

"I should have," she said, "but I was so tired, I fell asleep."

"I came over here last night, and I rang your bell and I peeped through the crack under the door. There was a light on."

"Jerry was reading in there last night."

"Jesus Christ, woman!" Ted pulled her into the pool of yellow winter sunlight by the window. "He'd dead, he's been dead for almost three years."

"I know that, Ted. I was at the funeral."

"Then what the hell is all this coming back business?"

Two absurd tears ran down her cheeks; she brushed them away impatiently. "Don't yell at me, Ted."

He bent, peering sharply into her face. "You eat anything yesterday?"

She made a vague little apologetic gesture, as if ashamed to have been caught out. "I don't like airplane food."

"Okay. Was there anything in the apartment for supper last night?"

"I told you, Ted, I was too tired."

"So first we feed you." The refrigerator was empty, but there were canned soups on the shelf.

"Obviously," Ted said, "you need me to take care of you. You're having soup for breakfast."

The bowl of shiny tomato-flecked liquid appalled her, but she ate it dutifully while Ted watched.

"Now that," he said, "is much better."

They sat at the tiny corner table, looking out across the tops of the trees into the flat plains beyond town, drinking cup after cup of instant coffee with canned milk.

The soft insistence of his presence was all around her again. Demanding. Promising. She shivered slightly.

"I really should get dressed." She automatically smoothed her uncombed hair.

"Don't bother," he said, "we're only going back to bed."

Later, limp and groggy with sex, they dozed lightly. Ann, turning over, glanced through the open door into the living room. Jerry stood there.

He was considerably smaller than life. As if he were a long distance away. As if this door were the beginning of a long transparent tunnel and he stood far down its length. He said nothing, he did not move, he seemed to be staring at a point directly over the bed.

He isn't looking at me, Ann thought.

Ted stretched and kissed her neck. "Want a cigarette?"

"Do you see him?" Like a light winking out Jerry was gone.

"See who, honey?"

"Jerry was there."

Abruptly Ted got up, then just as abruptly sat down again on the crumpled blanket across the foot of the bed.

Naked men look more vulnerable and stripped than women, she thought.

"Jesus Christ," Ted said, "why doesn't he come right in and stand by the bed and watch. And let me see him too."

"I think he will," Ann said quietly. "I'm sure he will."

Ted crossed the room to light a cigarette, his hands shaking ever so slightly. "God damn it, Ann, if I died there'd be somebody else and Jerry and I both would be off somewhere being jealous of him . . . Ann, listen to me now. I wanted to ask you this in Aspen, but you wouldn't come, so I'll ask you now. Let's get married."

"I am married," she said.

He ignored her. "I finish school in May, go to work for my father, have a quick rise in the firm, due entirely to my own merits of course. So we'll get the license tomorrow and get married on Thursday."

"Ted, it's not like that."

"It is now." He drew on his cigarette. "And I'm not going to let you out of my sight until then. Just to keep my place." He chuckled softly. "Anything moving around here will be me."

Though she expected him, Jerry did not appear.

They were married on Thursday. The ground whitened with the first serious snowfall of the year and planes came in late or not at all. The Unitarian chaplain obligingly rescheduled the ceremony twice until the last of the family had arrived (Ted's older brother Jess, who came the last fifty miles by bus).

After the ceremony, flushed and jovial with champagne, they scattered again: clutching tickets, staring at the heavy gray snow-laden sky, calling hasty good-bys at the airport.

Ann and Ted went to Mexico City for the weekend, returning for their Tuesday classes. The clock in the campus tower was striking midnight when they walked into their apartment building.

"Here comes Tuesday," Ted said.

In the elevator Ann noticed: It's something, it's something. I feel it. A breathing, a stirring. The edges of things are beginning to dazzle, to flame. To reassemble themselves in a different order . . .

The tiny black and white foyer outside the elevator was empty. Her neighbor's Christmas wreath still hung, dusty and crooked, above the brass nameplate. Her own door was sleek and smooth, waiting. The brass plate gleamed a bit too brightly, and the painted wood seemed soft as velvet.

Jerry is back, she thought, Jerry is here. I know it.

The door stuck. Ted pushed it harder and it flew open, crashing into the wall.

Ann rushed past him into the living room.

Jerry was waiting, in the big chair by the window.

Wearing yellow sweater and gray flannels. He was smiling directly at her.

I'm so glad, Jerry, she said silently, because it would only hurt Ted's feelings to hear. *You're not angry about Ted? You won't leave because there are three of us now?*

Jerry went on smiling his kindest, most radiant smile. The edges of his figure shivered and sparkled with points of light. *Not this time. Not again. I'll be here*, he said, *I'll be here.*

With a quick nod she hurried back to the entrance hall. Ted was just slipping the bolt across the door. "Why were you in such a hurry, honey? Anything important?"

"Come see," she said, "just come see."

The room shimmered and glowed all around her as she slipped her arm through his and led him into the living room to meet her husband.

The Long Afternoon

❦

LIKE THE WEEKS that had preceded it, the day was hot. There wasn't a speck of dust or a breath of air moving. Under the burning white light of the sun, things seemed closer than they were really. Hilda Marie Merrick, who was called Patsy, sat on the edge of the front porch and dangled her bare legs. She had been home from the hospital a week, and there was nothing to do. She lifted her right leg to stare attentively at the red polish on her toenails. She'd been up since eight, when the morning got too hot for sleeping. She'd washed her hair and set it too tightly; her head was beginning to ache. "When I woke up this morning, I wanted to die," she called over her shoulder.

In the living room, by the open window, her mother sealed the letter she had just finished and began writing the address. "Did you, dear?"

"Yes, I did." Patsy reached one finger to loosen the tightest of the curls. "Mother, do you know that there is not a single person left in this town that I would care to talk to. They have gone to camp, every single one of them."

Mrs. Merrick's voice took on a faint warning color. "The doctor told you no."

"I don't care what he said. I just don't care."

"Now you're being silly."

"I wouldn't hurt myself. I could be so careful."

"No."

There was the soft rubbing sound of pen on paper, and over by the hedge the ragged sound of a cricket.

"Do you know something?" Patsy said. "You would think that with the way they all came down to the hospital and stood around, looking all worried and wanting to do every little thing for me—a person would think that they wouldn't go off to camp and leave me where I haven't got a single person I know in town."

"Oh, Patsy."

"It is not often that eleven-year-old people have their appendix out, and as serious as mine."

"It wasn't serious."

"It was. I could feel it. You just don't know what it was like."

"Baby, how spoiled you got."

"You don't know." Patsy's hand felt lightly for the scar. "It's still sore."

Across the street a power mower started noisily, and from farther away still came the empty sound of a horse's hoofs and the singsong chant of a fruit vendor.

The street was paved on one side only. The city council had started to surface it months before, only to discover that they had overestimated the available funds. They had then announced that unless the people who lived on the street paid for it themselves, it would stay that way. It had stayed that way.

A small girl, not more than eight or so, came up the center of the half-paved road and in through the Merricks' gate, walking with the measured, scuffing tread of her age. Her hair was pulled back freshly into two pigtails, which stuck out from the nape of her neck; from each one dropped a ribbon. The starchiness of her dress was already beginning to wilt in the heat. One hand was stuck

into the skirt pocket. The other hand held a brown roll
—an old-fashioned leather music case. She climbed the
steps, smiled shyly at Patsy and Mrs. Merrick, and, with a
sidling glide, slipped in the front door. Between her thin,
nubby shoulders her dress was already stained by perspiration.

"I didn't look like that," Patsy said, "at her age."

"Yes, you did," her mother said.

"No."

Mrs. Merrick began putting the note paper back in the
box. "Why are you so trying, dear?"

"I was born that way." Patsy pointed her nose at the
white, hot sky. "Mother, I itch all over."

"The heat powder is in the downstairs bathroom."

"It's not that kind of a thing. I feel just like I could
shake myself once or twice and my skin would fall right
off. Like I'm not attached to it at all."

"The heat is bad," Mrs. Merrick said. Her gray eyes
had a misty look as they stared out at the lawn. And her
pencil was busy making little doodling marks.

From inside the house came the first hesitant chords of
the scale.

"Here we go." Patsy gave a long, whistling sigh. "Why
does Claude have to take pupils here?"

"Because there isn't any other place."

"Oh, hell's bells!"

Inside, fumbling fingers began striking G-major chords.
Patsy closed her eyes and tried seeing how long she
could hold her breath. Her eyes popped open when a
truck stopped, but she was so intent on holding her
breath that she didn't wonder about the large crate
two men unloaded. She went on counting.

The men balanced the crate on the edge of the steps
and wiped the perspiration from their chins. "Where you
reckon you want this?" one asked. He had bright china-
blue eyes behind the tight folds of lids squinched up
against the glare.

Patsy shrugged and went on with her silent counting.
Fifty-one, fifty-two, fifty-three . . . She heard the door

bell and then her mother's surprised murmur. She always manages to sound surprised, Patsy thought. And at that exact moment, without thinking, without deciding, she took a long breath of air. Fifty-eight.

"Patsy, honey," her mother called. "Come see—the new television's here."

She got up and ambled into the hall. Her mother was signing the receipt, on the top of the packing case. In the little room on the left that they called the music room she could see the bent small back of the pigtailed girl and the bent long back of her brother Claude. His finger moved directingly up and down, keeping time.

Patsy sat down in the hall, in one of the round-backed chairs that had belonged to her grandmother, and waited until the men had just passed her and were at the front door. "Mama," she said, "I'm growing again. I got to get a bigger bra."

The men coughed with laughter, and her mother closed the front door sharply after them. To Patsy, she said, "Just what are you trying to do?"

"Nothing." Patsy stared after the men, puzzled. She had not expected the laugh—a look maybe, or a wink. "I hate people."

"Young lady, you'd better find something to do," her mother said, and left her.

The little pigtailed musician departed, grinning broadly this time. Her dress was soaked with perspiration, her glasses were blurred and smeary, too, but she did not seem to notice. She had put her music away so hastily that the white edges showed ragged at the ends of the rolled case. Only one of the leather straps was fastened; the other dragged in the dirt. She skipped out the front gate and began to run back the way she had come, following the exact center of the street, so that one foot ran on concrete, the other on mud. It gave her a kind of lopsided, jack-rabbit pace.

"If there was any traffic, she'd get killed," Patsy said

with satisfaction. She had returned to the porch.

"But there isn't," Claude said. He swung his long leg over a chair and sat astride it. The Coke bottle in his hand dripped bits of ice to the porch floor.

"You didn't bring me one," Patsy said.

"This is the last."

"Now, that's not true. I saw a whole case."

"They're all warm." He held out the bottle. "You want the rest of this?"

"No." She threw back her head and stared at the bright blue ceiling. Wasps were building their round mud nests up against one corner. "You've got all sorts of germs I don't want to catch."

"Okay."

"You drink noisier than anybody I ever knew."

"More noisily," he corrected.

"Why do you have to wear those silly-looking shorts?"

He tipped his head back and finished the Coke with a gurgle.

"And those long socks are the silliest things I ever did see."

"Quit it."

"You're too thin to wear things like that—that's what Mama told you."

"One day," Claude said, "I'm going to strangle you."

"Mama did tell you you were too thin for shorts. I heard her."

He yawned.

"You got the biggest teeth I ever saw," she said. "Like a horse."

"Do you want to fight?" He pulled out his handkerchief and dried his hands. "I haven't got time now. Later this evening, huh?"

Patsy turned away. "I don't want to be here this evening. I won't be here this evening at all."

Mrs. Merrick appeared. She was one of those women who never step outside without a hat—in winter because it is cold and in summer because it is sunny. Now she wore a light-green straw with a wide, flopping brim.

"You're always wearing green," Patsy said accusingly.

"Idiot child, shut up." Claude balanced the bottle on one finger.

"Really, Claude," Mrs. Merrick said. "Don't be nasty to her."

"You heard her," Patsy said. "You heard what she told you."

Claude shrugged and blew through loose lips: "Ruuuuup."

"I wish I had eyes pretty as yours, Mama," Patsy said.

"Honey, you have lovely eyes."

"Brown." Patsy crinkled up the corners of her mouth in disgust. "Everybody's got brown eyes. And anyhow it makes me look like Claude."

"God forbid," Claude said softly, and his mother threw him a warning glance.

"Patsy, honey, don't you want to come along with me?" she said.

"Where?"

"I'm going to pick up the laundry."

"Nuh-uh."

"It would give you something to do," Mrs. Merrick said. "We'll be right back."

A ride across the little town to the Negro section, which was called Bridge City. Then a talk with the laundress while her oldest son brought out the bundle and put it in the back seat of the car and her other kids swung from an old tire hung from the branches of the big chinaberry tree.

"No," she said.

"Did Mary Beth finish her lesson, Claude?" Mrs. Merrick asked.

"Yep. Lucille won't be along until three-thirty."

"Why do I have to have a brother who gives music lessons?" Patsy demanded.

"Now, dear," her mother said.

"Why can't it ever be quiet around here."

"Hilda Marie, you are being mean, plain and simple mean, to your only brother," her mother said.

"I want to be mean. I want to."

Mrs. Merrick only waved as she headed for the garage.

"You *are* crazy," Claude told Patsy pleasantly and went inside to put back the Coke bottle.

Patsy threw her head far back over her chair, pressing until the wood cut into the back of her neck and little lights danced in front of her eyes.

"Fool jackass!" she cried at the top of her voice. "Crazy fool jackass!"

At lunch, Mr. Merrick, a short, very heavy man, looked longingly at the other plates and began his own low-calorie fare.

"I don't see how you eat that without salt," Patsy said. "And so dreadful to begin with."

"I don't either, kitten," her father said.

"You'd think Claude would put on some weight, instead of being a bean pole like he is," Patsy said.

"Like is not a conjunction," Claude said.

"Now don't begin that," her mother said.

"What grades did you get in English?" Claude asked.

"I got a B-plus, Mr. Jackass."

"That's enough," her father said.

Patsy moved her fork in circles around her plate, following the gold bands. "I reckon I am not hungry. I would like to be excused."

"You're not sick, dear?" her mother asked.

Patsy turned at the door, with one hand holding the frame. "I am dying," she said. "I am dying of loneliness with everyone away."

"What an act," Claude said.

Patsy retreated to a porch chair and propped her feet up on the railing. She was trying with all her might to see if she could pop the back hook of her bra by hunching her shoulders when he father came out and sat beside her.

"Dessert?" He offered her a plate.

She shook her head sadly. "Like I said, I am not hungry." She regretted the first word the minute it was out of her mouth, but he did not correct her.

He still held out the plate. "Chocolate cake."

She took it. "Mama said it wasn't polite to offer things with your left hand."

"She's absolutely right," Mr. Merrick said, "but I am not going to fight, kitten, so stop trying."

"I wish you would stop calling me that name. I hate that name more than anything."

"Hilda Marie?" he suggested.

She made a face.

"What, then?"

She did not answer.

"Don't forget to take the plate in with you, kitten, when you go," Mr. Merrick said, getting up.

"Daddy," she said. He turned.

"Can't I come to town with you?"

He put one foot on the step and leaned his elbow on his knee. "Kitten, you'd be in the office half an hour and you'd get tired and want to come home. And I'd have to stop and bring you."

"No," she said. "No, I wouldn't." But he shook his head and was gone.

In the shade of the big red honeysuckle, an orange-striped cat stretched lazily, and then it sauntered over to the deeper shade of the butterfly bush. The long, hot afternoon was beginning.

Claude came out and started down the steps.

"Everyody's leaving," Patsy said. He didn't answer or turn, so she followed him, scuffing her heels on the gravel of the walk. "Where are you going?" she asked.

His car was at the curb. "I'm going to see Joyce."

"Like that?" She pointed to his shorts. "I didn't think you'd want anybody outside the family to see you like that."

"Look, twerp . . . Why don't you find something to do? Anything."

"That's what everybody tells me. You going to play bridge?"

"Yes, I *am*."

"I could play with you."

"If you could play."

"You could teach me."

"No," Claude said.

"It wouldn't take long."

"Not on your life." He got in the car and pulled the door to.

She stuck her head in the window. "If I had a car, I could drive around and visit people way over in Jackson, if I had a car."

He switched on the ignition and started the motor. "Well, you haven't. Now move before you get hurt."

The car drove away. She stood and watched, swinging her right leg back and forth so that her sandal scuffed along the gutter edge. After the car disappeared, she stared down at her moving foot. Then, carefully, she bent her sandal back against the cement. Pressing with all her weight, she snapped the sole so that it flapped loosely as she walked.

In the side yard a mulberry tree was dropping its full purple berries into the grass. She heard them squish under her feet. From a branch just over her head she pulled one of the nubby berries, and put it in her mouth. It prickled for an instant and tasted of dust. Then the heavy, overripe juice flooded out on her tongue. She reached up for a cluster of berries this time. They crushed between her grasping fingers. She whistled softly between her teeth and wiped her hand across the front of her skirt.

Claude had left one of his hunting knives on the back porch. She picked it up and began tossing it idly into the ground, trying without success to spear a small fragment of wood. Tiring of this, she left the knife sticking in the ground and wandered over to the sunny end of the porch to inspect her geraniums—four little pots of earth, each with a couple of scraggly stems reaching up into the air. Only one had a leaf, a shriveled brown bit that wrapped itself around the dead stalk.

Patsy filled the watering can and poured a little water on each one. Then she went into the kitchen.

"Fanny."

The short, stocky black woman turned around. "Yeah?"

"We got any coffee grounds?" Even as she asked, Patsy was making for the coffeepot.

"What you want that for?"

"My geraniums." They had been on her bedside table at the hospital, and she had loved each single one. "Mama says coffee grounds are good for plants."

"Ain't nothing gonna help them plants. Watch out my floor!" Fanny said as Patsy carried a handful of dripping grounds. "They is dead."

Patsy sprinkled the grounds around the bare twigs, watered them again, and went back in the kitchen. She got herself a glass of water and leaned on the refrigerator, drinking and swinging her leg so that the broken sandal flapped slowly.

Fanny turned. She was perched on a high red stool at the sink, polishing demitasse spoons. "What I hearing?"

Patsy held up her foot.

"Might just as well throw them out. They ain't no more good than those plants of yours," Fanny said.

Patsy rubbed the back of her thighs against the cool enamel of the refrigerator. "This is the longest day."

"Iffen you want things to do, you could get that big silver pitcher from out the dining room and polish it up."

"Did Estes come yet?" He was Fanny's boy, a couple of years older than Patsy. He came sometimes to keep his mother company, if he didn't have anything else to do. "Did he?" Patsy demanded.

"No, he ain't, yet."

Patsy stood on one leg and curled the lifted foot around the other ankle. She watched Fanny's movements, narrowing her left eye with the effort of her perception. "Lord, but you sure are slow."

The hand stopped its motion. "You come all the way back here to pester me?"

"Nuh-uh. Fanny, why don't you give them to him?"

Fanny reached her rag into the jar of pink silver polish. "Give who to who?"

"You just don't listen to me. Give those spoons, the ones right there, to Estes."

"Now, why I want to do that?"

"He could sell them for a lot of money." Patsy squatted down on the floor.

"You mama say for you not to sit like that. She say it ain't becoming for a young lady."

Patsy pretended not to hear. "Don't you want to make a lot of money?"

Fanny turned around again. "And what you mama going to say to that?"

"She wouldn't know."

"And what the police gonna say when they see you mama's initials all over the tops of them spoons?"

"We could take the initials off," Patsy said, "or take them over to Atlanta, where nobody'd know."

"You been looking too much at that television. I told you mama that."

"That's got nothing to do with it."

"You looking at it all day in the hospital there, I told her it ain't good."

"You talk so much. Yack, yack, yack."

Fanny swung back to her work, so violently that she had to catch hold of the counter for balance. "I ain't even begun to talk."

Chewing her lip, Patsy gazed up at the crosspiece of the doorway. After a minute, she said, "I bet you anything I could chin myself on that."

Fanny whistled—"Euuuuuuu."

"Well, I could."

"And bust all that stitching the doctor put in your stomach. And pour your insides all out over the floor."

Patsy stood up, her arms moving nervously. That was a nightmare she had sometimes: the hole in her stomach opening up. Sometimes, when she woke up, she would reach inside her pajamas and run her fingers along the new scar, just to be sure that it still held together.

"Fanny, what would you do if I was sick right here?"

"Iffen you gonna get sick, you just plain better go out in the back yard, where it don't matter none," Fanny said calmly.

Patsy pounded her fist against the door. "You are just so mean that I am going to make my mama fire you, and then I'm gonna tell everybody about you, and you won't be able to get another job, and you'll starve to death. That's what I'll do."

"Man, man," Fanny said to the chrome-plated faucet of the sink. "She sure is changed. They must put something else in her when they took that appendix out."

Before she thought, Patsy said, "You reckon they did?"

"You reckon they did?" Fanny mimicked in a high-pitched voice. "You reckon they did?"

"Crazy fool jackass!" Patsy exploded as she banged out the door. "Crazy fool jackass!"

Fanny shouted after her, "They done fill you up with all sorts of garbage to make you act so ugly! That what they done!"

Tucking her hands in the back belt of her shorts, Patsy sauntered around the corner of the house, still whispering to herself, "Fool jackass, crazy fool jackass."

She spotted Jo Dillard's rumpled black head, almost hidden by one of the big old hydrangea bushes. The Dillards lived next door. "What are you doing by my house?" Patsy asked.

Jo turned her head slowly, and the clear, blue, five-year-old gaze focused first on Patsy's feet, then climbed her body, coming almost indifferently to her face.

"I asked you what you doing by my house."

The eyes climbed down the body again. "Digging," Jo said. She pointed with her left hand. "See?" Behind the hydrangea bush was a little hole she was making with an old wavy-bladed bread knife.

"What you doing that for?"

"Nothing. Digging."

"You're lying."

Jo did not answer.

"Tell me."

"Huh?"

"You tell me."

Jo turned back to her work. Two thin sinews stood out on the back of her neck, beneath the ragged fringe of her clipped hair.

"You are the ugliest-looking kid I have ever seen," Patsy told her. "You are positively the ugliest thing. And you get uglier every day. You do."

The eyes lifted, circled her face, and wandered off.

"And the way you do everything with your left hand— that's the silliest thing, too."

The child went on digging, her head bent.

"Tell me," Patsy's voice dropped, and she crouched down by the smaller figure.

The child watched the ground intently, fascinated by each small load of mud. A round white marble came to the surface. Two small, squarish fingers went down and picked it up; the hand closed over it.

"What you find?"

The knife continued to lift small pats of dirt.

"What did you find in my garden? Give it here."

The blade fell to the ground. Jo clenched both hands around the marble. Her fingers wove tightly together.

Patsy picked up the knife. She scraped it against the brick foundation and ran her finger over the wavy edge of the blade. "I am going to kill you," she said. "And a dozen policemen will come to take you away."

With a small whinny of fear, Jo scuttled home, her hands still clenched.

Patsy jumped up and, waving the knife over her head, shouted, "Don't come back! Don't ever come back!"

She tossed the knife up against the trunk of the hydrangea bush and walked away, wiping her dirty hands on her bare thighs. A window flew up, and Mrs. Dillard called, "Patsy, what are you doing! Patsy . . ." She pretended not to hear as she strolled to the back of the yard, rolling her hips under the tight white shorts.

In the quiet of the hot afternoon, she could hear the clicking of the dial phone. "Maybe she is calling the police," she told herself aloud. "And they will come and get me in one of the white cars with the chrome siren on top. And my scar will pop, and I'll bleed all over everything." She fingered her side; it was sore to the touch.

Inside her own house, the phone began to ring. She cocked her head, listening. She could almost hear Mrs. Dillard's angry words.

"She is old and ugly," Patsy said aloud. From a low branch a fat swallow beat a clumsy flight. "She is old and fat and ugly and I hate her."

Dragging her feet so that the tips of her toes brushed the crispy edges of the grass, she went around the two chinaberry trees, grown close together and circled by an old wisteria vine with ragged shreds of flowers still among its leaves. She was hidden from the house.

Her mother appeared on the side porch and called, "Patsy!"

"She is old and ugly and I hate *her*, too," Patsy whispered.

"Patsy, come here this instant. This very instant."

Patsy reached out and took hold of the sharp rough bark of the tree. "No," she whispered.

Fanny popped out the kitchen door. Through the vines Patsy saw the sun glint on her black skin.

"What she did this time?"

Mrs. Merrick opened the screen and came down into the yard; her heels made a sharp clatter on each step. "This is just too much."

"What she did?"

"Patsy!" Her mother folded her hands and rested her chin on them. She was really angry; that was a sure sign.

"Ugly," Patsy whispered.

Right in front of her were crosspieces of wood nailed to the trunk of one of the chinaberry trees—the steps leading up to the tree house. She tilted back her head. Vaguely, through the dense foliage, she could see the brown, weathered boards. Slowly and carefully, so as not to hurt her scar, she began to climb.

"Patsy! . . . Look in the back yard, Fanny." Mrs. Merrick started across the grass.

Patsy reached the platform, railless and tiny: only four boards wide. She sat down cross-legged on the wood that had been warped by winter rains and stained almost black by the falling berries.

"I won't ever come down," she whispered. The sound startled her, so she went on talking to herself silently. I'll live up here. Until I get old and die. I'll stay until I get old and older and die.

Below, hidden by the feathery leaves, her mother demanded, "Patsy, come here immediately."

I won't ever come down. I won't.

She clenched her fists and closed her eyes in determination. But already, under the lids, the tears were beginning.

The Land and the Water

❃

FROM THE OPEN Atlantic beyond Timbalier Head a few scattered fog horns grunted, muffled and faint. That bank had been hanging off shore for days. We'd been watching the big draggers chug up to it, get dimmer and dimmer, and finally disappear in its grayness, leaving only the stifled sounds of their horns behind. It had been there so long we got used to it, and came to think of it as always being there, like another piece of land, maybe.

The particular day I'm thinking about started out clear and hot with a tiny breeze—a perfect day for a Snipe or a Sailfish. There were a few of them moving on the big bay, not many. And they stayed close to shore, for the barometer was drifting slowly down in its tube and the wind was shifting slowly backward around the compass.

Larger sailboats never came into the bay—it was too shallow for them—and these small ones, motorless, moving with the smallest stir of air, could sail for home, if the fog came in, by following the shore—or if there was really no wind at all, they could be paddled in and beached. Then their crews could walk to the nearest phone and call to be picked up. You had to do it that way, because the fog always came in so quick. As it did that morning.

My sister and I were working by our dock, scraping and painting the little dinghy. Because the spring tides washed over this stretch, there were no trees, no bushes even, just snail grass and beach lettuce and pink flowering sea lavender, things that liked salt. All morning it had been bright and blue and shining. Then all at once it turned gray and wet, like an unfalling rain, moveless and still. We went right on sanding and from being sweaty hot we turned sweaty cold, the fog chilling and dripping off our faces.

"It isn't worth the money," my sister said. She is ten and that is her favorite sentence. This time it wasn't even true. She was the one who'd talked my father into giving us the job.

I wouldn't give her the satisfaction of an answer, though I didn't like the wet any more than she did. It was sure to make my hair roll up in tight little curls all over my head and I would have to wash it again and sleep on the hard metal curlers to get it back in shape.

Finally my sister said, "Let's go get a Coke."

When we turned to go back up to the house, we found that it had disappeared. It was only a couple of hundred yards away, right behind us and up a little grade, a long slope of beach plum and poison ivy, salt burned and scrubby. You couldn't see a thing now, except gray. The land and the water all looked the same; the fog was that thick.

There weren't any Cokes. Just some bottles of Dr. Pepper and a lot of empties waiting in cases on the back porch. "Well," my sister said, "let's go tell her."

She meant my mother of course, and we didn't have to look for her very hard. The house wasn't big, and being a summer house, it had very thin walls: we could hear her playing cards with my father in the living room.

They were sitting by the front window. On a clear day there was really something to see out there: the sweep of the bay and the pattern of the inlets and, beyond it all, the dark blue of the Atlantic. Today there was nothing, not even a bird, if you didn't count the occasional yelp of a seagull off high overhead somewhere.

"There's no Cokes," my sister said. "Not a single one."

"Tomorrow's grocery day," my mother said. "Go make a lemonade."

"Look," my father said, "why not go back to work on the dinghy? You'll get your money faster."

So we went, only stopping first to get our oilskin hats. And pretty soon, fog was dripping from the brims like a kind of very gentle rain.

But we didn't go back to work on the dinghy. For a while we sat on the edge of the dock and looked at the minnow-flecked water, and then we got out the crab nets and went over to the tumbled heap of rocks to see if we could catch anything. We spent a couple of hours out there, skinning our knees against the rough barnacled surfaces. Once a seagull swooped down so low he practically touched the tops of our hats. Almost but not quite. I don't think we even saw a crab, though we dragged our nets around in the water just for the fun of it. Finally we dug a dozen or so clams, ate them, and tried to skip the shells along the water. That was how the afternoon passed, with one thing or the other, and us not hurrying, not having anything we'd rather be doing.

We didn't have a watch with us, but it must have been late afternoon when they all came down from the house. We heard them before we saw them, heard the brush of their feet on the grass path.

It was my mother and my father and Robert, my biggest brother, the one who is eighteen. My father had the round black compass and a coil of new line. Robert had a couple of gas lanterns and a big battery one. My mother had the life jackets and a little wicker basket and a thermos bottle. They all went out along the narrow rickety dock and began to load the gear into my father's *Sea Skiff*. It wasn't a big boat and my father had to take a couple of minutes to pack it, stowing the basket way up forward under the cowling and wedging the thermos bottle on top of that. Robert, who'd left his lanterns on the ground to help him, came back to fetch them.

"I thought you were at the McKays'," I said. "How'd you get over here?"

"Dad called me." He lifted one eyebrow. "Remember about something called the telephone?" And he picked up his gear and walked away.

"Well," my sister said.

They cast off, the big outboard sputtered gently, throttled way down. They would have to move very slowly in the fog. As they swung away, Robert at the tiller, we saw my father set out his compass and take a bearing off it.

My mother watched them out of sight, which didn't take more than a half minute. Then she stood watching the fog for a while and, I guess, following the sound of the steady put-put. It seemed to me, listening to it move off and blend with the sounds of the bay—the sounds of a lot of water, of tiny waves and fish feeding—that I could pick out two or three other motors.

Finally my mother got tired of standing on the end of the dock and she turned around and walked up to us. I expected her to pass right by and go on up to the house. But she didn't. We could hear her stop and stand looking at us. My sister and I just scraped a little harder, pretending we hadn't noticed.

"I guess you're wondering what that was all about?" she said finally.

"I don't care," my sister said. She was lying. She was just as curious as I was.

My mother didn't seem to have heard her. "It's Linda Holloway and Stan Mitchell and Butch Rodgers."

We knew them. They were sailing people, a little older than I, a little younger than my brother Robert. They lived in three houses lined up one by the other on the north shore of Marshall's Inlet. They were all right kids, nothing special either way, sort of a gang, living as close as they did. This year they had turned up with a new sailboat, a twelve-foot fiberglass job that somebody had designed and built for Stan Mitchell as a birthday present.

"What about them?" my sister asked, forgetting that she wasn't interested.

"They haven't come home."

"Oh," I said.

"They were sailing," my mother said. "The Brewers think they saw them off their place just before the fog. They were sort of far out."

"You mean Dad's gone to look for them?"

She nodded.

"Is that all?" my sister said. "Just somebody going to have to sit in their boat and wait until the fog lifts."

My mother looked at us. Her curly red hair was dripping with the damp of the fog and her face was smeared with dust. "The Lord save me from children," she said quietly. "The glass is twenty-nine eighty and it's still going down fast."

We went back up to the house with her, to help fix supper—a quiet nervous kind of supper. The thick luminous fish-colored fog turned into deep solid night fog. Just after supper, while we were drying the dishes, the wind sprang up. It shook the whole line of windows in the kitchen and knocked over every single pot of geraniums on the back porch.

"Well," my mother said, "it's square into the east now."

A low barometer and a wind that had gone backwards into the east—there wasn't one of us didn't know what that meant. And it wasn't more than half an hour before there was a grumble of approaching thunder and the fog began to swirl around the windows, streaming like torn cotton as the wind increased.

"Dad'll come back now, huh?" my sister asked.

"Yes," my mother said. "All the boats'll have to come back now."

We settled down to television, half watching it and half listening to the storm outside. In a little while, an hour or so, my mother said, "Turn off that thing."

"What?"

"Turn it off, quick." She hurried on the porch, saying over her shoulder: "I hear something."

The boards of the wide platform were wet and slippery under our feet, and the eaves of the house poured water in steady small streams that the wind grabbed and tore away. Between the crashes of thunder, we heard it too. There was a boat coming into our cove. By the sound of it, it would be my father and Robert.

"Is that the motor?" my mother asked.

"Sure," I said. It had a little tick and it was higher pitched than any of the others. You couldn't miss it.

Without another word to us she went scuttling across the porch and down the stairs toward the cove. We followed and stood close by, off the path and a little to one side. It was tide marsh there, and salt mud oozed over the tops of our sneakers. The cove itself was sheltered—it was in the lee of Cedar Tree Neck—but even so it was pretty choppy. Whitecaps were beginning to run high and broken, wind against tide, and the spume from them stung as it hit your face and your eyes. You could hear the real stuff blowing overhead, with the peculiar sound wind has when it gets past half a gale.

My father's boat was sidling up to the dock now, pitching and rolling in the broken water. Its motor sputtered into reverse and then the hull rubbed gently against the pilings. They had had a bad time. In the quick lightning flashes you could see every scupper pouring water. You could see the slow weary way they made the lines fast.

"There wasn't anything else to do," my father was saying as they came up the path, beating their arms for warmth, "with it blowing straight out the east, we had to come in."

Robert stopped a moment to pull off his oilskins. Under them his shirt was as drenched as if he hadn't had any protection at all.

"We came the long way around," my father said, "hugging the lee as much as we could."

"We almost swamped," Robert said.

Then we were at the house and they went off to dry

their clothes, and that was that. They told us later that everybody had come in, except only for the big Coast Guard launch. And with only one boat it was no wonder they didn't find them.

The next morning was bright and clear and a lot cooler. The big stretch of bay was still shaken and tousled-looking, spotted with whitecaps. Soon as it was light, my father went to the front porch and looked and looked with his glasses. He checked the anemometer dial, and shook his head. "It's still too rough for us." In a bit the Coast Guard boats—two of them—appeared, and a helicopter began its chopping noisy circling.

It was marketing day too, so my mother, my sister, and I went off, as we always did. We stopped at the laundromat and the hardware, and then my mother had to get some pine trees for the slope behind the house. It was maybe four o'clock before we got home.

The wind had dropped, the bay was almost quiet again. Robert and my father were gone, and so was the boat. "I thought they'd go out again," my mother said. She got a cup of coffee and the three of us sat watching the fleet of boats work their way back and forth across the bay, searching.

Just before dark—just when the sky was beginning to take its twilight color—my father and Robert appeared. They were burned lobster red with great white circles around their eyes where their glasses had been.

"Did you find anything?" my sister asked.

My father looked at my mother, who was opening a can of beer for him.

"You might as well tell them," she said. "They'll know anyway."

"Well," my father said, "they found the boat."

"That's what they were expecting to find, wasn't it?" my mother asked quietly.

He nodded. "It's kind of hard to say what happened. But it looks like they got blown on East Shoal with the tide going down and the chop tearing the keel out."

"Oh," my mother said.

"Oh," my sister said.

"They found the boat around noon."

My mother said: "Have they found them?"

"Not that I heard."

"You think," my mother said, "they could have got to shore way out on Gull Point or some place like that?"

"No place is more than a four-hour walk," my father said. "They'd have turned up by now."

And it was later still, after dark, ten o'clock or so, that Mr. Robinson, who lived next door, stopped by the porch on his way home. "Found one," he said wearily. "The Mitchell boy."

"Oh," my mother said, "oh, oh."

"Where?" my father asked.

"Just off the shoal, they said, curled up in the eel grass."

"My God," my mother said softly.

Mr. Robinson moved off without so much as a good-by. And after a while my sister and I went to bed.

But not to sleep. We played cards for an hour or so, until we couldn't stand that any more. Then we did a couple of crossword puzzles together. Finally we just sat in our beds, in the chilly night, and listened. There were the usual sounds from outside the open windows, sounds of the land and the water. Deer moving about in the brush on their way to eat the wild watercress and wild lettuce that grew around the spring. The deep pumping sounds of an owl's wings in the air. Little splashes from the bay—the fishes and the muskrats and the otters.

"I didn't know there'd be so many things moving at night," my sister said.

"You just weren't ever awake."

"What do you reckon it's like," she said, "being on the bottom in the eel grass?"

"Shut up,'" I told her.

"Well," she said, "I just asked. Because I was wondering."

"Don't."

Her talking had started a funny shaking quivering feeling from my navel right straight back to my backbone. The tips of my fingers hurt too, the way they always did.

"I thought the dogs would howl," she said.

"They can't smell anything from the water," I told her. "Now quit."

She fell asleep then and maybe I did too, because the night seemed awful short. Or maye the summer dawns really come that quick. Not dawn, no. The quiet deep dark that means dawn is just about to come. The birds started whistling and the gulls started shrieking. I got up and looked out at the dripping beach plum bushes and the twisted, salt-burned jack pines, then I slipped out the window. I'd done it before. You lifted the screen, and lowered yourself down. It wasn't anything of a drop— all you had to watch was the patch of poison ivy. I circled around the house and took the old deer trail down to the bay. It was chilly, and I began to wish I had brought my robe or a coat. With just cotton pajamas my teeth would begin chattering very soon.

I don't know what I expected to see. And I didn't see anything at all. Just some morning fog in the hollows and around the spring. And the dock, with my father's boat bobbing in the run of the tide.

The day was getting close now. The sky overhead turned a sort of luminous dark blue. As it did, the water darkened to a lead-colored gray. It looked heavy and oily and impenetrable. I tried to imagine what would be under it. I always thought I knew. There would be horse-shoe crabs and hermit crabs and blue crabs, and scallops squirting their way along, and there'd be all the different kinds of fish, and the eels. I kept telling myself that that was all.

But this time I couldn't seem to keep my thoughts straight. I kept wondering what it must be like to be dead and cold and down in the sand and mud with the eel grass brushing you and the crabs bumping you and the fish—I had felt their little sucking mouths sometimes when I swam.

The water was thick and heavy and the color of a mirror in a dark room. Minnows broke the surface right under the wharf. I jumped. I couldn't help it.

And I got to thinking that something might come out of the water. It didn't have a name or a shape. But it was there.

I stood where I was for a while, trying to fight down the idea. When I found I couldn't do that, I decided to walk slowly back to the house. At least I thought I was going to walk, but the way the boards of the wharf shook under my feet I know that I must have been running. On the path up to the house my bare feet hit some of the sharp cut-off stubs of the rosa rugosa bushes, but I didn't stop. I went crashing into the kitchen because that was the closest door.

The room was thick with the odor of frying bacon, the softness of steam: my mother had gotten up early. She turned around when I came in, not seeming surprised—as if it was the most usual thing in the world for me to be wandering around before daylight in my pajamas.

"Go take those things off, honey," she said. "You're drenched."

"Yes ma'am," I told her.

I stripped off the clothes and saw that they really were soaking. I knew it was just the dew and the fog. But I couldn't help thinking it was something else. Something that had reached for me, and missed. Something that was wet, that had come from the water, something that had splashed me as it went past.

The Last Gas Station

WE HAVE LIVED here with our father for years and years. Joe, who's the oldest—then Mark, then me—says he can remember our other place real well: the house we used to live in, and the kitchen with yellow roses on the wall paper. He says there were tall trees, real tall trees where you could lie on your back and watch the sun spin in the leaves. (There's no trees that big around here.) He says that there was a high bluff where you could look down on a river that was twenty feet across. He caught crawfish in the pools there sometimes.

Joe tells that our father had a whole pack of spotted hounds, and when they went hunting you could hear them for hours, our father shouting and the dogs fighting and howling. Joe says on nights when the moon was full the country was plain crowded with animals running.

Joe says all of that—only thing he won't talk about is our mother. Now, I know we got to have had one, but Joe won't answer, and Mark, being younger, don't remember more than some old black lady who took care of us for a while.

Of course I don't even remember that, being the youngest. For all I know, I never been anywhere but here. Our gas station. Our house next door, sitting high on its foundations against the damp and the snakes. The highway, four lanes straight down from the north and straight off to the south, not a curve nor a bend in it. And all around everywhere, far as you can see, palmettos. Low and yellow green, and good for nothing except making fans. There's a fair number of snakes out there and some mice and rabbits but not much else. You can see it—the scrub's no higher than a man's shoulder —and that's all there is.

Once Mark told me that if I climbed to the very top of the roof and looked to the west, I'd see a big lake shining. But he was just fooling. All I saw was heat haze, and I don't have to climb a roof for that.

In one way it's a good thing we don't have our father's hunting pack any more. The scrub's full of sinkholes, and dogs are pretty like to fall in. I suppose that's what happened to Lucky—he was a dog we had for a while. He came off a Buick sedan—the people, they slowed down and threw him out a window. He bounced two or three times and landed on his back, but he wasn't any more than scared. That's why we called him Lucky. He was small and long-haired and he suffered from ticks during the spring and ear infections the rest of the year. Never was a time when both his ears stood up straight —always something draining out one or the other. But he sure did like running in the palmettos. And one day he never came back.

We went looking, Joe and Mark and me, but there was too many holes and too much ground. We never even found a sign of him.

We had a cat too, you know that? She got killed on the highway by a big semi, name of Beatons Long Distance Moving.

When Joe scraped her up with a shovel and tossed her way back in the scrub, I started crying. I really did love that cat. I kept on crying until Joe and our father beat the tears out of me. They said it wasn't decent.

After that I felt different about the highway. Before, I used to like it, especially the sounds: the tires whistling and singing on the wet, and hissing on the dry. The soft growling sound—kind of like a sigh—when some trucker tested his air brakes. The way horns echo way off in the distance. The thin little screech of car brakes, too, almost like a laugh. And something else—a steady even whisper. Day and night, no different. It ran along the whole length of highway, like electric wires singing. Or maybe kind of like breathing.

And I got to admit that sometimes the highway was a pretty thing too. When the moon was on it. When quick summer rains fell and clouds of steam rose up and cleared away leaving just a heat mirage in the distance. The wind was nice too. On a hot August day, those passing cars and trucks really stirred up a nice little breeze for you.

But I didn't like the highway anymore. Not at all. There just wasn't no getting away from it. If I didn't hear it or see it, if I closed my eyes and stuck my fingers in my ears, I still could smell it. The different exhausts, gas and diesel. The smell of oil that's burning clean and oil that's not. The paint smell of engines overheating with the load of their air conditioners.

Like Joe would say, the highway brought everything to us, and took it away too. Joe's always been the religious one around here, the one who put a Bible on the top shelf in the kitchen. He used to read a little from it now and then. It was a comfort to him, I guess, specially after Bruce left.

You see, when we first came here, there were four boys, not three. The oldest was Bruce. And this was how he come to leave.

Every December there was a big increase in southbound traffic. Out of that crowd there'd always be some who'd made the trip before, and who always made a point of coming back to the same places. Take this one car now; it had stopped every winter for four or five years. It was a man and his wife and their girl. She got prettier each year, her blond hair hanging long and loose down her back. The last time the man wasn't with them. They stayed quite a while, parked off to one side of the station, talking to Bruce. Afterwards Bruce was very excited: he smashed his thumb with a tire iron, something he don't ever do.

Anyway, right after they left, he marked a date on the wall calendar with a big red star, and on that day he packed his clothes in a paper bag and told us he was going north with them. Then he walked across the highway to wait.

I remember that: Bruce walking across the road, putting his feet down heavily, as if they hurt him, crossing the wide median, kicking at the pine trees the state planted there. (Funny thing, those trees, been there five or six years and don't hardly reach to your knee.) He waited a long time, swatting at the flies and slapping at the mosquitoes—they're both pretty bad sometimes.

Joe and Mark and me, we sat on the curb by the gas pumps and watched and waited with him. We only moved when a car came in. Then the three of us rushed to fill the tank, clean the windshield, and check the tires. (I always checked the tires because I was the smallest.) We worked so fast we even got a couple of tips.

The sun got hotter and hotter. Bruce kept taking off his hat to fan himself with it, and now and then he'd spit to clear the dust out of his mouth.

Along toward the middle of the afternoon, Joe said, "Maybe he won't get to go after all." And he went in the house to tell our father. Minute or two later he was back. "He said it don't matter none about Bruce."

Then a Mercedes pulled in, a 220 with special order extra green glass—made the people with their big sunglasses look just like frogs.

They wanted diesel fuel, which we never had.

"We may not make it," the man said accusingly to us. Like we had let his tank run low. "We just may not."

"She won't burn gas, mister," Joe said firmly. He

figures he knows a lot about cars because he's filled so many tanks.

"How far to the next station?"

"I don't know," Joe said. "I never been down that way."

They pulled out very slowly to avoid wasting any fuel. With a shrug Joe moved the sign that said LAST GAS a little closer to the road. It was one of those folding tripod things that we had to take in at night so the big trucks wouldn't backwind it over. It could make an awful racket in the middle of the night.

All of a sudden the three of us remembered and looked across the highway. Bruce was gone. We never even saw the car that stopped for him.

YOU'D THINK we'd be lonely living in a place like this. But we weren't. There was the cars stopping for gas. And once a week the company truck came to fill the underground tanks. That man always stayed to pass the time of day with us. Sometimes he'd bring the newspapers, and he'd always bring our groceries and take our order for the next week. We didn't ever go to town. Our father's car was parked behind the house, next to the cistern, a '59 Pontiac. It was up on blocks, nice and neat, and the hens liked to nest under it. Used to be, too, that the school bus picked us up, and made a big U turn through the highway median. But we stopped going to school, and the big tracks filled in and grass grew over them.

We had plenty to do what with running the station, and keeping house, and doing the cooking, and feeding the chickens, and hunting after their eggs, and repairing the roof, and keeping the screens patched. Our father, he didn't do anything. He was so tired that he could only sit all day long on the front porch. He used to chew tobacco, but finally he even stopped fooling with the plug.

One day Joe and Mark told me he was dead. "You come see for yourself."

I'd seen dead things before but never a man. Even so,

just the way he sat there, head a little on one side—and the big blue and green flies banging away at the porch screen to get at him—I'd have known by myself.

That night Joe and Mark (they wouldn't let me go with them) carried our father way far out into the scrub and dropped him into one of the sinkholes there. They took a couple of tire irons and a piece or two of rusted junk from the back yard—to make sure he stayed down.

Nothing changed after his death. Joe went on signing his name on the receipts from the company. He'd been doing it so long that nobody, not the driver of the gas truck nor the company office, seemed to notice the difference.

So, like I said, things went on, quiet except for that one busy season in the winter when all the campers and the trailers and the baggage-packed cars poured south over the road.

"Look at that," Joe said one day when four Pace Arrows and six Winnebagos passed, bumper to bumper. All the Winnebagos had little Christmas trees in the back windows. "Don't it look like something's chasing them."

And that was exactly the way it looked: drivers scowling, staring hard ahead, concentrating on the road, just like something awful was right behind them.

FEW MONTHS after that, Joe and Mark got in a fight. I didn't see the start; when I walked in the kitchen Mark had a hold of a broken bottle and Joe had his knife out, the big switchblade he kept from our father. I could tell that Mark was beginning to have second thoughts; he'd have turned and run only he was scared of getting that knife in his back. He just kept moving in the general direction of the door. Me, I was too scared to say anything.

Mark managed to back around the table, past the stove, and down the steps leading to the yard, pushing open the screen as he went. He had his left hand on the rail and he was trying to get down the three steps without taking his eyes off Joe. Well, we all knew that the railing was loose, been loose for years I guess, but neither Joe nor I knew that all you had to do was pick it up.

And that was very lucky for Mark. Because once he got to the steps, Joe closed on him, holding the knife low and flat, just the right position.

Well, Mark faked a stumble and Joe moved in. Joe was so busy watching the broken bottle he wasn't paying no attention to Mark's left hand. The long piece of two-by-two rail caught him square alongside the head. And he slid face down the steps into the yard.

Mark watched Joe for a long time. But whatever he was waiting for, it didn't come. Slowly, in an easy under-hand, Mark tossed the broken bottle at Joe's back, the way you'd throw something on a pile of garbage. The railing he dropped right where he stood.

He came back inside, walked straight by me into the bedroom. He pushed the mattress off his bed so that the whole set of springs showed. He kept his special secret things hidden in a black plastic zipper case stuffed down in one of the center coils. He took that case, and his good jacket from where it hung on a nail by his bed, and his special clean cap from the shelf.

"Cain killed Abel," he said to me as he left. And, "The end of the world is coming."

You see that he was really the religious one in the family.

He got a hitch almost immediately, a big truck with a load of cattle, going south. I never saw him again.

LIKE I SAID, Mark used his left hand. I guess that's why the side of Joe's head wasn't caved in. But he looked pretty terrible lying there, not moving, bleeding into the gravel, half his ear knocked off. I pulled him up the steps and inside; took me a long time and I couldn't hardly do it: he was a big man. I stopped the bleeding and kept ice on his head, but it was days before he came around. And then he couldn't do nothing but talk foolishness and vomit all over the kitchen floor.

He got well after a while and was just like always. Except for the headaches and the limp in his left leg. That never did feel right, he said.

Now I was really busy. I had to do the cars all by myself and of course I had to take care of him. That's why lots of things that should have been done, didn't get done. Like the light bulb over the round orange sign GAS. I wasn't tall enough to reach it, not even with our ladder; Joe didn't feel like fooling with it; and the sign stayed dark. I took to leaving the porch light on, so people could see where we were in all that empty stretch of road. I even found some reflectors and put them along the highway too.

We got along, one season after the other. Just Joe and me.

THEN something changed, really changed. All of a sudden there was too much traffic on the highway. Now, it gets pretty busy during the holiday season, but this was fifty times more. Thousands and thousands of cars, and this was the middle of the summer. The ground was shaking with their weight, all the windows were rattling in the back draft, like a storm blowing up.

We'd have four, five cars in the gas station at once. They weren't the usual crowd, waiting to get out and stretch, complaining because we didn't have a Coke machine or any rest rooms. They wanted gas and they wanted oil, forget the windshield, they wanted to be gone.

"Something's going on up north there," Joe said.

Nobody would stop long enough to talk. They were in that much a hurry.

Pretty soon our tanks were empty, regular and super both. And the truck from the company, the one that always came on Wednesdays, it didn't come. So I took in the sign that said LAST GAS and leaned it against the house wall, and at night I turned off the porch light.

Now the traffic raced by us without stopping. And on

the sides of the road abandoned cars began to appear. Nothing wrong with them, they were just out of gas.

The people from those cars, they'd thumb a ride if they could. If they couldn't, they'd start walking—not talking, nor anything like that—just following the highway.

Soon the roadsides were lined solid with empty cars, and then the left lane was closed completely by an eight-car smash-up. And then, well, then it began slowing down. Just as suddenly as it started, it was stopping.

This upset Joe, really upset him. "I know it ain't right," he said. He got more and more nervous, and that brought on his headaches, like it always did. In a couple of hours he was limping up and down by the empty gas pumps, holding his head with both hands.

All of a sudden he spun around, rubber heel squealing on the asphalt. "Now look"—he jabbed me right in the middle of the chest with his finger. "If they're going, we're going too. Let's get together right now. Before we miss the last car."

While his back was turned, I took off, running. There was this one particular sinkhole I'd known about for years—I'd found it myself. You could climb down into it (limestone is nothing but layers) to a nice wide shelf, under the overhanging ground. You were out of sight unless somebody happened to climb down after you. And I didn't think Joe was going to look for me in every single sink, not with the pain he had in his leg.

He sure did look for quite a while. He yelled and he cursed after me for hours and hours, before he finally gave up.

Even when I knew he was gone, I stayed hidden, just to be sure. I'd rather met a coral snake where I was than run into Joe on the surface, mad as he was. So I waited a long, long time; when I came out, it was late evening and the highway was empty and I thought: Maybe Joe really did get the last car. Maybe he really did.

• • •

THAT WAS yesterday. And there's things I didn't think about before that's bothering me now. Like, when I went to turn on the light, there wasn't any electricity. And food. Joe left everything for me, but it isn't all that much. And the quiet. I'm not used to the quiet. Nor the way winds sound in the dark, hollow and big. And most of all, being alone.

I should have gone with him. Sometimes I think I'll walk along after him, but it's got to be too far. I climbed on the roof to look off that way; I could see for miles and miles, and there wasn't a single thing moving.

And I wonder if there's anything there either, in that direction where all the people were rushing.

I sure wish I'd gone with Joe.

When the next car passes I think I'm going to run out in the highway so they have to hit me or stop for me. I know that's what I'm going to do.

If there ever is another car.

The Thieves

IT BEGAN to rain. Holding her purse over her head, Carrie ran the last few steps to the Lafayette Bar. Steve was waiting at the same table, the corner table next to the line of open doors at the sidewalk. He saw her, smiled, and half stood up.

She wondered how many times she'd come here in the two years she had known him. Hundreds of evenings probably—whenever he finished his work at the hospital early enough.

Rain dripped down her cheek. She shook her head violently, like a dog shaking his coat. She hated umbrellas and never carried them. Why couldn't he ever come to her apartment? Why did he always call her and say, "Want a beer at the Lafayette?" She'd suggested once: "I've got a refrigerator full of beer." "I like the atmosphere of bars," he said. "And I like that bar in particular."

It was a form of independence, she thought. Some men were like that. Were bred to be like that. A matter of pride. For them . . . And for me? She put that thought firmly out of her mind. It is a good relationship, that is enough. We have fun when we are together. And we are together so much . . . except for the last three days, she thought with a twitch of pain.

"My parents are coming to town for the weekend," he had told her. "They've never been here before, so I got somebody to do my work and I'm going to take off and show them around."

She had not been invited to meet them, but that would be his independence again. What was between them was none of his parents' affair . . .

She wiped the rain spots from her purse and went to meet him, heels clicking on the bare brick of the bar's floor. He leaned over and gave her a peck on the cheek. Without having to be told, the waiter brought her a beer.

He knew too, she thought.

The rain was falling in thick gray sheets, straight down, the color of fog. All along Bourbon Street drainpipes began to rattle and sing as they dumped thick arcs of water out on the broken, uneven sidewalks.

"And it never rains at night," Carrie said.

"Feel it turn to steam," Steve said.

Rain splashed through the line of open doors, ricocheting like bullets from the sidewalk. She could feel it on her legs, cool for a second, then a warm snaky line down to her ankles. She moved her foot from under the table and looked at it.

"You getting wet?"

"Just looking."

"We can move if you want."

"No." A raincoated policeman walked by, sloshing through the puddles. She leaned over and watched him. At the corner his shiny black coat merged with the shiny black street.

On the river a ship began blowing, urgent and mournful.

In the corner of the bar, there was a record player. The bartender changed the record, moving with slow deliberation. He turned up the volume.

"God," Steve said.

"What?"

"*Vesti la giubba.*"

"Oh," she said, "I wasn't listening."

"You've got the darndest habit these days."

"Like what?"

"Not listening. You just kind of disappear."

"I don't mean to."

"Oh hell," he said, "everybody's got a right to be peculiar."

"I don't . . ." She stopped. Don't whine, she told herself firmly.

On the river the tug hooted again, insistently. He cocked his head listening.

"Maybe some barges got loose."

"*Ridi, Pagliaccio . . .*" There was a scratch in the record.

"Your parents get off?" Her voice was sharper than she had intended.

"Sure. Why shouldn't they?"

She shook her head, smiling again. "Just asking."

They sat quietly, finishing one beer and beginning a second.

The same policeman sloshed wearily back along the walk. And on the other side a stray dog trotted along, hugging the wall, moving briskly.

"Where do you suppose he's going?"

"Who?"

"The dog."

Steve looked first at her and then out into the rain. "I don't know," he said, "looks like he's heading for the docks."

"I can hear the ferries," she said suddenly. "I can hear their signals just before they pull off."

"I wouldn't wonder," he said. "It's not more than two blocks away."

"Let's take the ferry across the river."

"What for?"

"Might be fun."

"In the rain?"

She thought about that for a moment and it was on the

tip of her tongue to say yes. But finally, under the steady prompting of his eyes, she said, "No, I guess not."

"For a minute you had me worried."

"If we had a tree house we could go and sit in it," she said softly.

"What?"

His new bottle of beer came and she watched him pour it carefully.

"I meant to tell you, Steve," she said, "I've been look-ing for another apartment."

"What's wrong with the one you've got? It's so handy to everything."

"You mean you live two blocks away."

"Sure that's what I mean. Unless you want to get away from me too."

No, no, I don't. I've even asked why you don't move in with me. The apartment is big enough. Your three room-mates could find somebody else to share their rent . . . Come live with me and be my love . . . "Of course I don't want to get away from you. I just don't think I want to live in the French Quarter any more."

"How come?"

"It was great for a while, Steve, but it's for when you're young."

"You're not that old."

"I'm getting old. And I just don't have the patience any more, not for the tourists and the queers and the Jesus freaks."

"No tourists ever come to this bar," Steve said. "Just regulars like us. And that's why I like it. Like a club, you know what I mean. Like progress hasn't touched it."

The record ended. Lazily the bartender changed it. "Oh God," Steve said, recognizing the first bars. It was the Intermezzo from *Cavalleria Rusticana*.

"I thought that was your favorite."

He made a face and did not answer.

The rain stopped with the same suddenness it had begun. They listened to the small sucking sounds of bricks absorbing water.

"Okay," Steve said, "let's go."

They walked the few blocks down Bourbon Street to the high iron gate that led to her apartment. She fumbled for her key, then dropped it. He picked it up, handed it to her.

"Sorry," she said. "I was born clumsy."

She opened the gate, noticing for the first time how rust came off in great smears on her hand. "I won't ask you up," she said, "I'm sort of tired today."

Steve hesitated and she wandered if he was about to object. But he only said, "I'll call you tomorrow."

It was very dark in the courtyard. The small lantern over the gate didn't penetrate the thick heavy leaves and the vines. She stopped once and peered down, then shrugged. The walk must be under water. She could feel it slosh through the open toes of her shoes. Here under the wide leaves of the banana trees it was still raining, a light continuing sprinkle. She looked up and caught a quick glimpse of the sky through a tiny opening. There was a star stuck in it, like a piece of ice.

She climbed the stairs slowly. On one—halfway to the first landing—the sharp point of her heel jabbed through the wood, and she had to slip her foot free, bend down and jerk the shoe loose. In the damp under the trees and between the thick moldy brick walls, boards lasted barely a year.

Her apartment was stuffy. She started the air conditioner, then methodically began to undress. Without thinking or desiring it, she hung her clothes away, brushed her hair, and gave her nails a quick buffing. The noise of the air conditioner bothered her, so she turned it off and opened the window. She took off the bedspread, folded it neatly, and put it away. Then she lay down, stretching herself carefully all over. She wanted to cry, but she told herself firmly that it was a silly thing to do, that it would only make her eyes achy and puffy and swollen in the

morning. She said this quite a few times, and finally, just
before she slept, she came to believe it.

SHE HAD been asleep for some time. And for a while
she thought that the sounds were part of a dream. A
rustling. And a scratching. For just a second behind the
closed lids of her eyes she saw her father, sitting on the
back porch on Sunday morning, reading, the newspapers
rustling under his hands. She could see the colors of the
funny papers. She could even hear the flat-toned ringing
of the Lutheran Mission down the block. And she could
hear her mother complaining: "He goes out in the yard
in his pajamas. A big Tocko he is!"

Even at this distance Carrie smiled and whispered to
herself, "And not for nothing is his name Tortorich."

She didn't think of her parents very often, and when
she did it was in terms of pyramids of fat, with a tiny
head balanced on top like a rock . . .

They had gone back to Ragusa while she was still in
high school. The strange country had become too much
for them, after nearly forty years. They were going home
at last. They left her with a cousin, to finish school.

At first, in the strange smells of her cousin's house, she
missed them. But when the year was done, and her cousin
brought out the little savings book with her passage
money marked in it in violet ink, she just shook her head.
And she never went. Her parents wrote, once or twice,
but then those letters stopped too.

She rarely saw her cousin any more, ever since that
day years ago when she had gotten her first job and moved
into her own apartment. She'd done well since then. She
had a fine job and a fine future. She was sharp and effi-
cient, too, the sort of secretary nobody made passes at,
though she was nice looking, with a lush, full figure. It just
didn't seem to occur to them.

Until Steve came. They had gone to bed on their
second date. That was a couple of years ago, when he'd

been a tall skinny medical student. He'd put on weight since them. You could begin to see the outline of a very heavy man in the making. Like his father, he said. His hair was thinning too, rapidly, though he was just her age. Sometimes when she stood above him, she could see the skull all pinkish under the thin blond hair. She always looked away quickly.

Outside her window the rustling continued. That would be in the garden next door. Somebody must be walking about down there in the bamboo and banana bushes, a tangle so thick that even the cats circled around it.

She opened one eye and looked at the small green luminous hands of the clock: ten past one.

The rustling stopped. Far off, and muffled by the thick high brick walls of the houses, a siren wailed. It seemed to stop on the other side of the block.

She paid no particular attention. Sirens were so frequent, you'd be up all night if you followed each one.

Now voices were coming closer, lights flickered on the ceiling.

Oh hell, she told herself. And got up slowly and went to look out the window. She propped both elbows on the sill and leaned her chin on her hands.

She looked directly down into five adjoining back yards, separated each from the other by the same thick brick wall that formed the houses. The two larger yards ran just under her window, met back to back at a wall edged by broken glass. Across the length of these and at right angles to them, were the three other yards, each of them with an almost identical adjoining cottage.

At the farthest house, two figures with flashlights climbed out the dormer window to the gentle slope of the roof. She heard muffled voices and recognized the light-gray uniforms of the police.

She lit a cigarette, and pulled a chair to the window to watch.

The rustling in the garden directly beneath her window had stopped. The police were exploring the second cottage roof now, even clambering to the top to shine their lights down the other side. A woman's voice called: "I saw him go that way there, for sure." And the police drifted slowly across the roof, looking like kids playing hide-and-seek in the dark.

Carrie thought: They guess he's up on the roofs. But he isn't. He's in the yard directly below.

She bent forward until her head rested on the screen and she stared down into the darkness. The top of the leaves reflected the flashlights dimly. Under them it was still and dark.

He must see me, she thought. He must see my cigarette.

The police walked slowly back and forth across the three adjoining roofs, their shouts stretching across space like lines of wire weaving a cage.

"We better look in the yards."

"Go around."

"He could be anywhere down there."

"He wouldn't jump down," a woman said, complainingly. "Not from the roof."

"Lady, I saw one go straight up a brick wall, like a fly, and grab hold of a second-floor porch."

He must hear them, Carrie thought, but not too clearly down below the walls and smothered under the canes. But he can see me. He's got to have looked up and seen me.

She let her eyes move slowly around the five little squares of patios, let her eyes feel their outlines like tangible things.

And she saw something else. In the fifth yard—which backed into the cluttered, overgrown one—a screen door scraped open. Her eyes, accustomed to the dark, made out the shape of a policeman's cap. He stood leaning by the door, and the gray of his uniform blurred into the old wall. He seemed to be turning his head about slowly, but he did not appear to hear anything, though the rustle in the canes had begun again. The man down there seemed to be dragging something.

A big police searchlight flashed on. She blinked and

shook her head, dazzled. The roofs were outlined now, sharp black and white; the old uneven slates made jagged black shadows like teeth.

In the reflected glare of the searchlight she saw the man below. She saw the back of his head and one hand. And all of a sudden she knew what it was he was trying to do.

He'd found something to stand on—in that garden it wouldn't be hard to find a rusted chair and a couple of wooden crates—and he was dragging them to the back wall.

Twenty feet away on the other side the waiting policeman heard nothing. But he couldn't miss someone who crawled over the wall and into that yard.

The hand was reaching higher and higher. She noticed it wasn't too steady or certain as it groped for a hold on the bricks.

She thought, They'll catch him and that'll be all . . .

It wasn't anything to her. Nothing at all. She pressed her forehead against the screen, so that dust fell tingling in her nose. And she lifted one finger and tapped sharply on the wire so that a little rattling sound dropped out into the night.

The hand jerked back down into the dark shelter of the bamboo.

She said, in a whisper, "Back of you, look back of you." There was no movement, no answer. "There's a gate. You didn't see it. Then go out the alley to Dumaine Street."

A pause, a rustling, and a small rattle.

The gate was six feet high, wrought iron with great squiggles of feathers and corn tassels. She saw a figure go over it like a cat, a large black cat, up one side and down the other, headlong. There was only a single grunt when he hit the other side.

Like a fly, the policeman had said.

The cigarette burned her fingers. She dropped it on the sill and poked at it with her nail until it went out.

Police now stood on the walls and turned their lights down into the overgrowth.

One said: "He could be down there."

"That house is on Dumaine," someone else said, "around the corner."

"You check it."

Carrie turned away from the window. She went into the living room, in the dark, and felt on the coffee table for her cigarettes.

She smoked quietly, studying the tiny coal, lighting one cigarette from the other. When the phone rang, she waited a long time before answering.

Steve said, "Where have you been?"

"Here. I'm always here."

"You sound funny."

"I don't mean to." She yawned slowly.

"Look," he said, "I'm coming over."

"I'm sleepy, Steve."

"I've got to talk to you."

"Okay," she said listlessly.

She sat, half dozing, thinking of nothing at all, until he came. It took him only a very few minutes; he must have run all the way.

"What's going on out there?" he asked quickly. "There are four police cars over on Dumaine Street."

"Yes," she said, "I know."

"They're checking the yard right under your window."

But he'd be gone, she thought, that dark figure who'd scrambled over the gate with such a hurt grunt. "He wasn't a very good burglar."

"What?"

"They were chasing him and he got away."

"Oh," he said. "Well, listen to me now."

"I helped him, but he wasn't very good, really."

"What in God's name are you talking about?"

She felt floating and pleasant. As if she had been drinking absinthe. "He made so much noise, he nearly got caught."

"I want a drink," Steve said. "You have any Scotch?"

"I don't think so, I didn't know you were coming."

"Okay, whatever you've got." He went into the little kitchen. The refrigerator door slammed and the icetrays rattled in the sink.

Words drifted across the front of her mind. As they passed she read them aloud. "Come live with me and be my love and we will all the pleasures prove . . ."

He brought back two glasses.

She ducked her nose down into the tickling of the rising soda bubbles, played with the pieces of ice with her tongue.

"Quit," he said. "That's too damn suggestive when I'm talking to you."

She put the glass on the coffee table and folded her hands and waited.

"I don't know how you guessed it," he said abruptly.

"Me?"

"You acted so strange, I should have realized."

She said nothing, went on studying the small patch of yellow light over the corner lamp. She did not remember turning it on. Steve must have done it when he came in.

"Look," he said, "there was something else all right."

"What else?"

"There was somebody else with my parents."

"Oh."

"A girl."

That was it, she thought. So simple. And she hadn't thought of it. She hadn't thought of it at all.

"I've known her ever since high school."

The way he said it made her think of football games in crisp clear northern weather, and proms with all the dresses fluffy and pastel, like so many flowers. And everything cool and crisp like an air-conditioned office . . . The only high school prom she had ever been to had been hot and crowded and steamy with perspiration. Dresses streaked and wilted in the heat. Her net skirt stretched and sagged; her heel caught and ripped it. Her skin developed stinging red blotches from the perfume she dabbed on it.

"My parents have been friends of her parents for years. Before she was born even."

And do I have continuity like that, Carrie thought. Of friendships carried from generation to generation. Did my parents give me a single thing but my blood . . .

"I guess they decided it would be a good thing if we made a couple. They had it all figured out. You know the way parents do."

A crisp clear world where boy and girl infants held hands between their carriages . . . She hadn't had a carriage at all. She had lain on a blanket on the floor on the front porch, fenced in by chairs turned on their sides.

"I didn't tell you before," he said, "because I didn't know if you'd understand."

"No," she said, "I probably wouldn't have."

"She'd been looking forward to coming, you know. It was a holiday for her."

"Is she pretty?"

"I guess so."

"Like what?"

"Dark hair, dark eyes."

"Oh," she said.

"I'd have told you before only I thought it would just hurt your feelings."

"But you feel better now."

"Well," he said, "yes."

"Are you going to marry her?"

"Now you are mad at me."

"I was asking."

"No," he said, "I'm not going to marry her."

"That's a shame when she was counting on it."

She stared at the pink azalea on the table, thinking: If I had a wall I could climb over it, but I don't even have a wall. I don't have anything at all.

She reached out and patted his head, gently, absent-mindedly, like a child. "Go home, little boy."

She did not hear the door. After a while she looked up and saw that he was gone. And the silence was no emptier than it had been with him there.

The Other Way

SANDRA LEE was late. It was nearly five o'clock when she got off the school bus. She walked through the narrow alley along the side of her house and heard the hollow echo of her heels on the brick. The philodendrons which her grandmother insisted on growing in the six inches of soil by the high board fence brushed crinkled leaves against her face, and she ducked her head to avoid them.

I been doing this every day of my life, she thought, since I been old enough to walk. And how many times does that make it?

She liked to think of numbers. She always counted things. The walk now, it had two hundred and sixty-eight bricks. And then you were at the kitchen door. She climbed the worn wood steps, the ones her grandmother still scrubbed with brown soap every day, rain or shine, hot or cold. The way she had done ever since she was a young bride just moved into the house. The steps now were a silvery gray color, the veins of the wood standing up hard and clear, the surface rough and uneven like a washboard when you sat on it.

She went in, letting the screen bang shut behind her. She knew who would be there—the same people were always there each day when she came home from school. There was her mother, short and heavy, dark brown and frizzled-haired, with only light green eyes to show her white blood. She would be standing at the enamel-topped table under the window beginning to fix supper, staring out at the line of fluttering clothes that ran from the back porch to the back shed. There was her aunt Norris, sitting in her wheel-chair, across her withered legs the endless balls of cord she used to crochet. She went very fast, the shiny little hook squirming about among the knotting thread. So fast that the finished product seemed to run smoothly off the tips of her black fingers. And there was the old lady, her grandmother. She would be at the wooden dining table, back in the dusky part of the room, reading the evening paper under the light of the overhead lamp, her gold-rimmed glasses sliding halfway down her nose. She had gotten those glasses from a lady she cooked for years ago, back when her children were still small; she found the glasses suited her fine and she had used them ever since. Now and then she would take them off, and stare at them, and you could tell that she was remembering back to those days when she was young.

Most likely too, they would be talking when Sandra Lee came in—the soft, muttered Cajun French. They always spoke it during the day when they were alone in the house. It was the only language her grandmother felt comfortable in. English came stiff and hard to her tongue, she said.

When Sandra Lee came, they stopped at once, for they would never speak French in front of her. She asked sometimes, but they only laughed and told her, "Layovers to catch meddlers, baby. No need for you to go talking the old folks' talk."

This was the same as every other evening. They stopped talking when they heard her foot on the step. They all looked up when she came through the door. Her mother asked: "How was school today?" and she answered,

"Fine," and put her books down on the table beside her grandmother's paper.

Then her mother would tell her what to do: go to the grocery, or get the clothes in, or wash your hands and set the table.

Today her mother said: "I won't be needing any help. But you could put the hem in that dress I ripped for you this morning."

"Growing like a Jerusalem weed," Norris said, as her fingers went back to their contortions with the strip of steel and the cotton thread.

So Sandra Lee fetched the dress, and brought it back to the kitchen and threaded her needle and checked to see just how it was that her mother had basted the hem.

"Who'd you eat lunch with?" her mother asked.

"Some kids." She began sewing, quickly, deftly.

"Like who?"

"Well, Peggy, and Amelie."

"What they have for lunch?"

"I didn't look."

"Lunch now," her grandmother said. "It used to be called dinner. When I was cooking we'd have four or five courses and never think anything of it. Excepting it was crawfish bisque. I guessed I picked ten tons of crawfish in my day."

"If John and the boys got them," Norris said, "we could make some again this spring."

And then Sandra Lee said what she had been saving up to say all afternoon: "I'm not going back."

They stopped what they were doing. They all looked at her. She could feel them looking through her.

"I'm not going back to that school." She found she was speaking louder than she intended. "I'm going where I was last year."

In the little silence they could hear the rattle of dishes and the television set in the house next door.

Her mother said slowly: "What do I got to tell your father?"

Her grandmother said: "Jesus Lord!"

"I thought you liked it. I thought you was happy there," her mother said.

And Norris said: "Alberta's quitting, no?"

She knows everything, Sandra Lee thought. And she nodded.

"And you plain don't want to be the only little black chile in the school."

"God, God," her mother said, chopping onions on the wood board with a steady, practiced thumping.

Norris said: "Alberta's a silly little ass."

"She quit yesterday," Sandra Lee said. "She wasn't there today."

"Was they mean to you?" her grandmother said.

"Did somebody say something to you today?" her mother asked. "Was somebody mean to you?"

Sandra Lee shook her head and began stitching in the hem, slowly.

Norris smoothed the folds of her finished crochet work against her knee. "There's more than what you saying."

"I don't want to talk about it," Sandra Lee said.

Her grandmother cleared her throat and spat into her wad of tissue. "Since when do you come to be short of words?"

"Since now," Sandra Lee said.

Her grandmother's little beady black eyes glared at her. "No mocking in my house, miss."

Sandra Lee bit her lip and began stitching furiously.

"How do I got to tell your father?" her mother whispered to the paring knife in her hands.

Norris gave her wheel chair a quick little spin, the boards under the linoleum creaked, and she was at Sandra Lee's side. She pulled the sewing from her hands. "You began out by talking," she said, "now you finish up."

"Don't they eat lunch with you?" her mother asked faintly. "You said they eat with you."

"Sort of. But it isn't just lunch."

"How?" Norris said. "Tell us how."

"Well," Sandra Lee said, "if I go sit at a table that's

empty they don't ever come and sit by me. But if I go sit with them, they talk to me and it's all right."

"Lord of mine!" her mother hissed her breath with relief. "What you expect them to do? They been going there for years and you just come. And what's it got to hurt you to go to their school and not them."

"Little jackass," Norris said bitterly.

And for a minute Sandra Lee wondered whether she meant her or her mother.

"We thought about nothing when we was young," her grandmother said suddenly, "beyond the color of our new shoes, and our men, and if there was going to be somebody to play the piano in the evenings."

"You just got to work harder," her mother said, "no reason you can't keep up. You won the scholarship."

"I'm keeping up," Sandra Lee said. "I don't have any trouble keeping up."

"You don't want to be the only one," Norris said softly. "Not the only black face all by yourself in all that white."

"I just don't want to go."

"My God," her mother said, "oh my God."

"*Tais-toi!*" Norris said, forgetting. "You are more foolish than your child."

Sandra Lee looked down at her empty hands folded across her lap.

"You are fixing to come running back to where you been," Norris asked. "No?"

"I don't belong there," Sandra Lee said, "that's all."

Norris snickered. "Where you belong, *chère?* Tell me."

"I don't know," Sandra Lee said miserably.

Norris snickered again. "You belong in Africa, maybe?" She held up the blue plaid dress. "You going back to Africa wearing this dress?"

Her mother chuckled and dropped the chopped onions into a frying pan.

"I'm just not going," Sandra Lee said.

"I won't, I won't, I won't," her grandmother mimicked.

"You going back," Norris said, "because there's no place else for you."

Sandra Lee bent her head and was surprised to see the splotches of water fall on her hands. She had not realized that she was crying.

"We won't say nothing about this," her mother said, "not to your father nor nobody else."

"I been trouble all my life." Norris looked at her withered legs. "From the day I was born, I been troubling others and there wasn't nothing to do about it."

"The Lord in his mercy," the grandmother said.

"But you now, you got two legs and a head on your shoulders, and you got no cause to be a burden."

"There's eight more months of school," Sandra Lee said, and she saw them stretch ahead like the shining curve of a railroad track, endless.

"You going tomorrow," Norris said as if she had not heard, "and all the days after. And when you come home in the evening, you are going to tell us what kind of a day you had, and what you did at lunchtime, and all that you learned."

Sandra Lee had turned her hands over and was studying the insides of them, the lines and hollows. Some people, she thought, they could tell what would happen to you from your hands, that the mark of the future was there, all spelled out, if you could just read it.

"And," Norris said, "you won't tell us no more of what you're thinking."

"No," her grandmother said. "No more."

The silence was thick and heavy until her mother said, "There's no milk for the morning, and I was forgetting about that."

"Yes'm," Sandra Lee said.

"My purse's on top the bureau."

Sandra Lee got up and walked toward the front of the house. She opened the purse and found a fifty-cent piece and, holding it in her hand, she went out the front door, the one that let directly onto the street.

The bricks gave out their gentle sound under her steps.

The houses passed one after the other, misted and shaded by fear and misery. She felt the pressure of her people behind her, pushing her, cutting off her tears.

She got the milk. For a minute she thought about throwing the bottle down in the gutter and running off in the other direction. Instead she looked at the black and white spotted cat that ambled loose-limbed along the walk, hugging the shelter of the houses. And so the moment passed, and when she looked up again, the other way was gone. The street in front of her had only one opening and one way to it, and her feet put themselves on that path, and she walked home.

"How was school?" her mother asked.

Sandra Lee put the milk in the icebox and closed the door. "It was fine," she said.

The Man Outside

THERE WERE horses on the streets in those days. You could sit on our front porch and listen carefully and you could hear the plop-plop of the hoofs and the rumble of the iron wheels of the carts in town—a mile away.

You might call our place a farm, though it hadn't been worked in years. Not since the time I was three years old and my father moved out of our house and went to live in his shack back in the woods.

It seemed to me once that I could remember when my father was living with us. Seemed I could remember the time when the fields around were full of white blooming cotton, and the east plot had corn growing. Seemed I could remember a hog pen too, lower down, in the bog where the pitcher plants stuck up their green flowers in the spring. And a sow that ate her litter, every one, and my oldest brother getting whipped for his carelessness.

But most likely I was too young to have seen my father. And if I remember my brother Dan yelling and running around the yard, without his pants, screeching with rage and fear, most likely it was my mother on the end of the switch.

(My brother Dan was a grown man when the First World War began, and working on the fishing boats down at Biloxi Bay. He had never much cared for fishing, or farming either, so he volunteered. He married a French girl, whose name I don't remember, and he was killed a couple of months before the Armistice. His wife wrote once to say that she had had a daughter, but didn't send her address. And my mother worried the rest of her life about that little French baby that had her blood and carried her name. It was the only thing I've ever seen disturb her. No . . . it was the *second* thing . . .)

My mother was what you would call a driving woman. For fifteen years she made a living for herself and her eleven kids off that farm, scratching away at the ground like one of her chickens. Without my father that wasn't easy, but I never heard her complain or say that she was tired. And only once I saw how scared she'd been. But that was later.

We lived in moonshine country, where most people had big fields of corn. Some of the corn went to the hogs and some of it went to the cows, but most went into likker. Practically every low swampy stretch that was wide enough and deep enough and tangled with old clumps of hackberry and poison ivy and swamp oak had one tiny little path cut into it. The sort you couldn't follow unless you knew where you were going. And at the end there'd always be a little still.

People would come from fifty miles away to buy the likker, and that was a long trip in those days. They came by train, the Smoky Bill it was called, to Plainfield and then they'd rent a carriage or some kind of wagon and drive the rest of the way. Lots of people did it, and corn whiskey was just about the biggest business for three or four counties around. There was even a special firm that came out from New Orleans and sold nothing but sugar—in any amounts, with no questions asked and no records kept. The business was that big.

Every so often there'd come a reform government in the state capitol, and you could see people drifting into town, casually enough. They'd wander around asking innocent questions, and the stills would finish up what they had going and lie idle for a while.

A couple of times those reform people talked to my mother. Once was a Saturday evening when she'd gone into town to deliver the pies she'd baked. She had gone to the drugstore and as she was coming out, with me tagging along at the end of her primly long skirts and high button shoes, a man I'd never seen before stepped up to her, politely tipping his hat.

"Move off, child," my mother said, and I went to the curb and stared up and down the red dusty street, waiting and trying to hear what they were saying. I couldn't. I caught only the last words and those only because my mother lifted her voice, indignant. "I am not a Judas Iscariot!" She stamped off down the street, her skirts swishing high around her ankles in her haste.

Even so, my mother would have nothing to do with the moonshining business, though there was a nice spot for a still on her property and she had had offers. She needed money the worst way, but she was a Baptist and she took it seriously.

She didn't countenance any hard likker, legal or not. We were all brought up to believe that the devil was a tall red man with a pitchfork in one hand and a bottle of whiskey in the other. And there was quite a to-do when my brother Roger, who must have been about fourteen at the time—a big, strong boy with the beard of a man —came home dead drunk and passed out in his bed. My mother got the wheelbarrow, the one that still stank of the chicken yard, and dragged or rolled him out of bed (by herself, though she wasn't a big woman) and carried him out to the front gate to the edge of the dirt road where there was a kind of little ditch cut by the rains. She dumped him out there, and left him, though it was a sharp night, with a little mold of frost on the ground.

When he did come up to the house the next morning,

so stiff and sore and cold he was limping like a cripple, my mother only glanced up from the pot of mush she was stirring. "Morning, Roger," she said. "You look like you had a bad night."

"Yes, ma'am," he said.

She brought us up carefully. Her girls wore cotton stockings summer and winter if they wore any of the shorter skirts. And if they didn't have stockings they had to have their skirts ankle length.

When you worked all day with chickens and walked the dirt roads, the hems got thick and crusted and heavy with mud and dragged at your feet. Once my sister Rosalie asked if she couldn't pin them up just for a little while, one wet fall when the mud and bramble burrs were caking and scratching. My mother looked at her—looked right through her—and didn't even bother answering. And that was the last said about that.

Maybe she was a little rough with the children. But maybe there wasn't any other way for her to do without a man working the place and the babies coming, year after year, in early summer, June usually.

It couldn't have been easy for her, after our father had his vision and stopped working and took his dog and went to live in the little shed down by the spring, right on the east side of the swamp. My mother went down each evening carrying his supper on a tin pie plate.

She would always leave us at our supper while she went down. She can't have stayed too long, because I remember hearing her come back, hearing the firm steady unhurrying tread of her heavy shoes.

For all of her energy, she wasn't a thin woman or a gaunt one. She was short, and inclined to be heavy. Her hair changed from light brown to gray, but her face was full and pink. Her mother had been German, and the blood in her showed. Even mud on her looked clean.

Her children were dark, every last one of them; they all took after their father.

I wonder now what she must have thought of him. But she didn't give a sign, nor say a word. She kept on bringing his food and bearing his children.

Not even my oldest brothers, Mark and George, knew exactly what happened. One day they noticed that they had considerably more of the chores to do, and their father didn't seem to be home for supper. Like kids, they weren't really very interested. They grumbled to themselves about the extra work, then they forgot about it. Next they noticed what was happening to the fields—they filled with dry stalks that rustled in the wind during the winter until even they fell down and blended into the mud and disappeared. And the fields turned into stretches of open ground covered by creepers and grass, the marks of old plow lines showing very faintly.

It was maybe six months, maybe a year, or maybe more, before the boys discovered where their father was living. They found his shack one day in early summer when they were heading for Taylor Pond to see if they could get any green trout. The shack itself had been there for as long as they could remember, only now the walls shone with bright new tar paper. The roof had been patched with sheets of tin and around the whole thing was a fence of chicken wire.

The boys tried to open the gate—they wanted to peep in the windows and see who was there. The gate wasn't a very good fit and it had warped besides; they were struggling with it when a big yellow hound came rushing out.

They recognized the dog. Their father's. It was in worse shape than they had ever seen, ears cut by brambles and coat tangled with burrs, but it was sleek and heavy. As if it'd been lying around for a week and hadn't been cleaned up after the last run.

The boys stopped fooling with the gate, not because they were afraid of the hound, but because they were no longer curious. They knew who was living there.

They backed off and tiptoed away, the hound watching them go, and them not talking until they were a half mile off. It was almost like they'd been to a graveyard.

They didn't go to the pond that day after all. Instead they went over to the Tickfaw River and caught some catfish, though it was a longer walk and they didn't particularly like the taste of cat.

So that was that. After a while we children forgot he was there. And things went on just the way they had before.

My mother baked, and we brought the cakes and pies and bread into town every Saturday. She made preserves and we'd comb the country for wild fruit. From the first blossom we'd know where the berry thickets were and we'd start praying for a good dry spring so the berries wouldn't blight and fall off. There was one particular spot, a kind of swampy one, where the bushes had plenty of sun and their roots were always damp—we'd be out before daylight, fighting the birds for every single berry. Poison ivy got in our scratches and we'd cool them by scooping up great handfuls of wet mud and smearing them on the spots until we got home. Then my mother would use a special lotion made of eleven different kinds of leaves and that would stop the itching.

We helped with the preserving, too, watching the long lines of jars stretched out along the kitchen table and over the window sills. And eating the hulls out of the bottom of the jelly bag.

Usually food wasn't any problem. There were plenty of wild greens and we grew a little garden too. Mark and George were good shots with the old Winchester rifle that hung over the kitchen door. The younger boys used slingshots. So we had deer and rabbit and plenty of birds: dove and pheasant and quail. All of us, boys and girls together, fished the streams for miles around. My sister Marjorie was very clever at spotting honey trees and we always had plenty of the sweet and faintly musky tupelo honey.

But winters were hard, no two ways about that. They

were short and very cold, with little skins of ice on the ground and air so damp you felt you were swimming under water. The house was never warm; the walls dripped moisture and the wind blew straight through. We put newspapers under the mattresses and newspapers between the blankets so that the whole night roared with crackling. Even so we went to bed right after supper, two and three together for warmth. Sometimes it seemed that there was a big lump of ice in the middle of my stomach that didn't thaw out until March.

But mornings were worst of all. There were things to be done and we had to be out doing, stumbling over our own feet because we were so sleepy. We all had our different ways of beating the cold. Like my brother John. On Saturday mornings he had to kill and pick and draw the chickens that were going to town to be sold that day. He had to work outside, in a special little fenced yard, where a charcoal burner heated a barrel of water. He was very good at the job and very fast, and he had added some improvements of his own, ones that saved him standing in the cold, stamping his feet and waiting. He had one in particular that he was very proud of. When he had slit the throat, instead of throwing the chicken in an empty barrel to bleed, he grabbed it by the feet and swung it around his head like a lariat. The blood drained out faster that way, he said, and he stayed warmer with the exercise. Sixty years later I can still see him—red blood spinning out, splashing like a sort of heavy summer rain on ground that was frozen hard into little ruts and hollows. (He became a car salesman in Pensacola, eventually, and never had chicken in his house.)

Once when my mother noticed him, she said quietly to no one in particular, "That is a great waste of energy." And later on she said to the kitchen sink, "I wonder if you couldn't do something with chicken blood. Seems such a pity to waste it."

That was the way she thought.

One day my father was gone. Really gone this time.

My mother said nothing. You would never think anything had changed. It was my sister Marjorie who came home from hunting honey and whispered to us that the shack was empty, and the door of the yard was standing open.

That evening we were all of us dying to get out. We often did that at night—after my mother had gone to bed, and we could tell by her heavy slow breathing that she was asleep.

But not this night. This night she sat rocking, alone in the kitchen, only moving every now and then to put more wood in the range. We could hear the thump of the sticks as she got them out of the basket behind the door and the clank of iron as she put them in the stove. Then the rocker began its creaking all over again.

We lay waiting, not even daring a whisper to each other, because she had sharp quick ears and could tell in a flash what the first whimper of a child meant. (She was always the first to tell when a fox or a weasel was bothering her chickens too; just the slightest flutter told her that.) We couldn't even creep to the door, because the old boards of the house would groan and sway under our weight. The foundations had needed repairs for years.

So we stayed very quiet and waited, and one by one we fell asleep. We never did know when she went to bed. Or if she did.

That same night the shack burned to the ground leaving only the fence posts. Pretty soon, in the damp and weather, those fell down and the brush covered it all up again. Until we weren't even sure any more just where it had stood.

Days went rolling into weeks and weeks into years. I remember worrying about my clothes, beginning to wonder how I looked. Beginning to fret at the old-fashioned pier glass that was so wavy you could hardly tell if your hair was combed. I was growing too, and I remember my mother adding ruffle after ruffle to the hem of my dress. They were all different materials, and my sisters thought the effect was very gay. I thought it was horrid. I had my heart set on a bright blue cotton in Keating's window.

I can still see that dress, as plain now as the day I coveted it so much my stomach was shaky. I can see how it was displayed, pinned up against a silver-paper wall. But I can't remember what my littlest sister looked like then.

And I can't remember the name of the boy who made love to me in the cotton shed on the Turner place. (My mother, being a practical woman, did not oppose sex before puberty for her girls.) He was a tall thin boy, with a beginning mustache, though he couldn't have been more than twelve then. I thought the mustache was terribly attractive.

He lived on one of the places close by, and he came every evening. He would circle close around the house, whistling like a night bird, a whippoorwill usually.

Sometimes my mother would look up and say, "Those are the saddest birds." She was too busy to notice that the call had an extra trill that no bird would make. He claimed to have learned it from an old Cherokee on the reservation at Wallace Falls some twenty miles away; he said it was a war signal.

I was impressed. War signals sounded romantic; and so did twenty miles. He might just as well have said ten thousand, like the old songs; I had never been either distance.

They weren't very successful, those early tries, more full of hurt than pleasure. I was kind of glad when I became a woman and stayed in the house and the cries of the whippoorwill stopped.

The next winter was unusually hard. I remember that my brothers couldn't go hunting for weeks on end, because there were no shells for the Winchester. Instead the boys set snares for rabbits. There were always plenty of them, and we had rabbit stew most of that winter. The walk to school was an endless trip of dripping noses and chattering knees. Until we finally gave up and stayed at home.

It seemed long, even to us. But then it was over, and my mother was sending us out to dig sassafras root and making us drink the pink tea. And all of a sudden the sun got hot and the days stretched out and, kid fashion, we forgot that we had ever been cold. We ate the wild watercress that grew around the spring and dug the young dandelion shoots out in the old pasture field and carried them home in our skirts.

That was the summer Albert Benton began coming to the house.

He was the foreman of a lumber mill in town, a short, squat, heavy-set man, with almost white hair and a face sunburned a bright red.

He came every Sunday, wearing a suit and tie, with his white hair carefully combed. He always brought something for us kids: a bag of apples, or peppermint candies.

After a time my mother began building a new room on the west side of the house. We were so excited that we just stood around and watched the Negro carpenter from town, until our mother chased us off with not so gentle swats. And every Sunday Mr. Benton inspected the week's work very carefully, plank by plank.

It did look kind of strange, all those new boards hung on the blackened paint-stripped main house. After all, any sort of addition was unusual in this part of the world. Most people lived in a house until it was ready to fall down with termites and old age before they built another one a few dozen yards away and moved into that.

Finally, one Sunday morning, my mother put on a new dress and gloves and a hat. "Elizabeth," she said to me, "go find the children." I scurried around the yard and yelled out over the closest fields, though I knew before

I started that I would find only the littlest ones, because it was fall and the pheasants and quail were in their prime and all my brothers had left before daybreak. My sisters were off hunting for field lettuce, which we called lamb's tongue. They wouldn't be back until evening.

I found only Marilyn and Junine and Jesse and took them into the kitchen.

My mother looked at us. "Where are the others?"

"Out," I said.

She folded her hands in her lap. I saw, all of a sudden, how old and rough and hard they looked against the new shiny material. I couldn't help glancing over to the net gloves that lay next to the little round bag on the kitchen table. And I thought how funny it was that a man's hands should wear lacy gloves.

"Well," my mother said, "they will have to find out later."

"Yes ma'am," I said. "Yes ma'am."

"I am going to get married," she said. "Mr. Benton is coming this morning. Now sweep the mud off the front steps."

Those were the words she used to tell us. Not "You're going to have a new father." No, she was a plain-spoken woman. He wasn't our father and he would never be. She had simply found herself another man.

Later that morning, Mr. Benton drove up—in a borrowed carriage this time—and got my mother and handed her in like a lady. We all stayed very quiet and listened to the hoofs on the dirt road. You could hear them for quite a distance, because it was Sunday and everything was very quiet.

He was a hard-working man, Mr. Benton. He'd be up early, as early as we were, joking with us over breakfast. Then off he'd go to town and his job in the lumber mill. He kept his own horse in a lean-to he'd built at the side of the kitchen, a small chestnut mare, a bit on the elderly side and quite a bit slow, but even-tempered and quiet.

He was a good, steady man, and things began changing. That spring, first thing I noticed, there was a hired man out with a mule plowing the east field. After that came a couple of Negroes planting.

One by one the fields filled up. Very slowly things got back to what they were when my father had lived with us. No, I guess they were better, a lot better. My father hadn't ever been one to make too much money out of the farm, he just managed to keep things going. With Mr. Benton it was different. He had a paying job and an all-year one, and whatever the farm made was extra. He had plans for that too. "Don't grow for yourself," he was always telling my mother. "Grow for money and buy what you need." That was a strange idea for us, because each of the farms around here always tried to be self-sufficient.

Mr. Benton just laughed at them. "With money," he would say, "nobody ever got hurt yet."

And I can see my mother sitting and looking at him, her full, smooth face coming alight with a kind of liveliness she didn't usually have.

They got the house painted, and my mother even started a little bed of cosmos along the new front porch, the first thing she'd ever done that was for beauty and pleasure and not for practical need. Then there was a young brown and white cow in the new pasture lot. My mother milked it herself twice a day and never let anyone else tend it. And each Sunday she and Mr. Benton went off to church, all dressed up, looking smug and fat and altogether satisfied with life. They even had their picture taken. That picture stood in a big gilt frame on the handkerchief table in the corner, the one that my grandfather had made years ago.

Then something happened, along one fall when the rains that bring in winter had started. (I don't remember the date exactly. But Mr. Benton and my mother had been married quite a few years. The three oldest boys had left home to find their own ways: Dan to try his hand at fishing, George to work in a department store at Leesville, and Mark all the way to St. Louis for a job with the telephone company. I was pretty near finished with school myself. So it must have been a good long time.)

This happened one evening, late evening. It had been pouring sheets all day, but along toward the time of sunset it slacked off, leaving just a light drizzle hanging like heavy smoke. The wet air was beginning to turn a funny fishy color, a sort of silver.

I was in the kitchen, helping with supper. I even remember that my mother was wearing a print dress and a big freshly starched apron that crackled as she walked. Everybody was inside, too, in that sort of weather. There was a new kitten in the box just inside the door; you could hear it mewing.

My brother Jesse, who would have been nine or so, yelled out from the front room: "There's a man standing outside the fence, right in the road."

Nobody paid attention to him. So he stood in the doorway and repeated: "He's standing still right in the road, looking at the house."

"Well," Mr. Benton said, "maybe he wants to stay out in the rain."

Jesse hopped up and down on one foot. "He's got a big old sack over one shoulder."

"Bogeyman," my sister Marilyn said.

"Tramps," Mr. Benton said. "Must have got thrown off the cars over by Ellenville."

Nobody bothered to look; they were more interested in supper. Marilyn and Junine, feeding the kitten in the corner, giggled softly, their heads close together over some private joke.

I finished the dish of potatoes, scraped clean, and began to quarter them. Then I noticed my mother. She stood in front of the range and her hands held a wooden spoon crosswise in front of her, just the way I'd seen people hold whips when they stood and talked on the main street in town. She was staring straight ahead at the wall, where a line of pots hung. They were mostly new, and some of them were copper, burnished so that they winked at you. And some of them were iron, blackened and greasy, and some were porcelain, mottled like a wild bird's egg.

I watched, the point of my knife digging little holes in the potato I was supposed to be quartering. She didn't so much as move her fingers for the longest time. Then she said very quietly, so that you could hardly hear it over the giggles of the kids and the bubbling of the pots on the range: "Make him go."

Mr. Benton looked up, puzzled, as if he'd heard a far-off sound and was trying to place its direction.

My mother turned around and walked crisply over to her chair, the black painted rocker that stood right by the kitchen table. And she sat down in it.

She didn't look particularly excited. She folded her hands over her stomach and began to rock, tapping her heels on the ground. And everybody stopped. You could hear breathing, and the whimpering of the kitten.

It was like hearing the roof fall, this sort of quiet.

She repeated: "Make him go."

Mr. Benton was on his feet now, scrubbing at the side of his cheek.

"Don't let him stand out there and look, make him go."

For a couple of seconds Mr. Benton figured out what she was telling him. Then he nodded to her and went out through the front door. My mother stayed in her chair, rocking the same sleepy rhythm. You'd have thought she was perfectly calm, if you hadn't seen her eyes.

When we finally collected our wits and thought about going outside, there was just Mr. Benton standing in the front yard, looking off toward the east. The road was empty, what we could see of it in the mist.

Jesse rushed up to Mr. Benton. "Who was that?"

"Nobody," Mr. Benton said. "A tramp."

"Where'd he go?" Jesse said. "Where'd he go?"

He made a quick move to dodge by Mr. Benton and dash out the gate. I suppose he had some idea of following after the man. But Mr. Benton grabbed him by collar and belt and swung him off his feet, carrying him on one side, the way you'd carry a bag of meal. He gave a swing and tossed him up to the porch. Jesse landed like a cat, on all fours.

"Kids," Mr. Benton said, "get on inside."

And we went fast enough.

My mother was still rocking, quietly.

"He's gone," Mr. Benton said.

"Who was that?" I asked.

And Jesse, taking courage from my question, asked, "Did you know him?"

"No," Mr. Benton said.

My mother said nothing.

Mr. Benton said: "There was nothing to get scared about."

"He went away," my mother said.

"You said to send him off."

"Yes," my mother said, and you could see that her eyes were coming back to normal.

Mr. Benton sat down, slumped way down in his chair, solidly, so that he looked a part of it. It seemed to me that he had never looked quite that way before.

All that was a long time ago, of course. It worries me sometimes, comes back to worry me. I suppose we could have asked my mother about that tramp, but none of us did, not even when she was an old lady sitting in a wheel chair, long after Mr. Benton had died. Just an old lady sitting on her front porch looking out across a yard that she had carefully planted in flowers.

We didn't know. And we didn't ask. Sometimes we would think that it was. And sometimes we would think that it wasn't. I guess we liked it that way.

Sea Change

⚜

SHE WENT to the observation deck to watch the plane take off, the way she always did. She watched it swing away from the loading ramp, windows like dots on its fat silver side. She tried to see into each window, trying to find a face, and couldn't. The plane eased around and began the long lumbering trip down the field. The big jets had to go all the way back to the very end of the runway. When they swung into take-off position, their tails seemed to hang over the low barbed-wire fence.

A small red private plane crossed overhead. The people next to her waved frantically, the children screeched, "Good-by, good-by. See you soon." "He can't hear you," their mother said. Their father said, "He better not be looking down to see you either." They walked away.

Her plane had cleared the buildings and the scattered service trucks, and moved upfield, a bit faster now, tail bobbing at each joint of the concrete. Another jet swung in behind; like two ducks they waddled up the runway, their shiny coats gleaming in the smoky sunlight.

She knew that by the time they reached the end of the runway she would have lost sight of her plane. She had never learned to tell one from another in that hazy distance. All the other times she had come, she had stood for half an hour in this same spot and watched plane after plane take off; that way she could be sure that one of them was his. And that he was gone.

She didn't really know why she waited. It was just something she did. Her eyes glanced from one speck to the next, trying to hold them in view for the seconds after they had disappeared. She tried to think of him up there, stretching, pulling out a magazine, settling back for a nap. Only maybe she was watching the wrong plane . . .

Now there was a cluster of planes down at the runway's end. The heat haze washed around them like beach ripples.

The top of her head began to tingle with the sun; she pulled a scarf out of her purse. In the sharp gusty breeze she had trouble getting it on straight. She finally tied it loosely under her chin, letting it crumple crookedly across the back of her har.

In the plane, he would be relaxed. Flying didn't bother him at all.

"Honey, when you've flown as much as I have, and in some of the planes I been in, with people shooting at you, or thinking of shooting at you, you get to think that a commercial flight is like sitting in a movie. No storm is going to be as bad as that ground fire coming up at you."

"I'm afraid," she said, *"I can't help it if I'm afraid of a lot of things."*

"When your number's up, it doesn't matter where you are."

"I just don't think that way."

"I have to, honey. In my business I have to."

Dust blew into her eyes. She let planes take off unnoticed while she blinked furiously. I'll have to cry a tear or two, she thought. And that was very easy. Tears came so freely she had trouble stopping them. The piece of dust washed away.

The haze and the planes were all the same silvery color. She squinted at them. And decided not to wait. Not this time.

She turned and pushed her way through the turnstiles, climbed quickly down the flight of stairs. She marched into the lobby, her heels clicking purposefully on the cement floors. Then quite suddenly she was very tired. Quite suddenly she felt the three or four nights of broken sleep, and tears, and the steady nagging ache in the center of her chest. The heart does hurt, she had thought over and over again. I always thought it was just a saying, but it's real. Your heart can hurt.

Now in the airport lobby her shoulders turned heavy and the back of her knees began to tremble. The tips of her fingers tingled and burned. She stopped to look at them. A porter, arms full of bags, dodged around her. "Sorry," she said.

She would sit down for a moment. The chairs in the center of the lobby looked smooth and clean, their slick green covers were chilly with air conditioning. She sat still and felt the cool slip through her dress and disappear against her sun-hot skin. As soon as one spot warmed, she shifted her body to a cool one. Once she even moved to another chair. The trembling left her legs, and she could breathe more easily.

"This isn't hot," he said, "not like out there. God, I never felt a sun like that. Or maybe it's the damp. And the funny plants. They got some vines out there, you'd swear they reached out and grabbed at you, they kind of wrap around you."

Here were only some plastic palms, standing on each side of the bar entrance. Two children played tossing paper balls into the sand-filled pots and sailed a folded plane over the shiny hard green leaves. Now and then they stopped to get some more paper from a rack that said Catholic Literature Take One.

"You've done two tours of duty out there. Why should you do a third?"

"They're short of people, honey."

"They're always short of people. Why you?"

"I guess it's like the submarine service. Those guys get

a lot of sea duty, honey. More than they should."

"It isn't fair."

"Things happen like that. You got to expect things like that."

She smoothed her pink linen skirt across her thighs. The building shook with the sudden roar of a plane. Funny, she thought, sometimes you didn't hear a plane and then sometimes you did. The wind must blow the sound around.

Would he have looked down from the plane to the observation deck and would he be upset that she wasn't there? The way the planes were taking off, he probably couldn't see anything at all.

She kept on smoothing her skirt, getting each little wrinkle out of the linen, working at it carefully, inch by inch, as if it were the most important thing in the world.

It hurts to worry this much, she thought. It really hurts like a cut, or a broken bone. It hurts more than my broken arm when I fell off the climbing bars in third grade. A lot more than that. It hurts so much that it can't hurt any more.

"I'm just scared," she said.

"I'll be all right. I've always been all right."

"Your luck's going to run out. You can't get away all the time."

"I'll be extra careful, honey. I've got a lot of experience in being careful."

"You'll get killed. I know you'll get killed."

The flat final sound of that voice, her voice, ran in her head. She heard it echoing among the bony arches, vibrating the white tunnels. Killed. He was going to get killed. This time, he would die.

She was so thirsty, her lips felt swollen. She would have to find a water fountain somewhere. She circled the lobby, then turned into the tile corridor that led to the landing gates. She kept swallowing, and each time her throat ached more.

He'd be killed. This time she knew he'd be killed.

She coughed, her throat was that dry. She couldn't

seem to moisten it. They said you were thirsty when you were dying. They said people screamed and begged for water, that was how you knew they were dying. Would he do that? He never asked for anything. Not before. It bothered her sometimes that he never even asked her for a cup of coffee, he'd just get up and fix it himself. Of course they hadn't been together very much during their three years of marriage, not in places they could call their own. There'd been a lot of different hotels and motels, and then she'd come back to her parents' house alone. That was the military life, he said, always coming and going. That was what you expected when you married a professional.

"I could go to Hawaii," she said. "I could get a job in Hawaii and it would be closer for you."

"Hawaii is pretty bad when you're alone. Anyway, it's not so far back here, not with all the planes. I can always get on one of them."

"But I want to."

"You stay with your parents, and I'll do the running around."

He never asked for anything. It wasn't in him to do that. Maybe he'd have learned if they'd had longer together.

She was halfway down the blue-and-yellow corridor, her heels clipping neatly. There seemed to be no planes unloading on this side. The tile-lined space was almost empty, with only a leftover smell of passing groups of people.

She asked a single blue unform, "Do you know where a water fountain is? I can't seem to find one."

"There's one downstairs by the taxi stand," the blue uniform said. "But the closest one's right there in the Weather Bureau."

"Thank you," she said, and walked toward the door he indicated. Then stopped abruptly.

"Anything wrong?" the blue uniform asked. "Change your mind?"

"No." She pointed to the door. It said clearly: No

Admittance. Authorized Personnel Only. "I guess I'm not authorized."

He pushed the door open and held it for her. "I forgot that some people still read signs. Fountain's right there."

She drank. The water splashed her nose and ran down her chin. She drank with little gulping sounds until she had run the water so long it was freezing cold and her teeth began to ache. Slowly she lifted her head, took a couple of breaths, then ducked for a last taste. Finally she turned away, reaching in her purse for a handkerchief.

He was still holding the door. "You really were thirsty," he said.

"I hadn't had a drink for a long time, thank you."

As she walked down the hall drying her chin, she thought: Why did I say that? It isn't true, I've been drinking like crazy all day.

"Don't gulp so fast," he said. "If you're thirsty, I'll get you some water."

They were sitting in the bar, the dark cool bar wth its soft vague music, wasting the few minutes before his flight left.

"I don't want you getting drunk when I'm going to have to leave. I'd worry about your driving home."

"I'm just thirsty, that's all."

"Drink water," he said, "drink all the water you want. It can't hurt you."

She went back to the lobby, found her old seat taken, and chose another, facing a high arched window and a fuzzy gray-white sky.

"Good-by, honey," he said. "Take care of yourself." She kissed him briefly. "Be careful."

But he wouldn't. She began smoothing the skirt across her lap again. He'd pushed his luck too far. He wouldn't be back. The pain inside her chest told her. He was dead, it was only a matter of the exact date . . .

She looked down at her hands which had stopped moving and lay palms up on her lap.

You always know, she thought, when to begin grieving.

The plane wasn't yet six hundred miles away and she was sure.

Her hands reminded her of boats drawn up on the sand, boats tipped over and dry, waiting for the tide.

And she was thirsty again, so thirsty. When she got home she would take the biggest glass in the kitchen and fill it right to the top with ice tea. That's what she'd do as soon as she got there. But first she'd have to catch her breath. She was really very thirsty, she hadn't had enough sleep in a long time, three or four or five nights, ever since she had come to realize that he was going off to die.

He laughed at her. "What do you want me to do, honey? Desert? Like in the movies?"

"We could go to Mexico."

"They'd catch us in Mexico."

"Well, there's got to be some place, if we changed our name."

"Honey baby, I've got to go back."

"You want to go back," she said bitterly, her tears a nasty salt in the corners of her mouth. "You really want to go back to the fighting."

"You're wrong, honey," he said quietly. His brown eyes were flat shiny marbles flecked with yellow. "I just do it."

She would rest a bit and then she'd get her car out of the parking lot and drive home and have supper with her parents and watch television with them. Just not yet. She just wasn't ready yet. She must have stayed too long on the observation deck, her head was still burning. When she was a child, she'd spent hours sun-bleaching her hair to the color of straw, but she couldn't seem to take that much heat anymore.

The big high window got too bright and too shimmering. She looked away, blinking.

There was somebody sitting next to her, a blue uniform was asking, "Do you feel all right?"

She had talked to a blue uniform in the corridor, was

this the same one? She hadn't looked at a face out there, she hadn't thought to.

"Of course I'm all right," she said. "I'm just tired and I stood in the sun too long."

"You look a little pale."

"Were you the man I talked to over there, who showed me the water fountain?"

"Yes ma'am."

"I was so thirsty."

"Maybe you did have too much sun. It'll do that, they tell me."

"I'll be all right. I'm always all right. I was just resting before I drove home."

"You'd better," he said. He had curly gray hair and a round face, a mouth that was too small and cheeks that were too heavy. A pleasant sort of face, the sort of face that would be easy to forget.

She lifted the hair up from the back of her neck, pushed it behind her ears. She seemed to be perspiring heavily. She took a handkerchief from her purse, found it damp and began flapping it in the air to dry.

"Here," he said, "use mine."

She hesitated and then accepted. She hated the feel of perspiration drying on her skin. She blotted carefully. The cloth smelled faintly of something—a flower or something like lavender. She couldn't quite place it, it was so vague.

"Thank you. I can go home now." She stood up and big black spots spread over everything until there were only little cracks of light and she peeped between them. For a minute she thought the light would wink out completely, but that time passed.

"It would be criminal to let you get in a car." He was holding her arm tightly. "You're not drunk so you've got to be sick."

She was still swaying a bit. "I almost fainted, didn't I?"

"You came pretty close."

"How silly."

"Look," he said, "why don't you come have a cup of

coffee with me before you try to drive?"

She hesitated, wordlessly.

"Look," he said, "I've got a wife and two kids in Cleveland. I brought a ship in a while ago and I'm going to take one out tomorrow. I meant coffee right there, over there in the bar where we can sit down because I don't want to drink it standing up and holding you up too."

She laughed. "Okay," she said. "I was upset."

"Saying good-by does that."

"Yes," she said, "it does."

He held her arm until they were inside the doors. Then he let go. One of the children's paper airplanes sailed between their legs.

"That's the third cup of coffee you've had," he said.

"I didn't notice."

"You drink it like you were hungry."

"I guess I didn't have any lunch."

"Or breakfast?"

"No."

"Any reason?"

"I'm dieting," she said.

She thought: Why did I lie like that? And why, after I've said those things, do I get so I believe them? As if I were somebody else and they really were true about me.

"Women always seem to be on a diet. Especially the ones who look fine the way they are."

She swallowed the last bit of coffee. "I think it's because clothes look better."

"Maybe so. Look, if you're going to have another coffee I'm going to have a sandwich."

"No more coffee, thank you."

"Skip it," he said, "if I'm going to eat alone I'd rather stand at a counter."

"I'll wait with you." She smiled slowly, knowing it was a good smile, that her teeth were white and even, that her lips were well shaped and firm. "It's the least I can do since you did keep me from smashing my head on the floor out there in the lobby."

He grinned back at her, and his grin was much younger than his face. "Let's change tables. There's an empty one over by the window."

He steered her carefully through the chairs. "I'm not dizzy anymore," she said.

"I hope not." He didn't drop his hand. "You know, you'd think I'd get enough of those ships out there, but if I'm around them I just have to get close enough to watch them."

He stared out through the sheet of glass, squinting a little in the glare.

One of the smaller jets flashed crosswise, on the runway, half obscured in the haze, and hopped into the air, climbing steeply.

"They're really very pretty, very graceful, and I guess that's why you like to watch them."

"That's certainly why I watched you."

The blue eyes were still out on the hazy distance. She was not sure she'd heard anything. "You noticed me because I asked you for some water. If I hadn't, you wouldn't have looked."

"You're wrong," he said.

"And when I nearly passed out, you were kind enough to worry. All that many people don't faint; you have to notice when they do."

"I see lots of people all day, without noticing too much."

"And you spent the last half hour feeding me coffee so that I could drive safely."

"About an hour."

"That long? Well, it's very kind of you to take so much trouble for nothing."

"Not kind," he said, "and not for nothing."

He left the planes and looked at her. She started to drop her eyes and slip away behind the lids, but she moved too slowly. Once she had started looking at him, she couldn't stop. His eyes weren't as blue as she had thought, there were black lines out from the pupils, lines like stars. And his hair had been blond, you could see the yellow tinge underneath the gray.

She knew perfectly well that he hadn't said anything. But she'd answered him.

"I'll have to call. I wouldn't want my parents to worry."

"And your husband?"

She looked at her wedding ring. "My husband is dead. He was killed in Vietnam."

"I'm sorry," he said.

And he might have said more but the waitress brought his sandwich and she got up to find the phone.

"It's right beside the door there," he said.

"I saw it, you don't have to worry, I'm not upset any more."

She ordered a Scotch and didn't finish it. The hot light turned into the beginning of a soft dusk.

Everything was slowing down, she thought, everything. And there would be a quiet time. A perfectly still minute. Perfectly balanced . . .

"Ready now?"

"Oh yes. It's almost time."

Later on things did stop and time ended, and she perched on a single spot, weightless and empty in herself. Quite detached from her body, her mind stole out, prowling like a cat in the shadows, searching. And it found that there was nothing on any side of her, that she hung like a point, like a star in the empty sky.

This is as far as I can go, she thought. This is the farthest.

And the cat that wore her mind found a dried empty shrimp shell mixed in the seawrack on a beach somewhere, empty beach, wet and cold, and began to play with it, to slap it back and forth with its paw. The shell rattled like a dry gourd.

"I wonder where that beach is," she said aloud. "I don't even know where that beach is."

"Hush," he said. "Don't talk."

And she saw her husband. Yellow stalks, heavy and bending almost double with grain fluttering slowly all around him. There was surf sound and spume mist in the air. He was lying on his back, he was lying on the water, it was supporting him, cradling him. There were snakes too, trying to crawl toward him, but the surface of the water was like glass, slick, and the snakes couldn't move across it. The water held him safe and floating. But all around him was red, and he was dead.

She wanted to cry but the glassy water was tears after all, and she had none left.

She stared at him and waited. Until she saw him move. And saw that the water was just water and it drained away with a falling tide, and the snakes were ripple shadows. He got up and climbed a little rise of ground and disappeared beyond a clump of trees. He'd been dead and he was alive again . . .

No, he'd been asleep. He was in a plane and he always fell asleep in planes.

She began to smile, at first, and then she chuckled aloud.

"Why are you laughing? What's so funny?"

"Because there wasn't anything left. And he came back."

"For God's sake."

Yes, she thought. Yes indeed.

Pillow of Stone

THE WIND was in the southeast, and the sky was a light, even gray, bright and hard like china, under which small broken clouds scudded, black and very low. The Gulf, usually brown-gray with river silt, was slate colored now and flecked with whitecaps. Surf pounded the shell beaches and rising tides littered them with brown and orange seaweed. Salt spray crusted the houses and coated the trees until the island was dripping wet.

Ann Marie Landry finished wrapping burlap around her three camellia bushes. She stared at them, wondering if the cover would hold. She would hate to lose them now, after all the trouble. Raoul, her husband, had brought over the soil on one of the fishing boats, black delta soil from her home; and she had watered them by bucket through the hot summer and the dry early fall. Now in December they were showing clear green shoots and even the buds were firm. They would flower soon, right in their season.

They were the only camellias on the island. The people here, her husband's people, had thought her foolish to come on her wedding trip with her bedroom set, her linen chest, and her plants. Now, seven months later, they asked about them, politely, the way they would ask about a child.

She arched her back, rubbing it with the palms of her hands. A little nagging ache; she must have strained it.

She decided to walk down to the beach because she was aimless and a little tired. She hadn't slept last night. The wind had been very noisy. The oleander bushes planted close to the house to shield off the heat of the summer sun slashed and banged against it. All around the woods, dead limbs of trees came crashing down. The house shook and quivered; now and then its beams creaked and talked. Raoul had not even stirred. Once when the dogs started howling she shook him awake: "What is it there?"

On an elbow he listened, fingers scrubbing at his bristly beard. "The storm makes them restless, some. They are always like that, *chère*, every time the wind comes to blow." And he was asleep again. She dozed, lightly, fitfully, until morning.

A few hundred yards to the beach—she shielded her eyes against the spray and the sand. The surf was breaking higher than ever. As she watched, a long black piling swung free and slid up the beach, grating its barnacles on the shell. There were some dead birds too, brought in by the surf, their white feathers streaked with brown seaweed and stained by the yellow sand.

Her cotton dress flapped and pulled at her body, and she shivered, though the wind was warm. She hurried back into the shelter of the trees. The branches still swayed crazily and their leaves streamed by, but the feeling that the wind was stripping her clean and bare was gone.

She walked quickly across the narrow island, scuffing her feet through the torn leaves that covered the white shell paths. She climbed the gently sloping back ridge, passed the last and highest of the stunted burned oaks, and stood staring down at the wharfs and the bay. She was looking at the shadow of the island: its lee was marked plainly by the smooth water. Beyond it, the arc of the bay was filled with white froth.

The fishing boats, the luggers, were gone. The men always took them to the safer harbor at Petit Prairie when the wind blew hard from the east quarter, even when it wasn't hurricane season. The line of black wharfs glistened wet and empty. A few frayed lines dangled from pilings and swung lightly in the wind. A yellow and white cat ambled along, loose-boned, fur ruffled in the wind. Some white gulls and a black man-of-war bird coasted lazily, high up, riding the spirals.

It would be near eleven-tthirty; she would have to be getting lunch. She turned and walked back, taking a different path. She passed old Mr. Delachaise, mending nets on his porch, and his two grandchildren, fixing traps on the bare swept earth of the yard. She passed Cecile St. Ange, chopping kindling by her kitchen door. Cecile waved her hatchet: "The electricity, she has gone off just a few minutes past."

"I will see that the kerosene lamps are full."

The houses were close together in this clump of trees. They were all one family, all the children and grandchildren and into the fourth generation of the old woman who still lived in the largest and roomiest house on the island —Justine Abbeville.

Ann Marie thought, With just a little work that house would be so pretty to look at, with roses growing up over the lattice, and wax plants set in a row on the porch, and chickens pecking loose in the yard . . .

Old Justine took no care of it. The shutters hung until they fell off, the porch steps cracked and broke. The old woman was very light on her feet. When a step rotted through, she picked her way delicately around it, like a cat. She and her house were decaying together.

This morning Justine Abbeville was puttering away in her front yard, tending her small round patches of bright annuals—zinnias, petunias, marigolds—set in beds of old truck tires. She was bundled in a gray wool sweater and several dresses. Their different patterned hems hung one under the other. The old lady was stooped and bent, wrapped up and knotted, almost. When she was sixty or so she had been up on her roof patching the tin, and she had fallen. Her back mended, but crooked.

Justine Abbeville beckoned Ann Marie over to her corner of the fence. Her bright little brown eyes, like birds' in the hanging wrinkled flesh of her face, stared: "You tell Raoul he will have a son by Easter."

Ann Marie nodded politely.

Justine rubbed her chin with a rheumatic stump that had been a hand. "He moves?"

"No." Ann Marie sighed. "Before too long I will see the doctor. The next time Raoul goes to Petit Prairie."

Justine snorted. "I can tell, me. Tell by looking . . ." She turned away abruptly.

Almost outside her own house. Ann Marie passed Rita Monet, whistling cheerfully, her long red hair whipping around her pale, freckled face. "Hi, little one," she said. "Somebody has told you the lights are gone?"

Ann Marie nodded.

"They been gone before," Rita said. "The telephone went too this morning."

The one phone on the island was in Raoul's store. It had been in only a few years.

"It blow for a couple more hours," Rita said, "then it come to raining, then it get cold . . . I go home and get myself a drink, me."

Ann Marie went into her house, a new house still smelling of paint. She lit the fire on her stove and shifted the pan of jambalaya on it to warm. She brushed the oilcloth of the table smooth and set out the plates, then she stood at the window and waited for Raoul to come down the path, through the grove of hackberries.

Each day for the past seven months she had done that, excited and happy. As happy as she had been last year at Petit Prairie, when she had stood inside the lace curtain in her father's parlor and watched for him to come down the street, in the days when he was courting her.

She had met him at the Christmas dance at Isle Ronquille, and all that night she had cried desperate tears into her pillow because she was in love. She had wanted nothing beyond marrying him. She had left her father's house and the little town where she had been raised. Without even a minute's regret, she had left her people and come to live on Isle Sebastian, the outermost of the Gulf islands. She had not been home once since her marriage. And she was content. She had her house and her garden and her chickens to look after, and there would be a baby along pretty soon. Maybe even by Easter, like the old woman said.

She shrugged and turned back to stir the jambalaya. Raoul was late. She decided to make a pot of fresh coffee while she waited, and so she did not see him come down the path. Suddenly he was standing in the kitchen door, saying, "Ann, *chère*."

Something was wrong. She carefully finished pouring the boiling water over the coffee grounds and put the kettle down on the back burner of the stove. Then she said: "What?"

"Your papa," he said.

She finished for him. "He is dead, no?"

He nodded. He stood in the doorway, not moving, waiting for her.

When she spoke it was not something that she had expected to say. "But the phone is not working. The phone was blown out."

He said quietly, as if he were talking about the load of an oyster boat, "Steve Robards told me."

He had a radio and a little gasoline-powered generator and an aerial up one of the tall palm trees. He spent all his free time talking to other operators. This morning, because no one was working, he got to his set early.

"Steve say your sisters send the message."

She did not cry, though she had always cried easily. "He saw the last of his children married and his wife in the tomb."

That wasn't what she had meant to say either. But

there was a singing in her ears, and she seemed to be turning into somebody else.

"Have something to eat first," she said, "then we will go."

"Ann, *chère*," he said, and came into the room, "there are none of the boats here."

"I have been down to the docks not an hour ago."

"They will not come back while the wind lies anywhere to the east."

She filled his plate, taking nothing for herself but a cup of coffee. "I will go."

"Time is nothing to him," Raoul said.

She stared down into her coffee, looking for words. "He will not rest . . ." Until the circle of his children was filled. Until they were about his body like a wall. All together. Without her there was a chink through which the unmentionable things could slip. His first night dead, but not alone . . .

She shook her head. "I will go, me. Or all my life my pillow is made of stone."

"There is only Lucien's boat." An old gaff-rigged sloop, small, and open. Some people said that Lucien Caillouet had won it in a poker game with a drunken vacationer from New Orleans. Against the boat Lucien had put up his wife, whose green eyes and enormous breasts made her the most beautiful woman anywhere along the coast . . . but that had all been years past. Lucien kept the boat in shape, after a sort, and he would take children sailing now and then. Presently the boat was moored in the shallows behind the Caillouet house. Unlike the valuable luggers, it was not worth taking to a more secure harbor.

"Would you go in Lucien Caillouet's boat?" Raoul asked.

She nodded.

"It will be rough and wet."

Always before she had been afraid of boats, had been afraid of being wet. Now it didn't seem to matter. She told him: "I will not notice."

She took what was left of the jambalaya and put it

between the halves of a long loaf of bread. She got a small bottle of water and a pint of whiskey. She found a canvas ice bag, its pale color spotted and splashed with mold, and packed them in there. She added a couple of sweaters and Raoul's navy jacket. And her good dress, her dress for the funeral.

The wind was about the same, but the sky had changed color. The low racing clouds had taken a greenish tinge. It was almost ready to rain.

Raoul went to move the boat to the lee behind the shrimp-packing plant. Ann Mare followed slowly. The network of small paths was empty. The news spread quickly and people had gone inside, deferentially. They had pulled back to let her pass, leaving the emptiness of her grief around her in a visible space.

She knew nothing about boats, and it did not occur to her to try to help. She sat very still, noticing for the first time, something, moving . . . like a bird, fluttering. She wondered how long it had been going on without her noticing.

Raoul said: "Keep down, *chère*. Don't stand up."

"Yes," she said.

"It will be a run, I think me, most of the way."

There was a small square of oilcloth on the deck beside her. She put it over her head, holding it under her chin, sniffing its comfortable smell of warm oil. She pulled it over her forehead like a visor and hunched herself down, both elbows on knees.

Raoul tossed off the mooring lines, pushed away the wharf with his foot. The old hull sighed with the motion of water under it, the soft lapping give of water. The blocks creaked as he hoisted the ragged sail. It filled with a soft plop, and then fluttered to a luff at the edges.

"There would be no beating with this boat," Raoul said softly. "God gives us a good wind for a sad thing."

She nodded her certainty. "He knows I have to get there."

Raoul glanced down at the rough splintered tiller in his fist, then up at the patched mildew-splotched sail. He fastened the top snap of his raincoat and settled down to finding the course and keeping it. He could see the rain squalls moving up out of the south, and he wondered if the low lumpy clouds were bringing water spouts with them. He put that thought from his mind, crossing himself as he did so.

At first, in the shelter of the island, there was just a gentle swell moving offshore and the slow white bubbles of their wake. Then the water on all sides of them prickled as it does with minnows feeding, and the first of the squalls caught them. The rain poured down, smacking hard as hail, exploding in little puffs. At that moment too, they slipped from under the lee, the sheets creaked with the strain and the hull shuddered and trembled as the canvas began to drag it along.

The bay water was shallow and there were no running swells under the wind, just quick nasty chops, short splashy slaps of water. Once Ann Marie looked out. She thought they must be moving quickly now, but she wasn't sure, because there was nothing in sight. The island had disappeared behind them, and the edges of the bay were all an even blurry gray, streaked by darker clouds.

And there was the flutter again . . . She drew up her knees around it, bent down her head, and waited for it to come back again.

She lost track of time. She crouched covered, in the bottom of the hull. When a squall passed, she did not bother looking up; she waited for the next. There was only sound and motion without time.

Finally they swung into the mouth of the bayou, missing the channel, bumping and scraping over the shoals. *"Sal au pri,"* Raoul muttered sotftly. They slid safely into the deep bayou water, around the little chenière that people called The Lady because she stuck out so stiff and proud against the marsh and the bay.

Raoul dropped the sail and put the outboard on the stern. It was raining steadily, and it was beginning to get a little cooler. She peered out from her cover now, watching as they moved along the empty bayou, the dark oily water flowing back to slap against the saw grass and the cane and the cattails of the marsh. As they went, following the snaky course, the day gave way entirely and night began, empty starless night of heavy rain and steady wind.

Her father's house was on another, smaller bayou to the east of the town of Petit Praire. Raoul lost the entrance in the darkness, remembered, and swung the hull about. He found it the second time, and in half an hour they had reached the landing.

In her father's house, the shades were up and every light burned: through each window stubby yellow fingers stuck out into the rain.

Raoul made the boat fast quickly. "They will not be expecting us."

The house was crowded with people; they shifted back and forth against the lighted squares. She wondered which room they had put her father in.

She got out of the boat slowly, her legs cramped and shaking. "The child is moving now," she said quietly.

Because he did not know what to say—because the night was stormy and the marsh grasses were crying, because there was a dead old man just behind the closed windows—he said nothing.

"Just now when I step on the ground, it moves again."

The rain was pouring down her hair, making it slick and black as patent leather in the light. "My papa he can rest, now I have come with one to take his place."

She began to walk up the gentle slope to the house. She walked carefully, feeling her weight against the ground . . . And how big was it now and what did it look like . . .

She would go inside and dry herself and she would light her own candle and put it with the others beside her father's head. She would sit, hands folded, in the formal circle in the parlor with her sisters. They would sit there, on the straight oak chairs with lions' heads carved on the backs, and they would wait the night through until the priest came in the morning. And if she ever felt like crying, there would be the faint flutter to remind her.

By the time she reached the door, she was smiling triumphantly.

Eight O'Clock One Morning

❦

MY MOTHER is standing on the front porch when we come down at eight o'clock one morning. The sunlight is shining clear through her fuzzy yellow hair, it's that bright a day. Soon as she hears us, she spins around and pops back inside the house.

"What you see?" I ask her.

"Go brush your teeth," she says. "Fill your mouth up with soap."

"But we haven't had breakfast," Rosalie cries. "Not even one bite."

"Go get it then," my mother says.

My old man is waiting in the kitchen, the way he is every morning. He always gets up early and has breakfast first, so that the three of us can have the table to ourselves.

"Hi kids," he tells us. "You all dressed up for school?"

"Good morning, sir," we say politely.

"That's fine," my mother says.

"Where's Taylor?" my father asks.

"Where is he?" my mother asks.

"He's coming."

Taylor is the youngest. He's five and starting kinder-garten today.

"Go tell Taylor to come down," my father says. "You, Carrie, go call Taylor."

As I leave I hear them talk about Taylor. It's a way they have of saying his name over and over again. They're crazy about his name, which is a pretty fancy name for a snuffly kid. They heard it on televison one night when my mother's stomach was bulging full with him. So that's why he's Taylor.

I don't go up, just stand at the foot of the stairs and yell after him. I keep yelling until he answers, which takes a while.

Then I go back in the kitchen. My mother is finishing lunch for the old man; she's wrappng up the sandwiches. She's trying to get him to do something too—you can tell by the tone in her voice.

"Just a little way," she is saying. "Go see can you find out anything."

"Okay," my father says.

But she can't stop. She rattles right on, as if he'd said no.

"I'd gone myself, only this man comes up to me—what's his name? Lives in the house with the pink shutters down the next block. He comes up to me while I'm standing on the front walk, trying to see what I can see, and he says: 'You go back inside, lady, there's going to be trouble.' And I see him tell the same thing to Marie Armand standing out in her front yard."

"Okay," my father says again.

My mother doesn't seem to hear him. "You wouldn't think school'd make all this trouble. There wasn't no trouble when Carrie started seven years ago."

"Eight," I tell them but they don't hear me.

"And there wasn't trouble when Rosalie came around to going."

"Yeah," my father says.

"Why it's got to be Taylor gets all the trouble?"

My father says okay again. I watch him go out the

door and put the lunch box on the front seat of the truck that is standing in the drive, the truck that says Harris Plumbing Company. That's my father and his brother.

"Where'd he go?" Rosalie asks. These days she talks in a high-pitched, whining voice she thinks she got from Marilyn Monroe.

"He's gone to look at the school," my mother says. "Now shut up and eat."

Just then Taylor comes in. "Shut up and eat too," my mother says to him before he can open his mouth.

In less than five minutes my father is back. "Keep the kids home," he says.

"My God," my mother says wearily, "them under foot all day!"

"You ask me to go look, I go look."

My mother gets herself a cup of coffee, and I know she is upset because she doesn't even like the stuff.

"There's plenty of police around the school," my father says, "and there's some other characters around too. So keep the kids out of it."

"Home all day." My mother rubs her hands together, sadly.

"Now listen, you kids," he says, "if I hear you been bad today, if your mama tell me one thing when I get back, you won't think you been so smart."

Rosalie asks me: "You think you can do my hair today?"

"Okay."

"No peroxide streaks," my mother says.

My father has fixed himself another cup of coffee too, and he sits down with it. He must feel something is wrong, or he wouldn't be hanging around like this. Other mornings he stays just long enough to see that we got our arms and legs.

All of a sudden, there's some yelling in the street: "Hu . . . hu." No words. Not that we can make out anyhow.

My father heaves himself up. And the telephone rings. His head snaps around like a mechanical doll's and he says, "Rosalie, go get it." Which isn't necessary, because Rosalie always answers the phone in this house.

He turns back to the window. Now, the way the house is set, he can't see anything unless it's right in front, and by the sound of it, the racket is a little way down the street. So he's looking at nothing. But he keeps on looking anyhow.

Rosalie calls: "It's for Carrie."

"My mother says: "Who is it?" And to me: "Sit down."

"Michael," Rosalie says. I go back to eating my corn flakes because I know I haven't got a chance in the world of getting that call.

We can hear my mother answer. "No," she is saying, "she can't come to the phone."

"What does that character want?" my father asks me.

"Ask Mama," I tell him, "I'm not talking to him."

He glares at me for a minute and then he breaks into a grin. He always did like his girls to talk back to him.

"A fine boy friend you got," he says.

"He's all right."

When my mother comes back, my father asks: "He's cutting school?"

"Wouldn't tell me nothing, but I can guess."

"To run loose on the streets . . . Keep these kids out of it."

"They're not going one step out the front door," my mother says.

There's more noise in the street—a kind of chant now. "Hu hu . . ." and this time I go to the window with my father. You can't see too much, like I said—just every once in a while three or four kids passing: they look like they'd be in high school. They are wearing black leather jackets, most of them, though it is a bright hot day, and they are walking right down the middle of the street.

"You know them?" my father asks me.

I shake my head.

"Not any of them?"

So I tell him that I haven't ever seen a single one of them.

"I figgered they wasn't from around here," my father says.

"What?" my mother asks. "What?"

"White niggers," my father says to the window glass. "God damn white niggers, spoiling for trouble."

In a couple of minutes a yellow Public Service bus passes. And a shower of things bang into it, ricochet off the steel sides, clatter down to the pavement. The passengers all duck down. You can see their hunched-over backs and the tops of their brown paper parcels. A window breaks and the bus drives on and all there is left is a pile of glass in the middle of the empty street.

Taylor begins to drink my father's coffee, which is right on the counter by him (he isn't allowed to have any for fear it will turn his skin yellow). And my old man is so busy at the window that he doesn't even notice. When he looks down and sees that the cup is empty, he just hands it back to my mother and says, "More."

My mother is putting things in the dishwasher, with short, jumpy motions. She knocks a chunk off a good plate when she bangs it against the sink.

My father says: "That was ice they threw."

"What?" My mother juggles another plate, but catches it in time.

"What they threw at the bus—it was ice."

"Where'd they get that?" my mother asks.

"Lots of places," my father tells her. "Everybody's got ice."

"I wouldn't like to get hit by a piece of ice," Rosalie says.

"Stupid kids," my father says, and I can't make out whether he is talking about us or the people in the street.

There are more of them now, laughing and yelling like Mardi Gras Day. One boy, with a blond crew cut, sticks his toe in the pile of broken glass and sends it flying all over the street. Some of the kids are carrying Confederate flags and some of them are carrying mops.

They're holding them straight up in the air, and they kind of look like heads on sticks, old women's heads with the hair hanging down.

I start to say something like that but I don't, because I see that nobody is going to hear me, nobody is going to listen.

"Oh my God," my mother says all of a sudden and she rushes off, yelling back over her shoulder: "I got to tell Mama she better not come for lunch."

"She must heard about this."

There was the sound of the phone dialing, little trickling sounds like water. "How would she know over there, way over there? I bet there's lots of people don't know."

My father just grunts and doesn't say anything.

My mother comes back from the phone and says triumphantly: "She didn't know anything about it."

Rosalie asks: "Can we make some fudge?"

"Anything to keep you quiet," my mother tells her.

They both get down on their hands and knees and start looking around in one of the low cupboards for the proper size pan. Taylor has found his kitten and he's feeding it catfood out of the can with a spoon. You can hear him singing to it.

Then it happens. I hadn't been looking out, so the first I know of it is when my father says, "Son of a bitch!"

But he says it softly so that my mother and Rosalie, who have their heads inside the cupboard rattling pans, can't hear him. And if Taylor does he pays no attention.

I look out. A diaper service truck (all white and blue painted) has pulled up in front of the Fortiers' across the street. The Negro driver must be awful brave or awful foolish or maybe he just doesn't know.

He has taken the clean diapers into the house and put the dirty ones in the back of the truck and closed the door.

When the kids notice him he is back in the cab. He has just started the motor and he is barely moving when they catch up with him. There are a dozen or so of them, and they dash alongside; some run directly in front and the truck stops. Two of them jump in the open door and grab for the driver, only they keep missing because another kid is beating away with an old mop. He is swinging it with all his strength at the driver but all he hits is the head of one of the boys who have hopped the cab. And all the time bits of things, rocks or maybe more ice, are rattling down on the truck.

My old man bangs through the kitchen door. I go after him, fast as I can. First thing I notice is how much noisier it is outside than it seemed from the other side of the glass. There's a lot of confused yelling, and the kid who got smacked by the mop handle is standing a little bit back, holding his head with both hands and roaring, louder than the rest.

My old man stops at his truck and takes out a short piece of pipe. Then he walks down to the edge of our lawn, right to where it meets the sidewalk.

The Negro driver has got the kids out of the cab now and has shut the door. Now they are standing in a circle pounding on the truck. I see the back window crack into a crazy star pattern when a rock hits it, but it doesn't shatter.

"Run over them," my old man yells to the driver. "Run over the bastards."

The driver can't hear him, not inside the cab. Some of the kids do and turn around, but they don't make a move toward him.

The driver is racing his motor, but he isn't moving. You can see his dark face peering out the windshield.

My old man says something very quietly under his breath and starts over to the truck. He moves to the front of it, and he takes hold of the first collar he can. He yanks on it; the kid goes sailing over backwards and he grabs for another. And I remember the picture on his dresser, the picture of him in trunks when he used to box at St. Michael's Arena. And all this time, over everybody else, I can hear him yelling: "Put it in gear. Run over them. Use the god damn truck."

Maybe the driver hears him, because after a while

he does shift (he doesn't have the clutch all the way in and the gears grind and scrape) and he begins to inch forward. Between the two of them, the slow-moving truck and the guy who is throwing people around, they get a little clear space. And then a little more.

Finally the truck slips through.

Everybody stands in the street and looks after it. Everybody except my father who comes stalking stiff-legged back to his own yard. The kids mill around muttering; some begin to drift toward us. My father straightens up, the length of pipe in his right hand.

They look at each other. Just stand and look. My father lets them do that for a minute.

Then he yells: "Get out of here." And he starts swinging the pipe around his head.

They disappear all right.

My old man comes up the walk, rubbing his shoulder and swearing.

By this time my mother is standing in the door and has both her hands slapped up against her mouth and Rosalie is behind her, trying to push her way into the door so she can see too. Back in the house you can hear Taylor singing to the cat and he doesn't know that anything has happened at all.

My old man puts the pipe on the lowest step and clears his throat and spits into the flower bed. He spits again, as if there's something in his mouth he can't get out. Then he turns and looks back down the street. And when he talks it is to the street.

"Niggers and white niggers," my father says. As if that explained everything.

The Lovely April

❧

MY FATHER sat on the edge of a baggage truck and waited for the afternoon train. The sun was getting low into the last quarter of the sky: there was no shade at all under the wall-less shed of the railroad station, except in the little room that had a sign, "Agent," in sun-cracked paint letters.

Hal Beecham came out of that office, tugging mail-bags. "Hi, Doc," he said. "You expecting anybody?"

"Yes."

Beecham cocked his head, listening. "There she comes, all right."

"On time."

"You waiting for somebody?"

My father laughed. The sound bounced around among the heat waves that were rising from the black asphalt street.

"You know what I'm doing here as well as I do."

Hal Beecham lifted his sandy eyebrows. "Me?"

"Sure."

Hal Beecham dragged the mailbags out onto the platform. "You never told me."

My father did not answer.

"Well," Beecham admitted, staring down at his dirty white buck shoes, "I reckon I did hear some talk."

"I reckon you did," my father said.

Beecham wiped the sweat from his chin. "People get to talking."

My father snorted, very softly.

"You know his name?" Beecham studied the broken dirty nails of his left hand.

My father snorted again. "Mr. Robin."

Beecham stared, his eyes squinting and his mouth pursed. "Mr. what?"

"That isn't his name. He just wants to be called that."

"I get it." He winked. "I get it."

"I bet you knew that much already, just from the town talking."

"I didn't know his name . . ." Beecham said shyly.

My father wasn't happy about the whole business. But he was doing it as a favor to Mr. Robin's father, who was an old friend and a man you couldn't say no to, anyway.

There were two houses on our block: ours and one other, a small one that hadn't been lived in for years. Mr. Robin's father had had the small one all fixed up so his son could live there, along with a cook and a colored butler. Although everybody always called Henry Stanford a butler, his job was really nothing more than keeping an eye on Mr. Robin. Because Mr. Robin did strange things sometimes, especially in the spring. "The lovely April," he called it.

His name was Mr. Richard Carlysle Peters. He was a little man, not much more than five feet tall, and very slight, almost scrawny, except for a little round stomach, like a pillow stuck out in front. He had a little face that could have been thirty-five or seventy; a little jutting cleft chin and a pug nose that turned up sharp at the end; the usual sort of blue eyes and lots of curly, almost tow-colored hair. He'd forget to go to the barber, and nobody remembered to tell him very often, so his hair was always sticking out in wisps over the back of his coat collar or curling into his ears. He had one little gesture: he would run his fingers over his ears and back to his neck, just at the hairline, brushing up the long curls, at the same time giving his head a little tossing jerk— just exactly the way a girl does when her hair gets in her way and she shakes it back.

Though Mr. Robin didn't look it at all, his family were important people. His uncle was governor of Carolina, elected just the year past. His father was a judge and about the richest man in the state. Mr. Robin was the exception. He wasn't nice-looking or smart or even clever. He went to school for a while, but he'd fall asleep in class sometimes and never pay attention, any time. When he was in the fifth grade (they'd promoted him because his father was an important man), he got roughed up by some bigger boys who'd yelled "pansy" at him. He would never tell who had done it, though it was almost a month before he got over the bruises and cuts.

One thing—Stan Watson, who was in seventh grade, a tough little kid, disappeared a week later. They finally found him in one of the small, old-fashioned freezers in the woods of a vacant lot behind the ice factory. The lid was locked.

Mr. Robin didn't go back to school. Each morning his mother would hand him the satchel with his books and stand by the front door and watch him trudge off down the street. She'd watch until he turned the corner and then she'd go back in with a sigh and send a servant after him. Sometimes he kept walking until he was out of the town. When he found a spot of grass that looked particularly soft he would put his satchel down very carefully and stretch out. He wouldn't sleep. He'd just stare right straight up at the sky. If there were clouds, his eyes would move very slowly, following them across the circle sweep of his vision. If it started raining, he'd find a tree with thick, twisted branches for a shelter. He never seemed to mind.

In winter he had to do something different; it was too cold to be outside. Mornings there was always a heavy frost, and he would walk looking back over his shoulder to see the dark tracks his own feet had made. Usually he'd head straight for the movie house—it was empty that time of day. He'd sit down at the piano in front and pick out little tunes with one finger. Nobody stopped him. After all, there was always his mother's servant standing close by, watching.

That was how he grew up. And somewhere in those years, nobody quite knew how, he got the name of Mr. Robin.

Until he was well in his twenties, almost out of them in fact, he kept up the pretense of going to school. He still carried the same little satchel. He had never opened it; by this time the lock was rusted and stuck. Each day, just as he came in the door, his mother would ask, "How was school?" and he would say, "Lovely." That was one of his favorite words.

Mr. Robin's mother died one hot July day. He went to her and said, "Mama?" in a kind of hesitant whisper, but she was too far gone to hear. His father took his shoulder in one hand and with the other pointed him stiffly out of the room. Mr. Robin left and was gone for two days, the days of the wake. Nobody knew where he was; nobody had thought to tell a servant to follow him, the way she did.

He turned up all rumpled and dirty, in time for the funeral. Nobody told him what to do or watched out for him, but he did everything exactly right. He washed and shaved and put on a white linen suit and a white starched shirt and a black tie. He brushed his curly light hair until it stayed in place and then to be sure he poured hair tonic on it.

People stared at him and wondered what was going on in his head, but he didn't seem to notice anything. He nodded to his uncles and his two cousins who'd come back from college in Stanton. Then he looked at the broad bands of black crepe on their arms and he said very quietly, "I want one of those."

After all the services were over, his father moved down to the hotel. For a week or so he stayed there, getting over the worst of his grief (he cried, people said; he cried for his wife, a hard shrewd man like that) and trying to figure out what to do with his son.

He finally decided to set his son up in a small town, where there was someone who could be trusted to keep a supervising eye on the whole thing.

That was how Mr. Robin came to us.

Of course, everybody in town was watching. They were surprised and disappointed, too, when Mr. Robin got off the train quietly and said how do you do to my father, calmly and just a little bored. That night there were lights in a house that hadn't been occupied for years, but the shades were drawn, and at nine o'clock the lights went out.

The next morning Mr. Robin's cook went into town to the grocery, while the butler, Henry Stanford, fixed a hammock between two pecan trees in the front yard. But Mr. Robin didn't appear. Maybe he was unhappy and sulking or maybe the change had just confused him; for five or six days nobody saw him.

Then on Friday afternoon, my mother found him in our kitchen. He was leaning against the doorjamb, his thin legs crossed, his arms folded, and his little mouth pursed. My mother stopped so suddenly that she almost lost her balance on the waxed kitchen floor.

Mr. Robin straightened himself and bowed very slowly from the waist. "Good evening, madam," he said, and his soft voice had just a hint of an English accent. (He had got that from his mother, along with his blue eyes and blond curly hair. She had come from Staffordshire.) "I am Mr. Robin."

"But I've met you before," my mother said. "The first day you came."

Mr. Robin sighed, very slightly.

"Do you remember?" she insisted.

"I forgot such a lovely lady." His soft light voice was really sad.

My mother smiled and one of her fingers caught up the stray hair at the nape of her neck. "What a nice compliment."

Mr. Robin smiled, too, and his blue eyes opened even wider. "Oh, I say that to everybody," he added earnestly.

My mother gasped and then laughed aloud.

Mr. Robin said, "I hope you don't mind my being in your kitchen."

Our cook, Oriole, had come in the dining room door and stood staring.

"It is so nice in here," Mr. Robin said. "Not lonesome like it is in my house."

"Oriole," my mother said, "would it worry you if Mr. Robin visited our kitchen?"

"No'm."

Mr. Robin bowed formally, the way his mother had taught him to do, years ago, when she had tried to teach him to dance.

And so all the rest of the summer, Mr. Robin hung around the kitchen.

Sometimes he'd move out to the yard and sit under the big sycamore. Leaning back against the white-and-brown-streaked trunk, he'd look even littler and fuzzier than usual.

But most times he'd be on the kitchen step, just outside the screen door. He'd sit quietly there, staring off across the narrow valley to the ridges over in the west. Even on the clearest day their edges up against the sky were blurred and indistinct: the summer fires were burning in the high slopes.

"The little people," he announced aloud one day.

"The what?" Oriole opened the screen door and stuck her head out.

"The little people."

"That what I thought you say."

"They are." Mr. Robin nodded toward the smoky ridges. "They're doing all that burning up there."

Oriole leaned against the door, one hand on her hip. "That right?"

Mr. Robin lifted his light-colored eyebrows until they arched up into his hair, peaked like gables. "What would you say if I told you I was one?"

Oriole laughed in her deep voice. "I say you plain better not start no fires around me." She held open the door. "You just come in and tell me some more stories."

"Poor little fellow," my mother said. "He's found somebody to talk to."

He had. He spent all his time back there. Once, because it was a dark, near-fall day, and fall days are always sad (like the dead cotton fields, brown and rattling with only a shred or two of white blowing in the wind), Oriole decided to sing "Garlands of Flowers." It was a Creole tune she'd learned from her first husband, who'd come from New Orleans. She sang it very well.

Maybe it was the day and maybe it was the song, but both Oriole and Mr. Robin began to cry. My mother heard the sniffling and went out to see. Mr. Robin rushed out, his blue eyes red and wet.

"We was singing a funeral tune." Oriole blew her nose and smiled and went back to work.

Oriole was a big woman, deep-black colored and bow-legged. She'd thrown out two or three husbands because they got funny and laughed at those bowlegs. That was one thing she couldn't stand—being laughed at. And when she said thrown out she meant just exactly that. She was a powerful woman, a match for a man in any sort of fight. You could see how her dress pulled over the lumps of back muscle; and when she kneaded dough you could see the muscles in her forearms knot and unknot like pieces of rope.

She had a little house a mile or so down the road, a good house with one room and a lean-to for a kitchen and a woodshed out back; but an old house: her mammy and pappy had lived there until they died. She owned the little piece of farmland, too, but that was just cut-out fields. And the only hard cash she had was what she got from my mother every Saturday morning.

All her husbands were big, good-looking fellows who could have had just about any girl they wanted. And there were lots younger and prettier than Oriole. She had a funny way with men. Days when she'd got rid of a husband—she'd had some legally and some not— she'd whistle in the kitchen like a mockingbird.

Along toward real fall, when it got to be too damp and windy for sitting outside, Mr. Robin caught cold. My father told his servants to make him stay inside for a week.

For that whole week there wasn't a sound from the kitchen. Oriole cooked and washed the dishes like always. But she didn't bother whistling or singing. And when she carried the dishes into the dining room she walked sort of stiffly.

It wasn't that she was in a bad humor, but she was so quiet and listless that my mother finally went back to talk to her.

"You're not sick, are you, Oriole? Do you want Dr. Addams to have a look at you?"

"No'm." Oriole kept right on fixing the meat for dinner, her black arms moving slowly up and down.

She looked out the window where you could see a few white specks of Mr. Robin's house through the thick trunks of the bare pecan trees.

"I ain't never missed a man yet."

"Don't you fret," my mother said. "He'll be all right."

"And I reckon he ain't even a man." Oriole blushed under her black skin.

By the end of the week, Mr. Robin was back in the kitchen. This time he brought something with him, a yellow upholstered stool that he carried over from his own kitchen. He carefully selected a place: under the window, next to the porcelain-topped table. And he settled down for the cold months.

That was the winter it snowed. Two days before Christmas the even gray sky broke. There was white snow covering the ground, making little drifts of an inch or so against the walls and the hedges.

Mr. Robin had Christmas presents from his family. They, remembering what he liked most of all, got together and filled a box—big almost as a laundry box, and so heavy that Henry Stanford grunted when he lifted it from the mail sack. There was only food in the box —candies and cakes and heavy jelly pastries wrapped carefully in waxed paper.

For a while, sitting on the floor in his living room, Mr. Robin studied his box. Then he put the cover back on and lifted it up and headed out across the snow-crusted yard.

He forgot his overcoat and his hat. It was very cold outside and there was a stiff wind. He began to run; by the time he'd got to our house he was almost exhausted. He kicked at the door.

Oriole opened it quickly. "Lord," she said. "Looks like all the devils in hell chasing after you."

She saw the box and grinned; her single gold tooth flashed. "You come on in."

While she cooked dinner, Mr. Robin sat on his yellow stool and ate most of the candy. He put the box down and his puffy blue eyes followed Oriole around for a few minutes. He got to his feet very slowly, gave a funny little clucking sound, and headed out the door. Oriole held his head while he was sick on the snow in the yard. They came back inside, shivering, both of them, from the cold. Mr. Robin sat down very weakly on his chair and leaned back against the wall and closed his eyes and hardly moved the rest of the day.

Pretty soon winter was over; and the spring rains were beginning. You could feel how excited Mr. Robin was. Then the rain stopped bit by bit and the sky got clear, the bright clear blue that is soft and hard all at once, the way the sky is only in spring. The ground began to dry and drain and very suddenly you could see things coming to life.

He was a different man in spring. His face suddenly got a peaked look; there was a little pointed chin where there had been a soft round one. His tousled curly hair fluffed up into little points around his face.

Some people began to wonder if his left foot was a hoof, until Mr. Robin one evening walked barefoot through the red clover field kicking at the round flowers so that the heavy dew splashed up in thick drops. His feet were small and fat and white and perfectly usual.

One afternoon my father came on Mr. Robin lying full-length on the ground in the wide rows between the turnips in our garden.

My father said, "Good afternoon."

Mr. Robin did not answer or move.

"It must be chilly on the ground."

"No," said Mr. Robin.

"Well," my father said, "how are you feeling?"

"I'm feeling fine," Mr. Robin said and his voice was as light and soft as the rustling wind. "I'm feeling real extra fine."

"It must be the weather." My father's eyes studied him carefully.

"I'm feeling extra fine."

That should have warned my father. After all, in the report he had of Mr. Robin in the big file in his office, there was a history of things that had happened when Mr. Robin was feeling fine.

The first thing that happened was the green paint.

The following Tuesday morning, about midmorning, he covered his whole face with green paint.

Henry Stanford practically passed out. Still laughing so hard he couldn't speak, he brought him up to my father's office. Mr. Robin was wearing an injured expression. His little mouth was pursed up into a perfect circle.

A few days later Henry caught him half a block down the street, his clothes on all wrong side out, his tie fastened firmly behind his neck and his black derby perched backward on his little head.

"For all the trouble," my father laughed, "he's such a nice little helpless fellow. You can't help liking him."

My father wasn't so sure about liking him a week later. Mr. Robin slipped upstairs into our bathroom and, using my father's own razor and soap, shaved off all his hair, until there was just a pink lumpy dome with ears that stood out like handles.

Oriole spent nearly two hours cleaning up the mess; there were soap-sticky wads of hair on floors and walls and doors.

My father got angry dark splotches on his cheeks. "What did you think you were doing?" my father asked Mr. Robin in a voice that was far from gentle.

Mr. Robin smiled right back at him. Smiled so bright that little wrinkles ran up over his face and crinkled along his bare skull and moved the little patches of adhesive tape covering the small nicks he had given himself.

For this, Mr. Robin was to stay in his house for five days.

Oriole didn't say one single word during the time Mr. Robin was gone. She just did the cooking and the cleaning she had to do, and then walked dismally home, stumping along on the dirt road like her feet had suddenly got too heavy for her.

"Sometimes," my mother told my father, "she's as crazy as he is."

My father grinned. "Maybe," he said, "only I don't think so. I just don't think so," he repeated.

My mother sat down in the rocking chair by the

window and tipped herself back and forth. "What's the matter, then?"

My father's grin got wider. "She's in love."

My mother stopped rocking so suddenly that her heels made a sharp click on the floor. "She's what?"

"She's in love."

"With Mr. Robin?"

My father nodded. My mother kept staring at him. You could see she didn't believe a word.

"Yes," he said. "That's it." He was not talking to her now. The words were directed to the polished leather of the shoes he had propped up in front of him. "She's in love. He's in love. That's it."

"But that poor little thing is hardly a man," my mother said.

My father puffed out his cheeks.

"That's what makes it so perfect for her. She doesn't like men."

My mother gave an unbelieving sigh.

Mr. Robin decided he did not like being kept in the house. The very first day he tried walking out six or seven times. Until the cook shook her finger threateningly and shouted at him. Then he retired to his room and sulked. He wouldn't come out or eat all the next day. And the following day he escaped. It happened like this.

Very early Sunday morning—before it had really got light and there was just this trembling uncertain glow, like always in spring—Hank Miller and his clanking little truck drove up to Mr. Robin's. (The town was too small for a regular garbage collection; Hank did most of the hauling.) He loaded the big cans on his truck and went inside to collect his money from Henry Stanford. Mr. Robin slipped into a can that was almost half empty and pulled the top on after him. He rode out with the truck.

About midmorning we located him. He had gone to church.

It was a dark church. The only windows were high up in the walls and covered with dark stained glass. The walls themselves and the pews were all dark wood that had been rubbed and polished for so many years that it gave out a dark light of its own.

And there was Mr. Robin. He was sitting in the very first row on the left side and he was sitting very quietly, not making a sound. Just wearing his black derby hat.

There was a sermon, but nobody listened. They were all watching Mr. Robin's hat. That was how we found him so quickly. Everybody's attention was like a finger pointing at him.

"Wait here," my father said. "I guess I better go get him."

His shoes had rubber soles so that there was just the faintest brushing sound. But at each row heads turned to him—it was like in passing each pew, he pulled a wire that swung all the heads. Up in the pulpit the minister was still preaching. Maybe he didn't quite know what he was saying.

Finally my father reached the front pew where Mr. Robin sat all alone. (Nobody ever occupied that pew; it was the one in which Jeff Davis had sat when he'd rode past this way during the war.)

My father sat down and pushed himself along the polished wood until he was next to Mr. Robin, who was looking straight ahead with a kind of puzzled intentness. Since he had no hair, the hat sat far down on his head, resting very gently on the back of his ears. If he were able to pull those ears flat against his head, he would disappear, and then there would be just the hat left sitting on the smooth waxed wood of the pew. Mr. Robin would be out somewhere, under a tree, staring up at the clouds. Or in our kitchen with Oriole.

My father slipped his arm through Mr. Robin's and he whispered something to him. For a couple of seconds Mr. Robin didn't move. Then he lifted both his hands and carefully, with elaborate ceremonious gestures, he took off his hat.

The whole congregation gasped. Even the minister gave a kind of gurgle and stopped.

Under Mr. Robin's hat there was his shaved bare head,

white as china but lumpy. And on top of that head was a pancake, a regular-sized pancake, and on it was a fried egg, all white and yellow.

It was very quiet. Seemed like nobody was breathing. Holding Mr. Robin's arm tightly, my father got up and rushed for the door. The pancake slipped to the floor with a gentle plop.

It seemed like that was all there'd be of Mr. Robin.

His father wrote and said that he was sending for him on the twenty-second, which was the coming Friday.

My father shook his head. "I'm glad it's over. It just wasn't working for him here."

"Poor Oriole," my mother said. "She'll miss him."

"No use telling her just yet," my father said. "Tell her after he's gone. It'll be easier."

The kitchen door swung closed just a tiny bit. Oriole had been listening. It wasn't going to be any surprise to her.

And the next day she asked my father to buy her little farm.

"All right," my father said. "But where'll you go?"

"I got people of mine I'd like to see."

My father stared at the black motionless face, its eyes shiny bright in the sunlight. "Let's just call it a loan," he said. "You can buy the place back from me when you want it again."

"I ain't going to want it," she said. "I ain't coming back."

So he gave her $350 for the little square of fallow ground and the little wood house. She rolled the bills and slipped them into the pocket of her dress.

"You're not gong to carry that money around . . ."

"Yes, sir."

"You'll get robbed."

She just grinned.

"Look," he said. "You're strong and you can take care

of yourself against most men alone, but what if there's two?"

Oriole pulled out the razor that dangled on a string around her neck.

"Okay," my father said and shrugged his shoulders. "Okay."

On Friday, the twenty-second, Mr. Robin's father came, a very tall, very thin man with white hair that was balding all across the top of his narrow skull. Hs eyes were large and a very dark blue, fringed with almost red lashes. He had no resemblance at all to Mr. Robin.

Judge Oliver Peters and Mr. Robin spent the afternoon in our living room. My mother got out the sherry and the little biscuits she kept for special occasions, along with the high silvery tones of her laugh.

While they were there, chatting politely, Oriole went to Mr. Robin's house.

"I came for them," she said to Henry Stanford, and pointed to the bags, all packed and ready, standing on the porch. "He said I got to get them."

And Henry Stanford looked at her, all fixed up in a new white dress that crackled with starch, and said, "Sure."

Henry noticed that she had a new bright blue wagon, with a young mule between the poles. He saw Oriole flip Mr. Robin's bags into the back, which seemed to be filled with household goods, pots and stoves and such.

As Oriole was driving off, he called, "Why ain't you taking a car?"

And Oriole yelled right back at him, "We ain't needing a car."

So Henry sat down again and dozed off. He was still dozing later on when my father and Judge Oliver Peters came to pick up the bags on the way to the station.

My father turned red with anger when he learned what had happened. But Judge Peters put one hand on his arm. "My dear doctor," he said. "There's nothing valuable in them. The bags aren't important; and the train is.

Send them along when you find them."

Mr. Robin and his father got on the train, after shaking hands with my father, and settled down in their seats. Judge Oliver Peters took out a sheaf of papers from his briefcase and began to study them—he had a very important meeting the following morning. Mr. Robin sat down very quietly and stared out the window. He and his father never did talk.

The train hadn't gone more than five miles or so before it came grinding to a halt. Oliver Peters fastened the papers together wth a big brass clip and put them inside the case. "What the hell is wrong now?" Holding his briefcase in one hand, he swung down the steps.

"You best watch out, sir," the conductor called.

Oliver Peters paid no attention. He kept right on walking, noticing now that he was passing little red warning flags, stuck at intervals along the track. When he reached the engine he saw what had happened.

There was a large gray granite monument planted squarely on the track. Oliver Peters walked over and looked at it. On one side, upside down now so that he had to twist his head to one side to read it, was an inscription: "This road was built in 1862 by General Cornelius Greenleaf, commandant of the Confederate arsenal at Cheehaw."

Oliver Peters looked around. There, a hundred yards to the north, was the road. The hunk of granite had been dragged from there to the tracks.

"Just you look at these mule tracks," a trainman said, pushing back his striped gray cap and wiping his forehead with one grimy hand.

"Why did they do it?" Oliver Peters demanded.

"Mister," the man said, "there ain't no telling."

The engineer laughed; he was a tall, thin man, with a long scar down one cheek and crisscrossing it the little blue scars of inexpert stitches. "They put out warning flags for us a mile back—just like the rule book says."

Judge Oliver Peters rubbed his forehead and frowned. He stood back and watched while the train crew found a heavy sapling and used it as a pole to topple the monument off the tracks. They left it lying on the roadbed.

Oliver Peters sauntered back to his compartment. He planted his chin on his hand and stared morosely out the window, watching the landscape begin to move. Half an hour later, he noticed that his son was gone.

My father said, "She knows this country with her eyes shut. She'll head straight for those high ridges."

It was late twilight now and even the heavy cement base of the granite marker looked soft and indistinct. Henry Stanford was searching the ground a couple of hundred yards away, following the imprints of the mule's hoofs.

"Hey," he called. "Here."

My father followed his shout down a little gully with soft, sloping sides, covered thick with red clover. Henry was pointing down at the ground.

"Look," he said.

In that light you had to bend far over to be sure what you were seeing—the beginnings of wheel marks, thin and not too wavering: a new wagon.

"She stopped here out of sight," Henry said.

We followed, far as we could, until we got to the stretches of pine where the needles were too springy to hold a trace.

It was night now, cool, the way they always are in spring, with a good wind off the hills and a flat, bright sliver of moon lifting up in the east.

"They could be traveling on a night bright as this," my father said.

We stood for a minute and listened to the sounds that came down on the spring wind: birds' flutter and the scurry of little animals and the swish of pines. You could almost hear the steady beat of the mule's hoofs and the creak of that new wagon, moving.

The Way Back

❈

THE OCEAN BEACHES were behind them, and the swampy stretches and the neon-frosted motels. The ground turned sandy, and rose slightly; the open stretches filled with palmetto. Then the palmetto began to be dotted with thin black pine trunks. Eventually the palmetto disappeared and the pine came in long clean rows, each tree neatly tapped for its turpentine.

"Do you want me to drive?" she asked once during the morning. "I can if you're tired, if you want me to."

"I'm fine," he said. "With the roads this empty, it's no strain."

The wordless morning hours slipped by. Neither of them spoke. The speedometer needle shivered at ninety, there was a steady clacking under the hood, a fluttering now and then as the light car held the road precariously.

She shifted in her seat, facing the window more squarely. This way, she thought, I can see how fast the trees pass. They go like blurs, I can't see any one tree. They're there but I can't see them. Like the scrub grasses on the side of the road—sage grass, shadow grass. I can see even less of them. When I look down I can't even see

that there is anything there. Makes me dizzy. I'd rather
look at the trees. The trunks are a black blur, and the
rows are so even that when they pass it's like I'm watching a wheel spinning. At least with the trees I can see
the tops, I can still make out the tops and they still look
like trees, passing.

But I can't make out one individual single tree. They
all go by as a mass, like the miles on the road, or the
seconds on my watch . . . And I can't remember a single
moment separately. All lumped together, all one, all
blended and fused, the outlines confused by tiredness
and lack of sleep. The colors all mixed. The sensations
all mixed. And nothing clear. Not one memory clear.
Not one thing I can reach back for and say: This was
so, and this. Except maybe the sound of surf, pounding.
Or was it surf? It could have been breathing. Yes, it
could have been breathing. And the pound of water,
white-crested water on the sand, that could have been the
thump of the heart under the sheltering arches of ribs.
And which was it? All blurred together. Like the weed
and the rock and the chitin that surf grinds up, flings up
in spume. All one, all mixed.

Abruptly they came out of the pine country and into
the little flat patches of strawberry farms. Square tiny
plots, still covered this time of year by strips of plastic.

"They haven't dared open them up yet," he said, "did
you notice?"

"How can you see them going this fast?"

"Sorry. Did I scare you?" He slowed, the needle
dropped to sixty, the blurs outside took shape and form.

"Not really . . . You mean all those plastic sheets?
This is only January; there's bound to be another frost
or two, don't you think?"

"The coldest weather is still ahead of us," he said.

"When they're expecting a freeze do you suppose they
put out smudge pots and old tires like they do in the
orange groves around Lakeland?"

"I don't know," he said, "but I could find out if you're
interested."

"I'm not interested. I just asked."

"That's a difference I don't understand." The blue eyes left the road, the light blue eyes with their strained, nearsighted look.

"You really should put on your glasses," she said.

"I don't like them."

"They do make you look different. It's surprising how much. Like another person almost."

"People sometimes don't recognize me with glasses."

"Well," she said, "they're big and round and black and they're sort of all over your face."

"Makes a difference."

"Lots of things do, I suppose."

The two-lane road widened with an abrupt flash of yellow lights to a six-lane throughway. The jarring asphalt turned to smooth light concrete; the car's squeaks and jangles stopped.

"How nice this is," she said.

"Haven't you ever noticed how highways always get beautiful near the state capital?"

"No," she said, "I never paid any attention."

"You didn't? Well, in any state. Any one at all. You always come into the capital on a beautiful big highway. Doesn't matter what the rest of the country looks like, Tobacco Road or not—and you ought to see some of those turpentine workers back there a way—but the state goes and builds a billion-dollar highway five miles out of the capital in all directions."

"Is that how far we are?" she asked. "Five miles?"

"No," he said, "I just picked a number. It's nearer twenty, I guess."

"Twenty miles is twenty minutes."

"Thirty or more. The traffic gets worse."

"So that's how long."

"I hate for it to end," he said. "I hate to have it end."

"Things do," she said.

"But this shouldn't."

"Shouldn't, but it does."

"I guess so."

"You know," she said, "I hate long good-bys. I'd just as soon have it be done quickly and be finished."

"Would you? I'd rather have it last."

"And there isn't anything to say. I never know what to say."

"Don't you? I wouldn't think you'd have any trouble."

"I talked a lot last night, didn't I? I'm sorry, I shouldn't have."

"I like to listen to you. I like anything with you."

"Yes." She found herself staring at the shiny knobs of the radio. "I do with you, too." The knobs began to pulse, to grow and shrink. She felt her own head nodding, back and forth toward them in their rhythm, yo-yo on a string. She let it bob up and down a few times, then at the top of a string, yanked back and broke the connection. When she looked at the radio again, she saw nothing but two shiny knobs, quite still. Ordinary pieces of unmoving metal.

The traffic got heavier. He swung around trucks sharply, the transmission slipping with a sharp knock. "Damn car . . . See what I mean? About the traffic. Just a steady line of produce trucks. Look, those are hothouse strawberries."

"Going to market."

"Where else?"

She gave his shoulder a pat and slipped farther across the seat, until she leaned her back against the door. "I'd better sit over here then, if we're coming into town."

"I hate to have you do that."

"Somebody might see."

"Yes," he said. "I just hate to have you do it."

"You might as well be sensible."

"Yes. Look, you see this turn, where the road branches and there's just that concrete divider in the middle, see how it comes up quick when you're almost right on top of it?"

"It looks dangerous."

"Most dangerous spot on the road. I've seen car after car smash right there."

"I can see how the concrete is all chipped."

They were coming into town. There were stores and bars and motels on each side of the highway, and now and then a shopping center: squat buildings in long rows with cars nuzzling their flat sides.

"Cars always look like beetles," she said.

"Only the VW's."

"No, all of them look like beetles to me when they're in the lots like that. Beetles on a log."

"Look now, are you sure you'll be all right driving back?"

"Three or four hours. Of course I will."

"I wish I could drive you."

"You can't."

"I know, but I don't like it."

"It's really all right."

The road ahead was a long sweep of concrete now, smooth, only dipping and banking slightly on the turns. Perfect and mechanical the way new roads are.

"It looks like tape from an adding machine," she said suddenly and laughed at herself.

"Why is that funny?"

"It isn't, I guess."

"I'll call you tomorrow."

"Yes, I hope so."

"I mean, it's all right in the morning?"

"My husband's plane won't get in before noon."

"I'll call you."

"I'll wait for it."

He left the road to turn down the gentle, descending bank of a cloverleaf. The hazy small sun jumped from one side to the other.

"We parked your car right over there."

"Seems such a long time ago."

"It was only night before last."

"But it looks so different now," she said. "I couldn't have found it again."

"You can't really get lost in a city this small."

"Everything looks different in the daylight."

"Look," he said, "are you going to be able to find your way out of town?"

"I found my way in. Only got lost once and I asked at a gas station, wherever that was, and they told me the rest of the way."

"Now look," he said, "you'd better follow me out. I'll take you to the highway east, the one you want. And I'll take you down a way, until you see the signs. Big green overhead signs, you can't miss them. Then I turn off to the right and you go straight. That's the road home for you."

"Just follow you."

"Yes," he said. "It's simpler, I think."

When he pulled up next to her car, she had the keys ready in her hand. "Don't get out," she said. "I can shift the bag without any trouble. And if you stay in the car, people are less likely to see you."

She stepped out. He, ignoring her, got out too and moved the bag from the back seat. They stood between the two cars, sheltered by the open doors, like small wings on each side. For a moment there was only the hiss of tires fifty yards away on the road, and a sharp, far-off squeal of brakes. Then something tapped her hair, brushed her cheek. She jumped, twisting around behind her.

"An acorn," he said.

She glanced up, and saw the high arching oaks in two solemn lines through the parking area. "I didn't notice them the other night. But I guess I was too excited."

"They were there."

Another acorn fell, bounced from the car top. He caught it, with a quick sidewise sweep of the hand, the way a boy catches a fly. "You see?"

She took it, her fingers brushing his palm. "Yes," she said, "I see." His eyes took color from the sky, she decided. Now they were cloudy gray, not blue at all. She held out her hand. "Good-by."

He took the hand, formally. "I'll call you."

She nodded and got into the car, not looking back,

not looking at him. She started the motor, bouncing her foot up and down so that clouds of exhaust rose in the heavy wet air. Then she backed out quickly and followed him to the road.

His ears stick out, she thought. I never noticed that before. He looks like somebody else from the back. So different. But then he looks different with glasses too. And different from face to profile. Maybe all people look like that. Maybe I do. I wonder, now. I wonder if I do. He looks different in bed too, his face gets longer and thinner. And how could that be possible . . .

There was traffic all around them now. Two cars in a stream of other cars. She followed more closely.

His car is a white car and so is mine, but there's another white car following me and I can see still another one in my side mirror. A world full of white cars—and how do you tell one from the other? How could I tell his from any other one, if I lost it now? What would be special about it? There wouldn't be anything, would there?

She shifted her grip on the wheel and felt something in her left hand. The acorn. She had been holding it all this time. An ordinary acorn, brown and green and dusty-looking. Nothing special about it either. But she held it. And settled back to driving the smooth, straight, car-speckled strip.

Then she saw the signs. Far off yet. But there. The place where he would turn off. Where the way back began. Right there.

But in a way, the road back didn't go back at all. Nothing was where you left it. Nothing was the same.

Except maybe the signs, the green and white signs. Approaching now. And this part of her life was nearly over.

And now that it was all over, she thought, could she say what it had been? Could she say what had happened? What had really happened?

Some time had passed. A day. Little more than one

day. Less than two. A bit of time. Passing. The endless
river. Passing.

And what else. What else on the surface of that river.
Not much when you thought about it. Some whispers.
Muscles contracting. Shudders. Spasmodic shudders, that
tore and twisted and wracked. But the muscles through
which they had run were smooth and quiet again and
carried no memory of the sudden convulsive movements.
No more than the time they floated and wasted. Impulse
and time alike. Gone.

And what was left. Something back inside your head.
Way back in your head, inside the shelter of the skull,
hidden by the bone. Encircled by the gray cells, fed by
the blood.

But it wasn't anything at all.

No more than the acorn she held in her left hand, the
green and brown acorn that had happened to bounce off
the roof of the car.

She looked at it again. Dusty thing. With the possibili-
ties of an oak tree. How unlikely, from something like
that.

The road signs were very close now. She could read
them clearly. He had turned his signal light on and was
looking in his mirror. She lifted one hand to show that
she understood. It was the hand with the acorn.

Following the soft, downward curve of the road, his
car swung to the right. She kept straight on, following
the rising concrete. An overpass. Of course. The two
white cars were peeling off like planes. She glanced to
her right once, answered a wave. And watched out of
the tail of her eye until the other car disappeared.

I will not turn my head, she thought. And did not.

I will not look back. Not for anything. I will just
drive.

Quite suddenly she had trouble seeing. The concrete of
the road turned the same color as the sky. Sharp gray
with prickles of bright metal like needles stuck in it.
Stinging like salt water in her eyes.

Concrete shouldn't dazzle. Not like that. And ground

and sky aren't the same. Why should they be the same color? The car ahead of her, it had been black just a moment ago. But it was gray now too, the shadowy hollow gray of a photograph negative. And that other car, she could see it, though it wasn't in sight any more, the car that had turned off the road, to go another way. Another way back.

All the gray colors. All the shiny, hard gray colors. Earth and sky and car alike. And why did it happen like that?

She scrubbed at her eyes, and that helped. She blinked and shook her head. Now she could see the sides of the road clearly—the dusty, straggly bushes, the scrubby grass. The hard gray light was fading. Colors came back, the sky was just a rain sky, the road was just concrete, cars were just full of people going some place.

She clenched her left hand over the acorn. Holding like that, she could feel the life inside it. Feel it move and twist against her flesh.

My own pulse, she thought. It's my own pulse I'm feeling. That's all.

But that doesn't matter either. Because one is as alive as the other. Life is the same in me as in anything else. Trees come out of acorns, no matter how unlikely that seems. An acorn is just a tree's way back into the ground. For another try. Another trip through.

One life or another. And what came out of sex now. Love maybe. But that wasn't as sure as a tree. Or maybe a tree was as unsure as love. One capsule or another.

She opened her hand and looked at the acorn again. Dusty green and brown. Tree colors. And the colors of love? Not colors at all. Lights like fireworks and spasms like death and absolute silence afterwards. Just silence and nothing moving. Just silence. That was all. The tree was still in the acorn, and love hadn't grown either.

The highway climbed another overpass. Cars cut in front of her. She grabbed the wheel hastily, swerved. The acorn fell. For a minute her fist felt empty and cold. Then the flow of her own blood warmed the spot. All the long drive back alone, she sat and listened to the singing of her veins, the pumping of her heart, and the steady rhythm of her blood.

And those sounds and movements of her body kept her from remembering: that kind of loneliness was the next thing to death.

Stanley

✤

IT WAS part of Stanley's job to open the greenhouse every morning. After the old man had taken his breakfast. It was part of Stanley's job to march formally along the slate-paved corridor that led from the west corner of the entrance hall and throw open the double doors into the greenhouse itself. Then he had to scurry rapidly among the welter of pots and trees, while the cool tips of climbing orchids and the furry tips of chain trees brushed his neck. Straight to the bird cage. Check the birds—first the floor: remove any dead ones quickly. Before the old man came.

Next the live birds—even more quickly now, because behind him he could hear the sound of the old man approaching. If any living bird looked sick or weak, Stanley had to reach out and grab it at once, snapping the neck in his fingers and stuffing the carcass out of sight. The old man must never see a bird die or flop about injured or unhealthy.

Sometimes, during the twelve years he had been a butler here, Stanley thought that they had arranged it this way just to make his job difficult. Why, for example, didn't they let him open the greenhouse doors before the old man came down to breakfast? There was plenty of time then, and there wouldn't be any of this last-minute business of disposing of the dead birds . . .

But it wasn't that way at all. Everything in the house had a fixed and ordered pattern. Unchangeable.

Exactly at seven-thirty every morning, the old man came down in the elevator with Mr. Murphy, the white night nurse.

White . . . Stanley sniffed. White like me, maybe. Just because he's got blue eyes, it don't mean he's white. His grandma was a nigger, sure as anything. All you had to do was look at the hands on him, and the nails. It didn't mean nothing that he had blue eyes . . . Stanley thought: I got to tell him this very day how I got a sister that's got blue eyes. Mr. Murphy, you ever hear how many niggers got blue eyes? . . .

But not now. Now was the morning routine. And the bird cage. It was a huge, flattened, watermelon-shaped affair made of reeds and straw. It reached right up to the high ceiling and down to the flagstone floor. The old man's daughter, who had decorated this greenhouse, had told Stanley that it was a fish trap of the sort that Brazilian fishermen use.

Maybe it caught fish, Stanley thought, but it was hell on birds. They died by twos and threes, every day since it had been installed four years ago. That made hundreds of birds in my hands, Stanley thought.

Only instead of taking the cage down, the old man's daughter kept restocking it. The pet shop in town sent out a new batch of birds every Wednesday afternoon. And if the old man noticed any difference in numbers according to the day of the week, he never said anything.

Finally, even the old man's daughter was convinced that it was not the fault of the birds but had something to do with her precious cage. So she found a man who knew about things like that. He had come two days ago—a short, bald man with thick glasses. Stanley watched while he emptied the cage and gave it a spray with some kind of powder and put in all new birds, of a more resistant species, he said.

Resistant to what, Stanley wondered. Except maybe the old man . . .

He looked on the floor of the cage. Nothing there. He studied the birds fluttering on their perches. Some of them were actually singing—he hadn't heard anything like that for quite a while. And even the silent ones looked all right. So maybe the little man with his powder had done some good. Stanley hoped so. He was tired of picking up the stiff, bony bodies. Sometimes he didn't have time to toss the small things out the side door, he'd have to slip them into his pocket. And once, one bad day when four or five of them had died, he'd had to tuck one up under his sleeve. A smelly swollen one at that. They puffed up quick in the damp heat of the greenhouse, quicker than outside.

This morning there was nothing to toss out. Stanley drew a sigh of relief.

The rubber-tired wheels of the chair were very close. Stanley straightened up and stood properly, hands behind his back, while the old man came in. Roberta the downstairs maid was pushing him, as she did every morning.

Stanley avoided her eyes, those yellow eyes like a cat, always staring at him. As if he didn't have enough trouble without getting mixed up with that broad. Never enough. Not for her. And he wasn't all that young any more, and with a wife of his own at home . . . he just wasn't up to things like that.

Roberta wheeled the old man to his accustomed place. It was a cleared space like a room in the very center of the greenhouse, completely surrounded by ceiling-high greenery, completely hidden from everything except the low whine of the ventilating fan and the nervous trickle of the little fountain a few dozen feet away.

Silent, the old man held up his hand and listened a minute. Funny, old as he was, and crippled and bent, like last year's kernel in a mockernut, he could still hear.

He listened and then nodded, his head trembling on

his thin neck. "Thank you, Roberta," he said.

She left, as the routine said she was to do. But she cut across the space at such an angle that she was bound to cross Stanley's vision. She wiggled her rear under her tight white dress. She did not look over her shoulder. She did not need to.

Stanley kept his face straight; he'd had lots of practice. Jesus, he thought, with Fred the mailman wanting to lay her real bad these past two, three months . . . you always did find him in the kitchen, hanging around, delaying his route, he was lucky they hadn't caught him at that. Why didn't she take on Fred . . .

Stanley stood quietly, in a version of what they would have called parade rest in the army. Almost, but not quite.

The old man sat in his wheel chair, not moving, not saying anything. Just breathing.

Which was quite an effort for him, Stanley thought. Quite an effort.

He whistled and rattled, the phlegm in the back of his throat fluttered; the sinews on the side of his thin neck, like small snarled cords, moved slightly, tightening and then loosening. His eyes were closed, those old bright eyes, hooded like a bird's, and quick as a bird's too, flashing open to catch you watching.

Stanley did not look at the old man. He simply stood, wiggling his toes inside his shoes to amuse himself. Thinking, in spite of everything, about Roberta. She had a cute ass, round and high . . .

The old man gargled and fluttered the steamy air through his lungs. The wet air, thick as a cloth, heavy, greasy as oil with all the flower and leaf scents on it.

Stanley no longer sweated profusely in the damp heat. When he first took this job—eleven, twelve years ago, he'd really forgotten just when—his shirts were always drenched with sweat when he finally was finished and came out of the greenhouse, and he'd have to walk around the kitchen with his coat off and his arms waving in the air like a clipped chicken to dry himself off. Some-

time he would even go and stand directly in front of
an air-conditioning vent, and let the cold dry air run
over him until he had a fit of shivers and had to step
away.

The heat in the greenhouse had bothered him once,
and so had the smell, the heavy sweet flower smells, the
dripping perfumes and musks. Flowers always reminded
him of funerals. But he'd gotten used to it. After all, this
was a good job. With only the old man in the house.

He was snoring loudly now, his square bony chin
resting on the carefully knotted tie.

Soft rubber-soled steps and a faint starchy rustle—
Miss Carter and her round white cap nodded to Stanley
over a low green distance. That meant Mr. Murphy, the
night nurse, was gone. Miss Carter pulled back and disappeared, her reddish blond hair fading against some
reddish blond orchids. She would wait in the hallway,
reading the morning paper, the one the old man had
glanced at during breakfast.

Same thing every morning . . . Stanley wiggled his
toes. Big toe, second toe, third toe, fourth, fifth. Now,
big toe alone, others flat and quiet. Now the little toe
alone . . . No, no luck. Still couldn't do it.

That was how Stanley spent his waiting time, learning
to move his toes separately. He would really practice
later on, when he was off duty and barefoot. He could
move the big toe alone, that was fine. But now he wanted
to move the little one.

It had to move, he thought, it was a toe, like the
others, it had to be movable, and he was going to train it.
Only so far, it wasn't doing any good. If the little one
moved, so did the others. He would have to keep practicing . . .

Abruptly the old man woke up. The thin head lifted,
the chin left the tie which now had a small wet saliva
spot on its smooth silk surface. His hand left the arm
of the wheel chair and reached out.

Stanley came alive. Thinking: the old man's morning

naps are just about the same length, how does he know, must have a clock in his head.

Stanley got the cigar box—it was only a foot or two away on a little table, but the old man never actually reached over and took hold of it, he only waved toward it with his hand and Stanley did the rest. He selected the cigar, slowly because the old man liked to watch. And he cut it, slowly too so the old man could see exactly how he was doing it. Then he tucked the cut end between the old man's thin, blue-tinged lips.

Stanley lit it for him, and put the silver lighter back on the table, noticing as he did that there were some spots of tarnish on its flat, shiny surface. He would have to bring that back in the kitchen to be polished, before the old man's daughter came. She was a great housekeeper, and she prowled around her father's house, running her finger along the tops of the shower curtain rods and over the bulbs in lamps, opening cupboards and searching drawers.

The old man began to cough; the heavy aromatic smoke spilled from his lungs. Stanley, standing beside him, stretched out his left arm stiffly. The old man bent forward, pressing against the arm with his thin bony chest, and coughed comfortably. His hands, which rested on his knees, did not move. His fingers, which held the cigar, did not loosen. When he was done, he rested silently against the arm. After a moment, Stanley straightened his arm gently, lifting him back into position. The coughing had given his face a little color. As Stanley watched, the pink drained off, leaving the usual putty color of old skin. Stanley took his arm away, the thin knotted hand lifted the cigar again, the old lungs filled. And emptied smoothly. No cough. Stanley stepped back, resumed his waiting, his toe exercising. The old man smoked quietly, and there was only the deep sound of his breathing.

They were both waiting for eight-thirty, when, as he did every weekday, the old man's office manager would arrive for his day's orders.

Standing quietly, again practicing moving his toes, Stanley almost did not notice the black shadow that passed over the glass roof of the greenhouse. A bird, he thought, flying low, a black bird, and pretty big. A crow, he supposed, or some kind of hawk. There'd been a red-tailed hawk in the big pecan tree down at the road yesterday. It must be cruising about now, looking for breakfast.

And then Stanley noticed the old man. He was sitting up straight; he almost never did that. (Only once, a long time ago—how long was that? Stanley thought . . . Eight years, when he had heard the news about his son-in-law.)

"Did you see that?" the old man asked. His thin, crippled body was poised against the air.

"Yessuh," Stanley said soothingly, remembering that it was bad for the old man to get upset. "A big crow or that red-tailed hawk I been seeing around here."

The old man turned to look at him, and the bright hooded eyes blinked at Stanley. "That was a condor. I didn't know they had them in this country. I never saw one before."

"Yessuh," Stanley said.

"Do you know what a condor is? Of course you wouldn't."

"Nosuh," Stanley said.

"We had them in San Ysedro, had lots of them. Wasn't a day you didn't look up and see one of the damn big birds sailing over looking at you."

"Suh . . ." Stanley said dutifully, wondering if he should call the nurse now. Whenever the old man started thinking about his days in South America, he got upset.

"And the damn fool Indians, you could kill them before they'd work like a white man . . ."

Stanley thought: I'll give him maybe half a minute more, and then I'll call for Miss Carter.

But this time the old man slipped off the subject. "Long ago, boy." His hand waved vaguely toward Stanley. "Gone too. Now I can't drink coffee, those days I used to chew up the beans in my teeth. Like an

Indian. Carry a gun and shoot a man soon as a snake, and always looking over my shoulder for bandits . . . That's gone, boy."

The old man dropped his hand and rested, remembering quietly. Stanley decided he would not have to call Miss Carter.

"Yes," the old man said so softly that Stanley had difficulty hearing him, "I had my time."

"Yessuh," Stanley said again. (The old man's daughter had told him, years ago, when he first took the job: Don't argue with him. Whatever he says, tell him yes. Whatever he says.)

"You wouldn't believe it now. You wouldn't believe the things if I told you. The things we did in San Ysedro."

He sounded sorry, Stanley thought. And it would be hard to be old and crippled, with nobody to remember the things you remembered. For there wasn't anybody left from that time . . . Stanley had heard about it: The old man had made his money in South America, fruit and coffee, people said. He'd gone down poor and come back rich. He married then, a man already past middle age, and had his children late, and settled down to a peaceful life.

But that meant that there'd be nobody who'd remember.

Stanley thought that it would be hard to be cut off like that. He and his wife now, they knew exactly where they would go when they got old and too tired to work. They'd go back to Ocala Springs, Mississippi, and they'd live in the house that Stanley's mother now lived in, the house that they were keeping for their old age. They'd known everybody in that town since they were kids, and when they got very old and sick and the shells of their bodies sat loosely around them, they wouldn't be alone. There'd be other people to sit on the porches with them and talk about things that had happened to them years before.

Like the time they were playing hooky from school, fooling around back on the old shell road that went to the Spanish fort, way back of town, where you could hardly find the road for the palmettos that overgrew it, and the still unmoving air smelled musky from snakes. They'd gone off the road somehow, and one of them— Charlie Edwards, it was—had got into a quicksand. By the time they found a plank to reach to him he was down to his waist in the stuff; he'd lost his pants and torn his shirt. When his mama found out what he'd been doing that made him come home half naked, stripped like a willow that's been peeled, she was too frightened to give him the beating he deserved. "Don't you ever forget," she screeched at them all, because Charlie was her only child and her husband gone, "don't you never forget what you done today. And how near you come to getting killed. Don't you never forget, not so long as you live."

They remembered all right, Stanley thought. His wife Louise, she had been one of those kids and every so often she'd say to him: "You remember that pit on the road to the old Spanish fort?" And in Ocala Springs they could always find other people who remembered. They wouldn't ever be alone, not the way the old man was. With just a lot of images in his mind and nobody really knowing what they were about . . .

Stanley heard the crisp footfall of Mr. Larsen, who was the old man's office manager. It would be exactly eight-thirty. Mr. Larsen was never either late or early.

The old man might be crippled and weak and alone, but he still ran his own affairs. Stanley didn't know too much about that. He left just as soon as Mr. Larsen arrived, so he didn't hear what they were talking about, but he knew from Viola, the cook, who'd been in the house for twenty-five years, that the old man was mean and sharp and feisty in his business. "Don't you let that body of his fool you none," Viola would always say. "He can't run no races, nor things like that, and he'd be no good to a woman any more, but there ain't nothing wrong with his mind, and he just sits in that hothouse of his thinking up ways to screw more people and make some more money." And when Stanley looked startled, as he did the first time he heard that, Viola just chuckled. "I reckon he is just about the smartest man God ever got around to making."

She'd been there longer than anyone else, and she remembered back to the time when the old man's wife was still alive, and his children were just married, back to the time before his strokes and paralysis.

Stanley left the greenhouse, closing the door behind him, moving from the warm moist air to the crispy cool dry air of the main part of the house, air that always smelled faintly of machine oil. They'd tried, but the service men had never been quite able to get that odor out of the air conditioner.

Miss Carter was sitting at her usual station in the hall; she dropped the newspaper. "Good morning, Stanley. How is he?"

"Same, I guess," Stanley said. "Feeble."

"More than yesterday?"

"No."

"Then it's a good day for him."

"Would you like me to bring you a cup of coffee?"

"No, thanks." She almost never accepted. "I'm just waiting to see if I'm needed, as usual."

Stanley went to the kitchen; he would get his own breakfast now. The room was empty. Viola must be off somewhere. Stanley hung his white coat carefully on the back of a chair. He poured himself a cup of coffee and shook some corn flakes into a bowl. He was eating that when Viola appeared. She was a short, wide woman, not fat but very muscular. "How is he?"

"Same as yesterday," Stanley said with his mouth full.

Viola clucked her tongue.

"You didn't expect no miracles?" Stanley teased her. "Nor anything like that?"

She sighed in answer.

Mr. Larsen left, and the old man's daughter arrived, as she did every single morning, weekends included, at ten o'clock. And the old man's daughter found the cigarette lighter with the spots of tarnish on it. She was so upset by this that she went through the house more carefully than ever, and insisted on taking all the linen out of the linen closet and looking it over, even the great initialed damask cloths that had belonged to her mother and hadn't been used since those days. Of course she found that they were blotched by brown age spots and so the whole staff spent the rest of the morning (while Miss Carter stayed with the old man) carrying the cloths to the back yard and stretching them on the grass in the full sun and spreading the brown age spots with a mixture of lemon juice and salt. While the old man's daughter stood in the shade of the big oak tree and watched. By noon they were all tired, and she went off to have lunch with her mother-in-law, as she did every day. She had always got on better with her in-laws than with her own father.

She kissed him good-by. "See you tomorrow, Papa."

"Edna?" That was her mother-in-law's name. The old man asked as if he didn't know.

"Of course, Papa, I always have lunch there."

"Terrible woman."

"I'm going," the old man's daughter said hastily.

The old man said: "No wonder that fellow killed himself with a mother like that to drive him to it."

The old man's daughter turned her round, middle-aged face to Stanley. In her eyes the old bewilderment at her husband's sucide. "Stanley," she said, trying to change the subject, "have you ever seen a father like this!"

"Don't involve the boy," the old man said.

A boy, Stanley thought; forty-six and I'm still a boy. And he felt a little rise of anger, white people were like that . . . But pretty soon it died away. The old man annoyed everybody, white and black alike. Look at his own daughter now, tears beginning in her eyes.

"I know you don't really mean that, Papa. See you tomorrow."

The old man said to Stanley with surprising strength

in his voice: "Silly woman, married a horse's ass of a husband."

But Stanley remembered the day when he had brought the news of that suicide. When he had brought the phone to the greenhouse and plugged it into the jack and rolled the wheel chair up to it. And all the time the old man was grumbling, "What the hell is going on, what the hell do you think you're doing . . . I don't answer the phone, not in here, you can damn well take the message or they can come out here and tell me . . . and why for Chrissake are you looking like that? You look like you're ready to puke. What the hell is going on?"

And Stanley not saying anything, just slowly going about the business of putting the old man in contact with the instrument.

Stanley already knew the message, he had heard it. He had just refused to deliver it. "No suh," he said firmly into the phone, "I couldn't tell him nothing like that. If you will hold on, suh, I will get him to the phone himself."

The old man took the receiver away from Stanley testily. "What the hell's going on?" he demanded into it.

Then he listened. His body stiffened; as if his spine would break. Stiffened and pulled away from the back of the chair, back arching like a bow. Just the way he did when one of his stroke attacks came. Stanley reached out to grab him, but something stopped his hand, and the old man's body stayed stiff and arched, but it didn't fall over or collapse. It just stayed there.

Finally he said to Stanley: "Take the phone back where it belongs." Quietly. He settled back into the chair. That was all.

Eight years later the old man's widowed daughter said: "Stanley, will you carry that package to the car for me?"

And Stanley, understanding that she wanted a word with him privately, said: "Yes ma'am."

They walked all the way to the front door before she asked: "Does he look all right to you?"

"Yes ma'am."

"Not pale?"

"He's got his good days and his bad."

"Not complaining?"

"He don't ever complain."

"He looks sort of strange to me . . . How're the birds doing?"

"All alive this morning."

"Fine . . . I guess I will ask the doctor to come by."

Stanley knew she meant the doctor for the old man, not the birds.

The old man was waiting for Stanley, bright hooded eyes in the wheel chair. "What were you two talking about?"

Stanley sighed silently. The old man always knew or he guessed correctly. So Stanley told him the truth. "She asked me if I thought you looked all right."

"Hah!"

"Said you had your good days and your bad ones."

The old man did not answer. He seemed to have gone back to sleep, and his hands on the arms of the chair were fastened like a bird's claws when it roosts.

The old man had lunch and went to his nap. Stanley and Miss Carter stretched him out on the huge tester bed with the maroon velvet quilt, stretched him out fully dressed, tie still in place, and covered him with a light cotton blanket because it was summer and even the air-conditioned house was warm. The old man fell asleep at once. He seemed very tired; he had dozed through his lunch and hadn't eaten a thing.

"I'll ask the doctor about that when he comes," Miss Carter said, and then they went their separate ways—Miss Carter to have her own lunch and read in the upstairs sitting room, near the old man's door in case he should call out, Stanley down to the kitchen.

Roberta was there, Roberta with her tight high bottom and her smiling eyes. Like a cat, he thought, eyes like a cat. He did not want to spend his lunch avoiding her glance. "Just fix me a sandwich, Vi," he told the cook, "I'm going to lie down."

"You want company?" Roberta asked wickedly.

"And what you do if I say yes, little girl?"

"Don't you want to see?"

"No," he said, "I don't want nothing. Except I'm tired standing and I want to sit down." He put the sandwich in a paper napkin and took a bottle of Coke out of the refrigerator. He ate his lunch sprawled on the bed of the room that was called his, way back in the servants' wing of the house. His room, even though he had never lived there.

He was still resting when the door bell rang. He heard it clearly, one of the stations was at the end of the servants' corridor. He did not move. Roberta or Viola or Miss Carter would answer.

He supposed it was the doctor . . . For a moment Stanley had a picture of the big black hawk ringing the front door bell. Like a comic-book illustration. Big black bird with a wing on the buzzer. And what had the old man called that hawk? A condor, or something like that. It wasn't like the old man to get mixed up in his facts, even sick as he was. But it wasn't like him to notice a bird either . . . Stanley finished the last swallow of his Coke. It was probably Dr. Andrews, a nice man, short and fat and cheery. Viola and Roberta thought he was courting the old man's daughter, and that they'd be getting married any day now, but Stanley wasn't so sure. The old man's daughter wasn't young any more and she wasn't ever very pretty, even if she was rich. Then there was that bit about her late husband. What man is going to like following to bed a man who took a shotgun and jammed it in his mouth . . . But Viola and Roberta swore that he would marry her anyway.

Stanley sighed. That was women for you. Always romantic, always looking for marriage and love. Seeing it everywhere.

Stanley reached out to the bedside table, felt around

on the shelf, then turned over to see. Nothing. And only yesterday he had put four or five new comic books there. He was sure.

It would be Roberta again, god damn her. She was always taking them, and yelling at her did no good. He'd tried that.

"But, honey," she would say, "but honey, living in like I do, this quiet old house, just Mr. Murphy in the evenings, and he ain't talkative, you know, I get so bored I don't know what to do, and so I go looking for something to read and when I see your books there I just know you wouldn't mind saving my life. After all, you live home, you got a lot to amuse you . . ."

Stanley sighed again. What could you do with a girl like that? Excepting maybe that he was a younger man . . . That was her trouble, part of it, anyhow. In a house with no young men around all day. Just him, and he was old and getting older. And Jasper the gardener, he was long past the age of chasing women. So it was no wonder the girl got bored. Maybe he'd better talk to her about Fred the mailman, he was a nice young guy now . . . But then again, maybe he'd better not. The less you talked about it with young girls like that, the better.

And Stanley rolled over on his back again, staring at the ceiling. Pity he wasn't young any more. Time was, a girl like Roberta looked real good to him. But that time, he said to the wallpapered ceiling, wasn't now.

And then his bell started ringing, the servant call bell in its shiny chrome case beside the door. Oh lord, he thought, what now?

They were impatient. The bell kept ringing. Somebody down in the pantry (where the house signal board was) was keeping his thumb pressed down on that button.

Stanley straightened his tie and put on his coat and went out in the hall. He was refusing to be hurried. Somebody's nonsense. As he walked along the hall, heading for the back stairs, passing the doors of the other rooms in the servants' wing, he noticed that the bells in all of them were ringing. The house was afire or somebody had gone crazy and clamped a hand across the signal panel, buzzing every single button . . .

Stanley stomped down the stairs into the pantry. It was Viola, all right. Viola standing there with her big hand over the signaling panel.

"Okay," Stanley said. "Okay . . . Stop ringing. Nobody's up there but me. You making enough noise to wake the dead."

Viola spun around and stared at him, her heavy-lidded eyes fluttering. Then, with surprising speed for such a big woman, she darted through the swinging door into the kitchen and through the kitchen to the servants' dining room beyond. Stanley followed, half-expecting to see flames and smoke.

Dr. Andrews was standing there, waiting. Stanley had the impression that they had been waiting for him. Viola flopped down at the table, her wide hips flaring over the wooden chair. Roberta was next to the window. She seemed to be backed up against the wall, as if she was afraid. She looked very pretty, Stanley admitted to himself. At least in that light.

And Fred came bouncing in the door, swinging his heavy sack to the floor. "Mailman!" he sang out cheerfully. And stopped.

Roberta said: "Fred, the old man's dead."

Before he took notice of what the words meant, Stanley thought: he's got it made, the lucky bastard. She never used that tone before.

Fred heard it too. There was just a flicker of understanding on his face.

Then Stanley heard the meaning of the words and he heard himself say quietly: "Oh my God."

Dr. Andrew nodded politely to Fred, but when he spoke it was to Stanley. "I wanted to tell everybody at once . . . He was dead when I came. He died in his sleep, I suppose."

"The cover wasn't even disturbed," Roberta said. Her usually husky voice was high and squeaky. "He didn't even move."

Fred's eyes glittered, and he smiled a comforting smile at her.

Damn the smug bastard, Stanley thought.

"Miss Carter is there now," Dr. Andrews said. "She'll stay. If the phone rings, she'll answer it. Don't any of you do it, understand? I'm going to tell his family personally, right now."

His family, Stanley thought. That is his daughter, so maybe there is some truth in the women's stories.

"Well," Stanley said in to the silence. "Well . . ."

Fred said: "Looks like I walked into something. I didn't expect nothing like this."

And Viola put her head down on the table and began to cry.

Stanley went into the front of the house and up the wide polished stairs. You could still smell the wax he'd used on the bannister earlier in the morning. On the second floor, Miss Carter was at her station. Only this time she wasn't reading, as she usually was. She was sitting bolt upright, on guard.

Stanley wondered . . . Now she was waking a dead body she couldn't read. But when she served a live one she could . . . But he'd stopped puzzling things like that a long time ago.

He went up to her and she said in a whisper (why whisper? he thought again, we never did when he was alive), "He looks so natural, he didn't even stir when he died. When the doctor went in I thought sure he was asleep . . . But he didn't look so good to me this morning."

Stanley didn't tell her any different. "I reckon that's why his daughter called the doctor."

Miss Carter sighed and fluttered the frizzy red hair at the top of her cap. "And he might been lying in there dead all the afternoon and us thinking he was just asleep."

"As soon dead one place as the other."

And he saw by her startled face that he'd said the wrong thing. So he added hastily, "Can I bring you anything? I mean, I know you can't leave, and I thought maybe I could bring you something, like a cup of tea."

She shook her head, and a pale red head's face swung back and forth. "Do you want to look at him?"

"Maybe Viola would."

"Well, tell her to come right up, before they come."

Stanley was halfway down the stairs before he realized that "they" meant the undertakers.

Much later, when the long summer light was finally ending, Viola and Stanley stood on the back drive waiting for her husband to pick her up. It was over. The old man's daughter, with Dr. Andrews, had come and gone. Stanley had to admit that the old man's daughter looked more relieved than upset.

Viola rested her fat buttocks against a gatepost and sighed. Her eyes were red with weeping.

Directly over their head were two lighted windows and a shadow that occasionally passed by them. Roberta was dressing. Fred had promised to stop by tonight, after the house had quieted down. It was the last chance for a while. They'd be bringing the old man back tomorrow, there'd be a couple of days of wake and then the funeral. And a lot of work for the staff. But not tonight. Tonight the house would be empty and quiet. Mr. Murphy wouldn't be back, the old man had no more need for a night nurse. Roberta would be staying alone. Except for Fred, of course.

The old man sure set that up for him, Stanley thought. As much as if he'd arranged it. And Fred didn't even know it.

And Stanley said aloud: "You know what a condor is?"

Viola turned her head slightly from watching for her husband. "A what?"

"Just about the last thing the old man said was to ask if a black hawk was a condor."

"Yeah?" Viola pulled a handkerchief from the front of her dress and blew her nose loudly.

"I never heard of it, but that's what he asked about."

"You never can tell what they going to say." Viola folded her pink square carefully and tucked it away. "My papa now, when he was dying, the last thing he says is: 'There a fly on the ceiling. No, there two flies on the ceiling.' And then he died. So you can't tell what they going to say."

The night moths were beginning to come for the heavy opening flowers of the moonflower vine by the door. They bumped their pollen-laden wings on the screen of the porch there.

"It's a bird," Stanley insisted. "Like a hawk."

"Red-tailed hawk in the big oak. Saw that yesterday."

"That's what I told him."

"Didn't believe you?"

"Said it was a condor."

"He was remembering, I guess." Viola rubbed at her swollen eyes. "Bet he was talking about the old times in San Ysedro."

"Yeah," Stanley said.

"That was a long time ago," Viola said. "I used to hear him talk about it sometimes."

"How old you suppose he was?"

"Him? Way in his eighties somewhere."

Stanley lit a cigar. He had taken one from the old man's humidor, and now he smoked it slowly, the way the old man would have.

"His?" Viola asked.

"Yeah."

"You know," Viola said, "kind of hard to think it's all over."

"Yeah," Stanley said. "You going to stay on and work for her?"

She had asked them to stay in a formal little speech, with Dr. Andrews standing at her side. "If you want to stay your jobs will be here. You can go on just as you did before, without a change."

"You going to work for her?" Stanley repeated.

Viola shook her head. "I don't reckon I will. I been

here nearly thirty years, and I reckon that's enough."

"I don't figure to stay," Stanley said. "I don't see much to staying." He puffed the cigar that had belonged to the old man. "I feel right bad about him. I didn't expect to feel so bad about him."

Viola didn't say anything.

"I wasn't really expecting him to die. You know, not today. Not with him talking about the old days in San Ysedro and how he'd be carrying a gun ready to shoot anybody."

Then Viola's husband came. She shifted her weight wearily. "See you tomorrow."

"I'll be going along," Stanley said. But he didn't, not for a while. Not yet. He wasn't in any hurry. He hadn't called his wife to tell her the news, so he would have to go through all of that. She'd have to know every detail, so she could pass it along to her sister first thing in the morning.

Stanley looked at the little red glow on the tip of his cigar. He was upset, no doubt of that. And he didn't know why. It was something he just couldn't put in words. Or in thoughts. He tried to come at it, but it twisted and slipped and faded away, leaving just an echo where it had been.

Because he was restless and didn't quite know where he wanted to go, Stanley walked back through the darkened house, cool and smelling of polish and wax. He crossed the front hall, through the living room, through the second slate-floored hall, and went into the greenhouse. It was too dark; he switched on the light by the door. Not nearly bright enough. But the only one out here, except for the fluorescent tubes over the African violet plants. Stanley looked toward the north end of the greenhouse, and he could see the bluish glow.

The old man had loved those African violets. He'd inspected them every few days, measuring with his eye the size of the blooms . . . Would his daughter keep them now? Would she keep the greenhouse? Or even the house itself? Would it be sold and slip away and be painted another color and have different people living in it, people of different blood from the old man, who had built this thing of wood and brick and his energy and money . . .

Stanley wondered. Viola was quite sure that the old man's daughter would marry Dr. Andrews now. That the old man was the only thing standing in the way. That they would then move into this house, and it would go on that way. "Only thing," Viola said, "I'm thinking about her age. She's pushing forty, and she's just about through with breeding. Kind of pity if she's too old."

Stanley wondered. Maybe so. Maybe not. Viola didn't know everything. She just knew a lot.

Stanley sat down in one of the iron chairs with the blue striped cushions, and looked at the spot where the old man's wheel chair always stood. He tried to imagine it standing there, to imagine the old man sitting in it. And he had trouble with his memory. He couldn't quite bring it to focus. Like a jigsaw puzzle in a way. He just couldn't bring the color and the shape of the pieces into line. It was there in his memory all right, only broken up and scattered. He couldn't seem to fit them together. Not now, not when he wanted to . . . Of course he could go into the upstairs hall and look at 'he wheel chair and get that all settled and sorted out right, but that wasn't the whole thing. He couldn't fit the pieces of the old man together. He was dead now and gone. And he hadn't left behind anything, not even a clear image. Not anything.

Stanley looked around the shadowy greenhouse. He half expected to see a ghost or a spirit or some sort of sign in the tangle of light and shadow. Once he had believed in ghosts and once had seen them all the time. Ghosts in the shape of people he'd never met. Ghosts in the shape of old people he'd known who had died. Ghosts in the shapes of small animals, cats mostly, that purred and rubbed around his legs. Spirits in the shapes of dark shadows and light shadows. Of winds and voices out of a sunny blue sky.

So he would have not been too surprised if he'd seen something of the old man in the dark greenhouse.

But he didn't. He looked and he looked. There wasn't anything.

Not even that, Stanley thought. There wasn't even that left. It was like the condor that the old man had seen in the red-tailed hawk. He'd seen it, and nobody else had.

The condors and the mountains and the shooting and the anger and the murders—all the things that the old man had left in his memory, keeping them green and fresh and alive until the day he died. All those things were gone now. He'd taken them with him.

Stanley tried again, staring at the spot where the old man used to sit, trying with his thought to make him appear, make him come back from wherever he was.

And it wasn't any use. He was just gone.

Stanley stood up and left the greenhouse, walked through the empty rooms. Empty except for Roberta. And he shivered. You're getting old, he told himself. Sitting in the dark, not even trying a good-looking piece like Roberta. Once upon a time you'd tried all the broads . . . just like the old man, he thought abruptly. And stopped. He hadn't thought of himself as like the old man, not in any way. But there it was.

He felt in his pocket to be sure that he had the house keys. Under his searching fingers the skin of his leg prickled and twitched. Jumpy, he thought.

He went through the house, turning off all the lights as he did every night, all the lights except the one in the hall and the one in the kitchen. Then he went out, carefully locking the door behind him.

A warm night, bright and clear. Sweet smelling and heavy with jasmine and calycanthus and sweet olive. Dead man's bush, the old people called it.

He'd go home now, Stanley thought, and he would tell his wife all the things that had happened during the day and he would bear with her impatience at his delay. And after a while they would go out on their porch to drink beer and talk about one thing or another. And pretty soon they'd be thinking back to the time in Ocala Springs when they were children together. She was always very good at remembering, far more than he was. But when she reminded him, then he'd recall whatever it was she was talking about, and he'd know what it had been like and how it had felt and smelled and tasted. All the things of that time years ago in Mississippi when they were children.

They'd sit late into the night, and he'd get over the creepy feeling that he had right now. She was a good woman and with her and her talk, he could remember all sorts of things. With her he wouldn't be lonely.

Roberta would have company tonight too. As Stanley left, he saw Fred's car turning into the drive.

ABOUT THE AUTHOR

Shirley Ann Grau was born in Louisiana and spent part of her childhood in Alabama. With her husband and children, she divides her time between winters in Metairie, a suburb of New Orleans, and summers on Martha's Vineyard.

BESTSELLERS

	Title	Code	Price
☐	BEGGAR ON HORSEBACK—Thorpe	23091-0	1.50
☐	THE TURQUOISE—Seton	23088-0	1.95
☐	STRANGER AT WILDINGS—Brent (Pub. in England as Kirkby's Changeling)	23085-6	1.95
☐	MAKING ENDS MEET—Howar	23084-8	1.95
☐	THE LYNMARA LEGACY—Gaskin	23060-0	1.95
☐	THE TIME OF THE DRAGON—Eden	23059-7	1.95
☐	THE GOLDEN RENDEZVOUS—MacLean	23055-4	1.75
☐	TESTAMENT—Morrell	23033-3	1.95
☐	CAN YOU WAIT TIL FRIDAY?— Olson, M.D.	23022-8	1.75
☐	HARRY'S GAME—Seymour	23019-8	1.95
☐	TRADING UP—Lea	23014-7	1.95
☐	CAPTAINS AND THE KINGS—Caldwell	23069-4	2.25
☐	"I AIN'T WELL—BUT I SURE AM BETTER"—Lair	23007-4	1.75
☐	THE GOLDEN PANTHER—Thorpe	23006-6	1.50
☐	IN THE BEGINNING—Potok	22980-7	1.95
☐	DRUM—Onstott	22920-3	1.95
☐	LORD OF THE FAR ISLAND—Holt	22874-6	1.95
☐	DEVIL WATER—Seton	22888-6	1.95
☐	CSARDAS—Pearson	22885-1	1.95
☐	CIRCUS—MacLean	22875-4	1.95
☐	WINNING THROUGH INTIMIDATION— Ringer	22836-3	1.95
☐	THE POWER OF POSITIVE THINKING— Peale	22819-3	1.75
☐	VOYAGE OF THE DAMNED— Thomas & Witts	22449-X	1.75
☐	THINK AND GROW RICH—Hill	X2812	1.75
☐	EDEN—Ellis	X2772	1.75

Buy them at your local bookstores or use this handy coupon for ordering:

FAWCETT PUBLICATIONS, P.O. Box 1014, Greenwich Conn. 06830

Please send me the books I have checked above. Orders for less than 5 books must include 60c for the first book and 25c for each additional book to cover mailing and handling. Orders of 5 or more books postage is Free. I enclose $_____ in check or money order.

Mr/Mrs/Miss_____

Address_____

City_____ State/Zip_____

Please allow 4 to 5 weeks for delivery. This offer expires 6/78.   A-14